Island Secrets

Stories from the Coast of Maine

Catherine J.S. Lee

SEA SMOKE PRESS
Eastport, Maine

 SEA SMOKE PRESS
P.O. Drawer J
Eastport, Maine 04631-0911
U.S.A.

Copyright © 2022 by Catherine J.S. Lee
ISBN 978-0-578-36028-7

All rights reserved.

No part of this book may be reproduced, stored in a retrieval system, or transmitted by any means, electronic, mechanical, photocopying, recording, or otherwise, without prior written permission of the copyright holder.

This book is a work of fiction. Names, characters, places, and events are the products of the author's imagination and any resemblance to actual events or places or persons, living or dead, is strictly coincidental.

First Sea Smoke Press Edition, January, 2022
Cover design and photo by Catherine J.S. Lee
Author photo by Robin Farrin
Printed in the United States of America

*For those who go down to the sea in boats,
and for those who love them.*

*And for those who treasure the times they spend
on summer islands.*

ACKNOWLEDGEMENTS

I AM GRATEFUL to the following publications in which these stories, or earlier versions of them, originally appeared:

"Borderline," *ShatterColors Literary Review*
"Everyone Knows This is Nowhere," *Prick of the Spindle*
"Quarry Secrets," *Summer Stories Anthology*
"Relentless Tide," *SNR Review*
"Sea Change," *Potato Eyes*
"The Season of Beginnings,"
The Binnacle and *The Rose and Thorn*

I am especially thankful for those who helped me on my journey to make this collection the best it can be. Any lacks, flaws, errors, and deficiencies in it are mine and mine alone.

Ruth Cash-Smith
Joan Connor
Jack Driscoll
Robert Froese
Melodie Greene
and my fellow workshop members in the charter class of the Stonecoast MFA in Creative Writing Program at the University of Southern Maine.

AUTHOR NOTE

THE STORIES IN THIS COLLECTION were written over several decades, and the majority are from the days before our world became so instantaneously connected, when people talked on landlines and payphones and CB radios rather than cell phones, when "social media" was not yet a thing, and when commercial fishermen had less technology and fewer safety measures at their disposal.

In order to stay true to the spirit of the stories and the times in which they were set, I have chosen to leave these story elements as originally written rather than modernizing them.

I hope, dear reader, than you find something worthy in these stories, anachronisms and all.

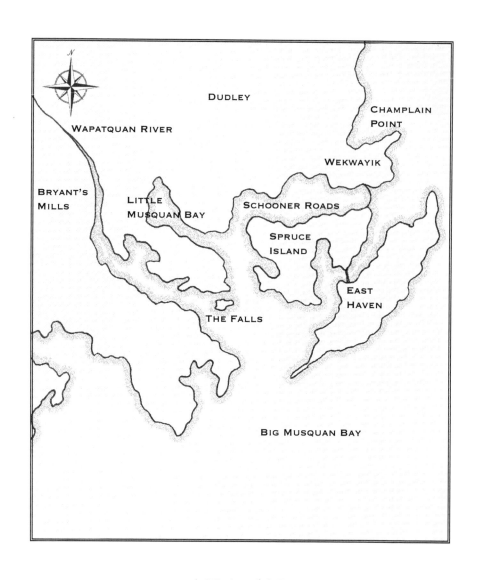

*A Fictional Map
of
Way Down East*

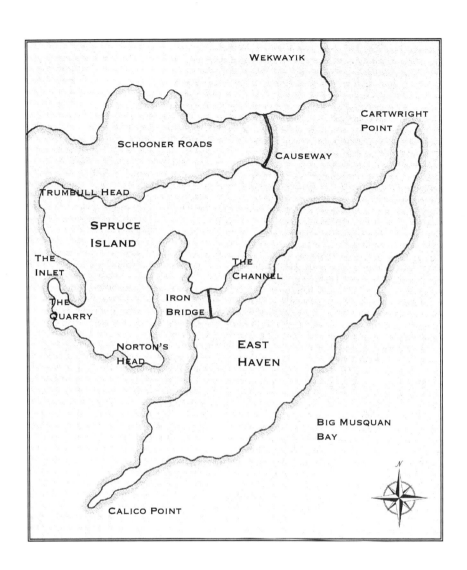

A Fictional Map of The Islands

CONTENTS

Never Love a Fisherman	1
Summer Wages	21
Island Secrets	38
Relentless Tide	61
Quarry Secrets	80
Island to Island	86
Leaving Wapatquan	101
Sea Change	106
Borderline	123
The Season of Beginnings	144
Everyone Knows This is Nowhere	148
Gone Like Sea Smoke	174

NEVER LOVE A FISHERMAN

LOST IN THE WATERCOLORS for her latest children's book, Rainey Faulkingham jumped at the sudden jingling of the doorbell, then shook her head at the smear of blue across what was supposed to be a golden beach. For the first time that afternoon, she noticed the clumped snowflakes swirling past the window. Was the boat in early? Had Justin forgotten his house key? Rainey dipped and blotted her paintbrush, dashed downstairs, and yanked open the front door.

Standing on the porch was Sheila Mac Caswell, whose husband Leon was the sternman on the urchin dragger Justin and his brother ran. She seemed flushed and sweaty despite the December cold. "Something's happened to our guys, Rainey," she said as she closed the door. "Something terrible."

Her heart skidding against her ribcage, Rainey grabbed the newel post to steady herself. Had it finally come, the moment she dreaded every time the *Delores Dawn* left the breakwater for the fishing grounds? Queasiness overtook her, and it wasn't just from her five-month first pregnancy. "How terrible?" she said, torn between needing to know the worst and wanting to pretend that her world was still safe and normal.

Sheila Mac undid her muffler and fingered her silver cross. "I stopped at Abbott's to get gas after I got back from Mayfield. Marcie and Bernadette were there and came over and said how sorry they were, and they hoped everyone was saved, and they'd do anything they could for us, and—oh, Rainey, they didn't know I didn't know."

Rainey felt as though a hive of bees buzzed in her head, and wondered if that were how a stroke felt. The summer-resident outsider who married into the fishing community, she wasn't prepared for her nebulous fears to become reality.

"Call Delores," Sheila Mac said. Delores was Justin's brother's wife. Despite their husbands working together, she and Sheila Mac clung tightly to an old feud that went back to high school days, before Rainey knew either of them.

"Sheila Mac's here," Rainey said when Delores answered. "She says—she says—" Rainey leaned against the wall.

"Something's happened to the boys," Delores said. "By my father's blood, I felt something was wrong today." Her unknown father was rumored on Spruce Island to have been a Gypsy, an idea Delores had long embraced. "I'll be right over."

In the living room, Sheila Mac was on her knees. The Baptist preacher's daughter, she had a habit of falling into frequent prayer. Rainey, raised a Quaker, believed prayer was a private matter, but she clasped her hands across her belly and bowed her head anyway.

"Keep our husbands safe if that's Your will, Heavenly Father," Sheila Mac said. "And if it's not Your will, please reconsider and keep them safe anyway. And please forgive me for anything I've said or thought that offends You. In Jesus' name, Amen."

Rainey murmured, "Amen." Sheila Mac, thick-bodied with unshed weight from six pregnancies, leaned on the arm of the velvet sofa and heaved herself to her feet.

When Delores pulled up a few moments later in her battered SUV, Rainey and Sheila Mac piled in. The street wasn't plowed yet, and in an hour it'd be starting to get dark, a week from the shortest day of the year.

"Everything seems so unreal," Rainey said as snow floated down like thick confetti. The words had barely left her lips when she felt a flutter under her ribcage, so tiny she wasn't sure she hadn't imagined it. Tears welled up, and she blotted them on her gloves.

"My baby kicked," she said. "I just felt my baby kick." If his child chose this moment to quicken, Justin had to be okay, and she held that thought against all doubt as they made their slow way to the mainland through blowing snow.

NEVER LOVE A FISHERMAN

☙

Rainey was the fourth generation of her family to summer on East Haven, a summer colony of sailboats and large cottages, in a house that was a slightly smaller replica of their three-story Victorian home in the Philadelphia suburb of Chestnut Hill. She had figured she'd summer there forever—but that was before Justin.

She was three years out of college when they met. Her first children's book had already been published, and with the story for the second in final draft, she went to Spruce Island one day to take some photos of the working waterfront to guide her illustrations. She was at the Cannery, a seafood restaurant with lobster traps piled high on the end of the wharf, when a trim fishing boat with a dark blue hull came in and three men started offloading lobsters.

Two of the men ignored her, but the third, a tall, sinewy man about her own age with sun-streaked brown hair pulled back in a ponytail, kept glancing her way, smiling when he caught her eye.

"Wait a minute," he called as she started to put her camera back in her bag. He held up a lobster. "Would you take a picture of this?" The broad smile shining between his mustache and goatee was the warmest thing she'd seen in a long time.

Only half of the lobster he held was the usual dark, red-speckled green. The other half, divided along the length of its carapace, was a sort of stormy blue. "That's a rare one," he said. "We're giving it to the aquarium over in Falmouth, New Brunswick."

"Why is it like that?"

"I don't know." His eyes were the color of warm cognac, and looking into their clear depths made her feel weak in the knees. "A freak of nature, I guess."

"I guess." Rainey smiled and nodded, unable to think of anything else to say. Ever since her college sweetheart had broken their engagement a week before graduation, she'd avoided men, even those who telegraphed their interest with every glance and smile.

He returned the lobster to its crate. "Your first visit to Spruce Island?"

"No," she said. "My family summers on East Haven."

"I'm—" he began, but was cut off by one of the other men, who called, "Justin, come on. We still got to work on that trap hauler."

She watched the boat until it was out of sight, then headed home to East Haven. Her parents were on the back verandah, playing bridge with the Harlows from next door. Rainey went straight to her studio on the third floor and sat on the window seat overlooking the channel with Spruce Island in the distance, feeling blindsided by a desire she hadn't felt in a long, long time.

※

The road to Demby's Point, which jutted into Little Musquan Bay, was still unpaved. The transplants who had built their mansions on the shore figured it would keep the locals from crossing their land to harvest the clam flats, but what was one more bumpy road in a hardscrabble life?

Despite its swift fall, the snow was already packed down by tire tracks. Cars and pickups lined both sides of the road, but Delores found a parking spot right at the edge of the beach. Thirty or forty people were clustered in small groups above the high tide line as searchlights from two Coast Guard vessels sliced the murk into snowy yellow cones on the gelid, white-capped water.

Karen Wallace, another fisherman's wife, stepped out of a huddle of people and reached up to hug Delores. "Anything we can do for you," she said. "Anything at all."

After Karen, others approached them. No one said it would be all right, or offered other platitudes that seemed so useless now. Realists all, knowing the chances for survival, they confined themselves to saying that Walt and Justin and Leon were good men, a real loss to the fleet, and would be missed.

They'd been shivering on the frozen shore for a half-hour or so when two divers emerged from the water with a limp form between them.

"Stand back," someone yelled. "Give them room."

In the sweep of the searchlight, Sheila Mac cried, "Oh, Lord! Leon!" She fell to her knees in the snow and tidal mud, beating at the hands that reached out to pull her to her feet, rocking back and forth as the divers laid Leon's body on a sled-like stretcher. "Dear Heavenly Father, forgive us, forgive us for all our sins," she wailed.

In the instant before the EMTs covered Leon's body, Rainey saw his face, eyes blank, rockweed and sea-wrack caught around his neck and in his red hair. Was she going to see Justin like this, before the horrible day was through? Nausea overtook her, and she vomited as everything started to slide out of focus. The next thing she knew, two women were guiding her up the beach to Delores' SUV.

"What happened?" she asked.

"You fainted," one of them said. "But we caught you before you fell in the mud." They settled her in the front seat and wiped her face and smoothed her hair.

"Thank you," Rainey said. "Thank you so much."

Alone, she stared out into the snowy dark. It wasn't the beach before her that she saw, but a vision of Justin, cold and pale as marble, seaweed shrouding his hair, foam on his lips, brandy-colored eyes staring sightlessly into the vast black sky.

∝

Rainey was uploading pictures to her laptop the morning after first meeting Justin when she thought of taking him some photos of the bicolored lobster. After working on sketches for her book for a couple of hours, she cropped and printed some eight-by-tens and changed her clothes four times before deciding on a simple jeans skirt and white-on-white embroidered camisole. A quarter hour earlier than the boat had come in the day before, she put the photos in an envelope and drove across the iron bridge to Spruce Island. She could see a blue-hulled fishing boat heading towards the Cannery.

"Let it be him," she whispered, "please let it be him."

She reached the wharf before the boat did. Although she'd never before gone solo to a bar, she squared her shoulders and walked into the restaurant's Capping Room. At a small window table with a view of the wharf, she ordered a glass of Riesling, lingering over it until the boat came in and they offloaded their catch. When they started loading empty traps back onto the boat, she walked down the wharf, feeling as giddy as a love-struck teenager.

"Hello," she called, and they all turned towards her, Justin, a man who looked like his older brother, and a third with red hair and freckles. "I brought the photos of that lobster," she said.

Justin took the envelope, and they all looked at the photos. "Very thoughtful," he said. "Thank you."

"They'll have to believe us now," said the redheaded man.

"We're just about done here," Justin said. "Let me buy you a drink."

"That sounds fine," Rainey said.

After loading the rest of the traps, Justin took off his oilskin overalls and the black rubber boots that the wags on East Haven called "Spruce Island Nikes."

They walked back up the wharf to the Capping Room. "I'm Justin Faulkingham," he said.

Rainey nodded. She tried to smile, but the smile felt as though her lips were trembling. "I'm Rainey Sheffield."

"Rainey," he said. "I like it. And what do you do, Rainey Sheffield?"

"I write and illustrate children's books."

He nodded but didn't say anything else, and Rainey began to suspect that he was just as shy as she was. She sat in the chair he held for her. He ordered her a glass of Riesling and himself a draft beer.

"Have you always lived on Spruce Island?" she asked. She liked questions. Her nerves usually vanished when the focus was on her companion.

"My whole life," he said and the adventure of getting acquainted began.

❧

By the time Rainey stopped feeling dizzy, the sleet had tapered off, and a crescent moon cast its pale glimmer over the snow-laden spruces. Sheila Mac was gone with Leon's body to the funeral home. In the yellow glare of the searchlights, Rainey could see Delores standing at the edge of the tide, her dark hair whipping in the wind.

Rainey picked her way down the slippery, frozen beach. "Do you think they're out there?" she asked. She knew the odds were about a million to one, but she couldn't let herself think about that. Maybe in some cosmic way, her belief in her husband's survival would keep him safe until rescue. "I feel like Justin's still alive," she said. "If he wasn't, I'd feel it, I know I would. Don't you feel like he and Walt are out there somewhere?"

Delores put her arm around Rainey's neck and pulled her close. "I don't know, hon. I don't think so. I learned long ago how to live without hope." The moonlight casting shadows across her strong-boned face really did make Delores look like a wise Gypsy. "Rainey, don't you know hope's just another form of denial?"

Rainey shook her head, but she knew she'd be mulling those words for a long, long time.

◊

Near midnight, the Coast Guard called off the search for the night. "Go home, everyone," the chief petty officer said. "We'll start again in the morning."

"No. Please." Rainey knew she was begging, but she didn't care. "You can't stop now, while there's still a chance. Please."

"We have to, ma'am," the chief said, bowing his head before he turned away. Rainey watched the Coast Guard boats pull out while Delores explained that this was the way it was. The chief had to balance the well-being of his crew against the chance of finding still alive those who were lost, and searching in the dark with only their spotlights to guide them in finding drowned bodies wasn't an efficient use of men and time and equipment. Rainey listened, her head starting to ache as they walked arm in arm up the beach.

Delores was turning the SUV around when Rainey saw something in the sweep of the headlights. "Stop," she cried, and Delores hit the brake pedal. Rainey jumped out and hurried back across the slippery beach. She didn't realize she was in water up to her knees until it started pouring into her rubber boots. The cold bit into her legs with sudden fierceness, leaving her feeling as though all the breath had been sucked out of her.

Delores was thudding along the beach, wailing now. All Rainey's hopes that Walt and Justin had managed to save each other evaporated as she grabbed Walt's frozen wrist so he wouldn't float away before his wife reached him. They slipped on the slick mud as together they pulled Walt's body above the wash of the tide. Rainey's chest and throat had constricted so hard she could barely draw a breath. She knew what that feeling was; she'd had a whole summer of panic attacks after Lowell broke their college engagement.

"What are we going to do?" she said breathlessly as Delores picked seaweed from Walt's hair. "I'm so, so sorry."

"Take the car," Delores said. "Stop at the first house and call Mister Evans at the funeral home. Tell him to come get Walt."

"I'll walk," said Rainey. "I don't know how to drive a stick."

Delores, still squatting beside Walt's body, looked up at her. "Whatever," she said. "Just be quick. I know it doesn't matter now, but be quick anyway. Please."

☙

Rainey's wet feet felt as though they'd turned to frozen blocks of wood. Evergreens and pale, ghostly birches grew thick on both sides of the road, and the high, cold moon hid its face behind long, ragged clouds as sleet again began to fall. Rainey followed tire tracks she could barely see in the black void of the night.

She struggled, shivering and out of breath, to the top of the first hill. To her right, lights twinkled, impossibly far away.

She kept walking, struggling for breath, fighting the panic that had her tightly in its grip. It seemed as though hours had passed since she left the beach. She felt about collapse when she came to a set of wooden gates standing open to a house with white Christmas candles in the windows and several cars in the yard. Warmth, she thought, shaking with relief as well as cold. Warmth and a phone and someone to help. Sleet needled her face as she stumbled towards the light.

Through the windows, she could see a party in progress. A party, going on a quarter-mile from where men were dead and a woman waited on a frozen beach in the storm. People celebrating the holidays, people who didn't know how easy it was for one's whole life to be washed away, people whose money and connections insulated them from all the world's harsh realities. It seemed impossible she had once been one of them.

When she pushed the bell, a woman in a red cocktail dress opened the door, smiling as though she were expecting a last-minute guest, but then her expression changed to confusion.

"I need to use your phone," Rainey told her. "A boat went down. One man is dead on the beach and another's missing. I need to call the funeral home. Please."

A man in a plaid dinner jacket hovered behind the woman's shoulder. "So that's what all the traffic was."

"How terrible," another man said.

The woman gestured for Rainey to come inside and said, "Let me get you the phone."

More people had come into the hall now, murmuring quiet words that Rainey couldn't make out. Phone in one hand and phone book in the other, she made the call.

"Thank you," she said before turning back into the storm. In the interval before the door clicked shut, she heard someone say, "Wasn't that Rainey Sheffield? How tragic."

ଔ

They had planned their wedding long-distance, Rainey in Chestnut Hill for the winter, Justin on Spruce Island. Since there was no Quaker meeting house near East Haven, her parents offered to host a garden wedding, but Justin was uncomfortable with that idea. "My friends won't come," he told Rainey. "My friends won't cross that bridge for anything. It's an old feud, Spruce Island and East Haven. I don't mean to be selfish, but I don't want that vibe at our wedding."

She knew what he meant because she was hearing it, too. Although her parents accepted Justin, others in the family had not been shy about giving their opinions. She was marrying beneath herself by becoming the wife of a fisherman. Justin was a fortune hunter who wanted her for her money.

She spent November and December alternating between tears of frustration and tears of anger, until her mother said, "You love him and he loves you, and that is the only thing that matters. Trust your heart, Rainey. Always trust your heart."

In the hours not spent planning the wedding or working on her book, Rainey embroidered a lace-edged white satin pillow with those words: *Always trust your heart*. Each time another controversy arose, she sat on her window seat and stroked the pillow's silk stitches, listening for that inner guidance.

ଔ

The undertaker came for Walt's body, and after walking up and down the shore looking for a sign of Justin, Delores and Rainey went back to Spruce Island. "It's not a good night to be alone," Rainey said when they pulled up in front of her house. "Do you want to stay?"

For a few moments, Delores was silent. Then she said "I know it's late but I really should go see Monkey and Rita. Monkey's going to take this hard. I hope he doesn't have another heart attack."

"I should go with you," Rainey said. After all, Monkey and Rita were Justin's parents, too.

"Better you get warm and dry so you don't catch cold with a baby on the way." Delores drummed her fingers on the steering wheel. "Look, how about I go see them, then grab my PJ's and toothbrush and come back. You're right, it's not a good night to be alone."

While she waited, Rainey changed into her nightgown and robe and made a saucepan of cocoa. Maybe the hot milk would induce a night's sound sleep, the way it had when she was a child. "I made cocoa," she said when Delores let herself in, already in her pajamas and robe, clutching a pillow and a canvas bag.

"Great." Delores took a bottle of coffee brandy out of the bag, but before she poured it into the steaming mugs, she said, "What was I thinking? You can't have booze while you're preggers."

"You go ahead," Rainey told her. She ran her thumb up and down the handle of her mug. "I'm starting to feel I have to be extra careful about this baby. It might be the only—" She broke off. Delores had no children to comfort her. "Did you ever want kids?"

"Yeah, I used to think I did," Delores said. "But Walt got the mumps when he was twenty and that ended that. It wasn't meant to be."

"I wish I was like you," Rainey told her, and picked up the pillow she'd made in another lifetime. *Always trust your heart.* "I wish I was strong and wise and able to accept things the way they really are."

Delores slid along the sofa and put her arm around Rainey's shoulders. "It's a hard life when you're brought up to it. When you're not—I don't know. You got to find something inside yourself to carry you through."

How, Rainey wanted to ask, *how do you find something within yourself when you're totally hollow inside?* Instead, she nodded and sipped her cocoa and wished for the sweet oblivion of sleep.

෮

They were married outdoors on Spruce Island's Trumbull Head on the longest day of the year. Nature cooperated brilliantly, providing a spectacular sunset that gilded the ocean rose and peach and gold. Lupine in purple and pink and white rioted on either side of the high, rocky headland, and as though they'd been scripted, two bald eagles soared on the thermals high above as Rainey and Justin made their self-written vows.

The reception was held under an elegant white canopy provided by a caterer from East Haven. Despite the place cards on the round tables, Rainey was disappointed to see that the Spruce Islanders were clumped together on one side and the East Havenites and Philadelphians on the other. At the head table, she sat between Justin and Delores, her matron of honor, and wondered what it would take to bring the two sides together. Were she and her new husband to be caught in some sort of eternal no man's land, condemned to not belonging to either group?

"Why can't everyone get along?" she murmured.

Justin was joking with Walt, his best man, and didn't hear her, but Delores did. "My wedding was real small and simple," she said, "but in one way it was just like this. There were a lot of people on Spruce Island thought Walt shouldn't marry me. Some of them said I was trash and they couldn't trust my Gypsy blood. They said I'd be the ruin of Walt. Once, one of his uncles even spit at me on the street."

"*Spit* on you?" said Rainey. "People really do stuff like that?"

Delores pushed lobster thermidor around on her plate. "Oh, they do. But we survived. Everyone getting along is a dream, Rainey. Concentrate on the two of you and let the naysayers go to hell."

Later, dancing their first dance as husband and wife, Rainey thought she was going to swoon from happiness. Justin was the only man she'd ever love, and they'd grow old together, their marriage a long and happy one. That was the way it was meant to be, and the naysayers were, as Delores advised, not worth thinking about.

○₹

The morning after the sinking of the *Delores Dawn*, Rainey and Delores had just sat down with their coffee when the phone rang. Already feeling like an overstretched rubber band, Rainey picked it up and steeled herself for the news she didn't want to hear.

A candle-flame of excitement blossomed when an unfamiliar female voice said, "This is Mayfield Hospital calling." But then the voice went on, "Sheila Caswell asked me to call Rainey Faulkingham. Is that you?"

"Ye-es," Rainey said as sudden tears sprang into her eyes.

"I'm putting her on the phone," the voice said, and the next thing Rainey heard was Sheila Mac saying, "Rainey? I've got to tell you something. I can't carry it alone any longer."

"Delores is here," Rainey said. "They found Walt's body."

Sheila Mac didn't say anything. Rainey held on, waiting. "Well," Sheila Mac said at last, "I am sorry. Walt was a good man." She paused again. "Okay. Here it is. I was three months pregnant. And last night, I had a miscarriage."

Her legs suddenly too weak to hold her up for even one more second, Rainey slid down the hall wall until she was sitting on the floor, feeling as though her brain were sloshing around inside her skull like a slurry of half-frozen ice. "I'm so sorry," she said.

"It's God's will," Sheila Mac went on, her voice very flat. "And He's right. I have six kids already, and it's going to be hard enough being a single mom to them without a baby who'll never know his dad. I accept that."

No one could take the death of a husband and child so calmly. No one. Sheila Mac had to be in shock.

"Like I said," she continued, "I'm going to lose my mind if I don't tell somebody this. You're the only one I know who won't judge and won't gossip. Promise not to say a word. To anyone. Especially to Delores."

"Okay," Rainey said, although she hated the burden of other people's secrets.

"Not a word to anyone. Ever. Understand?" Sheila Mac's voice had lost its flatness and taken on a desperate edge.

"Yes. All right. You have my word."

"Leon was going to leave me," Sheila Mac said. "Can you believe that? After seventeen years of marriage and six kids, after going together since we were freshmen in high school? He said he felt like he'd never had any freedom. You know what 'freedom' means, Rainey? It means he wanted to fornicate with other women."

Rainey didn't know what to say.

Sheila Mac kept talking, leaving Rainey relieved that all she had to do was listen. "I said divorce was out of the question. And I told him I'd never have relations with him again, because how could I be sure he wasn't contaminated by some other woman? And then one night, I'm not sure how it happened, I didn't mean for it to happen, but we—it was lust, it wasn't love. That's when I got pregnant. And get this, when I told Leon, he said he'd stay with me till the baby came. Wasn't that big of him? But now God's taken our baby. To punish me for my sins."

Rainey spread the fingers of one hand over her belly. Justin's baby hadn't kicked this morning. Fear began to nibble at the edges of her mind, fear that she could be next, that she was too weak and helpless to protect the life growing inside her.

Sheila Mac said, "Are you still there?"

"Yes," Rainey answered. "Yes, right here."

"So then I started praying that God would punish him. Oh, I knew it was wrong. But I'd lie awake nights and imagine awful things happening to him. He swore before God till death us do part, and he was going to keep that vow. I didn't mean for anyone else to die, Rainey. I didn't mean for the boat to go down."

"That's not God's way," Rainey said. "I may not know the Bible like you do, but I'm sure of that. What happened was beyond anyone's control."

"God's gonna judge me for this," wailed Sheila Mac. "God's gonna send me straight to the lake of fire." Rainey pushed herself to her feet. The bees were back, buzzing loudly inside her skull, and she knew there was no way to make them stop.

◌

The search went on for two more days. Unable to concentrate on her children's book, Rainey lay on the sofa waiting for the call that never came. At least once a night, she awoke crying and drenched in sweat, shivering over some bad dream she couldn't remember, but waking to a worse one, life without Justin.

The morning of the third day, the day of Walt and Leon's funerals, the Coast Guard called off the search. The officer in charge told her they'd searched for Justin Faulkingham's body from Ross Bay in the south to Falmouth, New Brunswick, in the north, and there was nothing more they could do.

"You're just going to forget him?" Anger, frustration, and disappointment mingled in a confusing muddle. "He's out there somewhere. Don't you have to keep looking? Isn't that your job?"

No, she was told. It wasn't. Looking for survivors was one thing, but continuing to look for a body was—sorry, ma'am—an expensive exercise in futility.

❧

Days turned into weeks, but Justin's body never washed ashore. The deadline for her book arrived, and Rainey begged for an extension, too paralyzed to pick up pen or paintbrush. Delores returned to the school cafeteria, and Sheila Mac was busy with her children and her father's church, but they'd had closure in a way she hadn't. They knew where their husbands were, sleeping safely in the crypt at Sunrise Cemetery. Justin could have been smashed to pieces on a rocky ledge, or eaten by dogfish, or taken by the tide and washed up on the shores of Nova Scotia, where no one would ever be able to identify him or send him home.

Her parents offered to come to Maine, but she knew what that meant. They'd open the house on East Haven and try to get her to stay there with them. It was the last thing she wanted. Then come back to Chestnut Hill, they said in every phone call. Raise your child in a place that isn't a cultural wasteland. Sell your house and come home. We miss you. She almost did—after all, her parents had been in their forties when she was born, and they weren't going to live forever. The more time they'd have with their grandchild, the better.

But when she thought about leaving, about locking the door for the last time on the sweet little 1850s cottage she and Justin had worked so hard to restore, she couldn't do it. She couldn't leave the roses and clematis running riot over trellis and arbor, the oak tree that had cast its shade over summer picnics on the lawn, the tiled kitchen where Justin taught her to make clam pie and fish chowder, the bedroom where their child had been conceived, the nursery they'd been planning before that terrible day. It was her home, the place where she'd known true happiness. The place where she'd once believed that all her dreams were coming true.

Valentine's Day—the fifth anniversary of their engagement—came and went, and Saint Patrick's Day and the vernal equinox. Hyacinths and crocuses blooming along the front walk heralded the slow coming of spring, while the plow ridges of dirty snow rotted in the new warmth of the sun. Her book was still stalled, her brushes untouched in her studio as the extended deadline passed. She stopped going to East Haven for haircuts, instead tying her hair back into a ragged ponytail. She discovered why Spruce Island women cherished the comfort of tee-shirts and sweat pants. She spent hours compulsively cleaning the house, trying to scrub away her pain along with the non-existent dirt. *I'll get myself back together when I find out what happened to Justin,* she'd tell herself. *Or in a few weeks, when my baby comes. Then I'll get my life together. I will.*

She was scrubbing the kitchen floor one afternoon in early April when Delores stopped by. She and Rainey kept in touch, but without their husbands to link them together, Sheila Mac had severed all ties, which made Rainey feel both sad and glad. Sad that Sheila Mac was no longer part of her life, but glad not to have to be reminded of the terrible confession.

"I have something to tell you," Delores said when they were settled on the couch with their coffee. "I don't want you to hear gossip about this, and I don't want you to think I'm a terrible person. I'm not good at being alone, Rainey, and I never have been. I met a man. There, I said it. I met a man, and I like him a lot."

Rainey spun her wedding ring. "If you're happy, I'm happy for you. I'd never think you're a terrible person."

Delores picked up her coffee mug and put it down again without drinking. "We, um, got together last night for the first time. It was so different, being with someone else after sixteen years with Walt. Sheila Mac will say I'm a slut, but it felt so good. So right. I need someone in my life and in my bed. I can't help that, and I know Walt would understand."

"I see," said Rainey, although she didn't see at all.

"His name's Graydon Maddox." Delores laughed, looking like the schoolgirl she must have been half a lifetime ago. "He's so perfect for me. He lives like a Gypsy—isn't that neat? He's a long-haul trucker, our school's Trucker Buddy. Do you know what that is?"

"No," Rainey said. "I don't."

"He sends postcards to the geography classes from everywhere he goes, and he visits the school twice a semester to talk to the kids. Yesterday he came to the cafeteria looking for a cup of good coffee, not that yucky teachers' room stuff. We got to talking, and—"

The doorbell jangled. The only person who ever rang her bell these days was sitting beside her, and Rainey had a moment of panic that her parents had come and were about to find out what a sloppy mess their daughter was.

Delores said, "Do you want me to get that?"

"No. Thanks. I'm going." Rainey opened the front door to find the Spruce Island police chief standing on her porch. Her heart fluttered madly. A policeman at the door was never a good sign.

"Are you Lorraine Sheffield Faulkingham, ma'am?" The chief turned his Smokey-the-Bear hat in his hands and looked at her and then down at the floor.

"Yes," Rainey said faintly. "Yes, I am."

"Could I step inside, ma'am?"

Rainey moved back to let him enter, stumbled, and felt Delores' hands on her shoulders, steadying her.

They went into the living room. The chief waited until Rainey and Delores were seated on the sofa, and then sat stiffly in one of the matching wingback chairs. "The remains of Justin Faulkingham have been located, ma'am. They've taken him to Evans Funeral Home."

Rainey felt Delores's arm slide around her. The room faded in and out like a strobe-lit dance club, and everything got small and distant, as though she were seeing the world through the wrong end of binoculars.

"Where? How?"

"Are you sure you want to know?" Delores said.

"Where?" Rainey repeated. "How?" She had to know. No matter how terrible it was, she had to know. The chief hadn't gotten far—just to the point that someone named Dewey Mullis was walking his tree-line above the beach at Demby's Point and saw something a little farther into the woods, something that turned out to be a body—when Rainey was gripped with a pain of such white-hot intensity that she doubled up, pulling her knees against her belly and gasping for breath. Sweat beaded her forehead as the pain ground into her, and when it was over, she lay back against Delores, limp and shaky.

"Are you all right, ma'am?" the chief asked, leaning forward. "I know this is difficult."

"He froze to death," Rainey said. "So many people on the beach that night, so many people at that party where I went to use the phone, and right then, right there, my husband, my husband survived the sinking and was freezing to death in the woods."

Delores brushed Rainey's hair back from her forehead. "I'm so sorry."

The pain struck again, harder, and Rainey almost bit through her lower lip. No one had ever told her that bad news could tear a body apart. She drew a deep breath against the agony. Then she felt her bladder let go, soiling her sweatpants and spreading across the velvet sofa cushions. Embarrassed, she tried to tell them she was sorry, but Delores was saying, "Look, her water broke. We've got to get her to the hospital," and at last, Rainey understood.

CR

It was all a blur after that. An ambulance ride that made her sick to her stomach. Nurses in colorful scrubs in the hospital birthing room. Her doctor's calm voice. Delores holding her hand and telling her to breathe. At last, someone said, "Push, PUSH," and she pushed for all she was worth. They put the baby at her breast, a tiny baby with a halo of silky blonde hair.

"A girl," one of the nurses said. "A perfect little girl."

"Yes," Rainey echoed, "a perfect little girl." She felt the tears start, joy mixed with sorrow. Nothing was perfect. Her baby would never know her father, would always have that big hole in the middle of her life. Nothing could make up for that. Still, here she was, this fresh new life, opening a door to the future whether Rainey wanted it opened or not.

CR

Early the next afternoon, Monkey and Rita came to see their first and only grandchild, and so did Rainey's parents, who'd caught a flight that morning from Philadelphia. After they all left, Rainey took a nap. She was awakened by Delores, standing at the foot of the bed and tweaking Rainey's toes through the waffle blanket.

Delores pulled a chair close to the bassinet and traced the baby's cheek with her index finger. "She's a beauty. What's her name?"

"We had planned to call her Ashlyn. But I want to name her after Justin. Justine Ashlyn Ainsley Faulkingham. Do you like it?"

"I do. And how are you feeling, now that your daughter's come and you've got some closure?"

Rainey looked at Justine and then at her wedding ring and then out the window. Delores had a way of reading people, and Rainey didn't want her to see how lost she still was.

Delores leaned forward and grasped Rainey's hands. "I know you're hurting. But now you have to get your spark back. For your daughter. For Justin's daughter."

"I know." Rainey heard the quaver in her own voice and felt tears welling. "I know I need to, but I don't know how."

"No one said picking up the pieces would be easy, Rainey. It's as hard as anything we're ever asked to do."

Rainey reached out and laid her pinky across her baby's palm and watched the tiny fingers curl around it. "Here's what I can't get past. We think we have it all mapped out, and then it all gets swept away. So why make plans? Why try to accomplish anything?"

"Because that's how life works," said a voice from the doorway. Rainey looked up to see Sheila Mac standing there. "Is it okay if I come in?"

"You got something to add to this conversation, you might as well park your carcass," Delores said. "Which is a lot smaller than it used to be, I see." Sheila Mac looked trim in a pair of black capris and a pink sweater.

"Yes," she said, smiling. "Thanks for noticing. I'm so busy, I don't have time to stress-eat like I used to." She bent and looked at Justine. "Beautiful baby. Now listen to what I'm telling you, Rainey Faulkingham. You have to keep going as though it's all going to work out. Because it will, in God's good time. Faith, Rainey. You have to find your faith."

"Sheila Mac," Delores said, "I swear, you might as well take up the family business."

"Funny you should say that." Sheila Mac clasped her hands and smiled widely. "Last month, Poppa told me he'd like to retire in a couple years. I've been called to take over his pulpit. I'm going to Bible school up in New Brunswick next fall, and then I can get ordained. They're really nice people up there. They're even helping me get visas for the kids."

"Wow," Rainey said.

Delores chuckled. "You with a career. That's pretty damn amazing."

"I thought I was going to have a nervous breakdown after Leon passed," Sheila Mac went on, looking straight at Rainey. "But with the Lord's help, I overcame my troubles. Now I ask myself, What would Jesus do? And here's one thing I've been thinking about—Jesus would've made peace with Delores a long time ago."

"Sheila Mac," Delores said, "you amaze me. I didn't think you'd ever be able to pull your life together. And I can't quite believe you're admitting you might have been wrong about things."

"Some things." Sheila Mac wagged an index finger at Delores. "Not everything, but some things."

Delores nodded. "Okay. That's a start." She stood up, then bent and kissed Rainey on top of her head. "You look tired and you've got a lot to think about. I'm going to take Sheila Mac to Dunkin Donuts for coffee, and see if she can live up to her good intentions."

"Ha-ha," Sheila Mac said. "'I can do all things through Christ, who strengtheneth me.' Even be friends with you, Delores Faulkingham."

CR

The next day, Rainey's parents picked up her and Justine at the hospital. "You're welcome—more than welcome—to stay with us," her mother said as they drove down route one, and Rainey knew they wanted to pass straight through Spruce Island and keep going to East Haven. It was tempting—to be cared for again as when she was a child, to have a life that was fixed and predictable and therefore safe. But this was a decision she'd made already in the long days before Justine was born.

"No," she said. "No, I want to go home. My home. Spruce Island."

"But—" her mother started.

To Rainey's surprise, her father put his hand on her mother's wrist and said, "Let it be."

Home at last, Rainey carried Justine up to the nursery. So many details left unfinished, the nursery half-painted, the children's book stalled, Justin's service as yet unplanned.

For a while, Rainey watched her sleeping daughter, marveling again at the perfect tiny fingers, the delicate convolutions of Justine's ears. The time was past when she could indulge herself in sorrow, sorrow that would leach like corrosive into her daughter's world.

What was her heart saying? Wasn't it telling her it was time to take a first small step, to pick up her brushes and meet that final deadline before her book contract was revoked? What kind of parent would she be if she let circumstances defeat her? If she didn't trust her heart.

Sheila Mac had said that was how life worked. *And she was right,* Rainey thought. *We make our plans and we do the best we can with what we've been given. It's like getting on a plane to Paris and ending up in Jamaica—not what we expected, a different world, a different beauty, but still a trip worth taking.*

At the door of her studio, she hesitated, willing herself to enter. The last time she'd crossed that threshold, to answer Sheila Mac's doorbell, she'd been a young wife with a husband and all the hope in the world. Now she was older, it seemed many ages older, a widow with a child.

The watercolor she'd been working on that day was still taped to its backing board, the accidental streak of blue trailing across a golden beach. I'll have to start this one over, she thought, but first, on a whim, she found herself beginning to paint a wave that curled across the sand. It wasn't what she'd intended, but she decided she could use it anyway. It would be her secret, the book's hidden symbol of her new beginning.

Justine slept on and Rainey painted as the studio's clear north light took on the soft colors of a spring late afternoon. *It's good to make plans,* she thought. But in the times when life had to be lived in the turbulent wake of plans destroyed, there were only two choices— drift aimlessly, or swim as hard as you could until you reached safe harbor. *Keep swimming,* she told herself. Setting the revised painting aside, she took up a fresh sheet of watercolor paper and began to sketch her book's next illustration.

ଚଓ

SUMMER WAGES

I WAS NINETEEN THE FIRST time I punched my father. It happened ten years ago, back when I knew way more than I do now. Everything seemed clear cut and simple then, but I learned that summer that clarity in matters of the heart is only an illusion.

In March, Dad got laid off from his job at the paper mill, but I didn't find out until summer break from college. We didn't want to worry you, Cal, my sister Dori and little brother Rico said when I asked why they hadn't told me. But that was typical—even important things in our family were never discussed. My mother died when I was twelve, and after that, the glue that held us together just seemed to dissolve, and we forgot how to take care of each other.

ଙ

The sign was the first thing to catch my eye that late-May day I returned home, a Haskell Realty sign on the front lawn of our big white-painted Federal where, counting us kids, four generations of Callahans have lived. Dori and Rico weren't home from school yet. Dad was alone, sitting in front of the television when I came in. Wile E. Coyote was taking his usual lumps on the "Bugs Bunny/Roadrunner Hour," but Dad and his best old friend Jim Beam didn't seem to be enjoying it much.

I felt ready to burst with questions about the *For Sale* sign, but with Dad we always had to pick our times carefully. Even so, he frequently either ignored us or threatened us, depending on his mood. I could see right away he was drinking heavily, slugging down the bourbon with ginger ale chasers straight from the bottles.

"Hello, Dad," I said, and he glanced at me without interest before turning back to the cartoon. "Where's Captain Asa?"

"On the back porch." Dad stared at the TV, dismissing me.

I walked out back. Asa, my tri-color beagle, lay on his cedar-chip denim dog bed, chin on his paws. He looked up at me bleary-eyed, but his tail gave two excited thumps. He'd been my dog since I was three, and until I left for Bowdoin the fall before, he'd slept on my bed almost every night of his life.

Home at Christmas, I'd noticed he was slower and stiffer, but now he seemed as ancient as my grandfather in his final days. I knelt beside him and rubbed the roots of his ears. He crooned a little earsong back to me, but I was freaked out by the way he felt under my hands, so fragile and insubstantial.

I wondered if Dad had made him stay out here alone that cold, wet spring. Had he been lying there missing me, ignored except for having his dishes filled? My eyes began to smart, the end of my nose twinged, and I knew I was on the verge of bawling. My dog had gotten old and feeble and my father had turned into a drunk, and I still didn't know the worst of it.

※

Dori and Rico brushed it off when I mentioned the *For Sale* sign. The house had been on the market for two months already without so much as a nibble, they said, so why worry? It wasn't like Spruce Island was a tourist or retirement town, where real estate moved quickly.

It must have been hard for my brother and sister not to be rattled by Dad, hard as ignoring a great gruff grizzly bear lumbering around the house, but I decided to try to follow their lead. We fell back into our usual routines, Dori cooking, me washing up, Rico doing the vacuuming and dusting. We kids ate our meals at the scrubbed pine kitchen table, while Dad had his on a tray in front of the TV. Our chores finished, we usually retreated to our rooms, where Rico sketched and Dori wrote wish-fulfillment stories about Lacey MacQuinn, star lawyer, and I lay on the bed with Captain Asa and read, or wondered what was to become of us now that just about the only money coming in was Dad's unemployment, which wasn't much, and what Dori made at her summer job.

The really important matter was getting myself a decent job before the hordes of high schoolers made the competition way too intense. Dori was already waiting tables at the Chart Room, the most popular tourist-trap seafood restaurant on neighboring East Haven. She offered to get me in, but I couldn't face washing dishes all day, or bussing tables and taking my chances on being shorted on tips by a squad of teenage servers.

I tried the IGA, the stevedoring company, the ship's chandlery, both convenience stores, and the gas station. For two days I endured rejection. No one had job openings.

Finally, the only place left was the big aquaculture operation on the southwestern side of the island. The kids who'd worked down there when I was in high school had made processing salmon sound exactly like working in a slaughterhouse, and the discomfort of rubber boots and rubber aprons and rubber gloves would be hell, but the pay was good and they seemed to be always hiring.

The unsmiling woman in personnel looked over my application to work in the processing room, then said, "Turn around." I must've been slow in reacting, because she snapped, "Turn around. I want to see that ponytail." It was a good one, thick and down to the middle of my back.

"Can't use you in processing," she said, which I thought was barefaced reverse sexism because I knew at least two girls with longer hair than mine who worked there.

"You're not hiring me because of my *hair*?" I asked, but she said, "I'll hire you. But it'll be to work on the cage sites."

A vision came to me then. Sunshine on the water. A salty breeze on a humid day. Seabirds cruising overhead in the blue cloudless sky. What could be closer to heaven?

Driving home from my interview, an idea lightbulbed in my head. If I could get work at Quoddy SeaFarms, so could my father. He always liked being out of doors.

He had plenty of reasons why not. After thirty years in the heat of the paper mill, he wasn't about to work outside. He hated the water and he hated fish. And on and on, until I tuned him out. I decided then he was just a loser, but now I can see that he must have thought he no longer had a future. And he must have been scared, just plain scared, about starting all over again at fifty. Maybe giving up seems the only choice sometimes.

Later that afternoon, Rico came bicycling home with a permit that would allow him to work until he turned sixteen in August and a job as a spooner scraping out salmon innards in the wet end at Quoddy Sea.

I said, "We ought to be able to keep the house with all three of us working."

Rico gave me a chill when he answered, "Don't count on the house. Dad wants out and the money's just an excuse."

"Why?"

Rico kept his back to me as he squeezed chocolate malt syrup into a glass of Coke, but he couldn't keep the quiver out of his voice. "Dad says it's foolish to pay taxes and insurance and upkeep on an ark like this when he could get a nice new trailer on a piece of land upcountry."

I understood why he was upset. Rico bicycled everywhere, and the wilds of Dudley or Bryant's Mills were just too far away from his friends and hangouts. It wasn't fair—two more years and we'd all be gone, and then Dad could do what he pleased.

"Look," Rico said. "I know that look. Don't make waves. Next fall's going to be just him and me. I don't need any extra shit."

"What sort of extra shit?"

Rico just shook his head. That ended the conversation. Captain Asa and I went out on the back porch and sat in the sun, and if he wasn't thinking along with me, he sure did look like he was.

ഇ

For a big operation like Quoddy SeaFarms, a cage site is both vast and intricate. Wooden walkways maybe a yard wide surround huge nets full of fish, with more nets over the top to foil marauding seagulls. Two cages wide and twelve long, twenty-four cages are linked together to form a floating world bigger than a basketball court. The feeders on each site shovel over a ton of food a day to salmon and sea trout neatly separated by age and size.

The site farthest out, closest to Swift Island, was my new responsibility, mine and Stence Merrow's. He was in his late twenties, a member of that species of Downeaster that Dori had dubbed the "cowboy clammer." That's not a putdown. Stence was the salt of the earth, a good old boy in a jacked-up pickup truck who worked hard and played harder.

Stence and I had our own skiff for getting to the cage site. That first day, motoring through the slight chop off Trumbull's Head with the wind whipping my hair loose from its ponytail, I found it easy to believe that our problems could be solved and that everything was going to be fine. At six-thirty, the sky still retained the luminous clarity of an early-summer morning, and it spread across the sea until I felt like I was motoring through light itself. In a world so beautiful, how could anything be wrong?

As soon as we reached the site, I stepped onto a rocking wooden walkway that all of a sudden seemed about as wide as a rail on the train tracks. I stood with my arms outstretched, keeping my balance the way a toddler would. Stence laughed. "Everyone feels like that at first. You'll get your sea-legs."

He strolled along as nonchalantly as an ironworker on high steel. I couldn't help but envy his competence, his sure movements, and the sense that he had found his place in the world and was master of it.

"The feed barge'll be right along," he told me as he straightened up after securing the skiff. "Let's get you used to this." His way of getting me used to the undulations of the site was to walk me around it, slowly at first, and then faster and faster. Before we got going at more than a leisurely amble, my heart was pounding so loud I could feel it in my head and I was panting as though I'd just run the 440. I knew well that the water temperature of the bay would kill a man from hypothermia in less than thirty minutes. The sweet calm of the boat ride had completely evaporated, and all that kept me going was the thought that if I couldn't cope with this, I'd be no better than Dad, and Rico would be trapped upcountry.

By the time the feed barge hove into view, I'd figured out how to stay loose in the knees and hips and rock with the walkway as it bobbed on the swells. The feed barge's crane swung the first pallet of feed bags over the walkway, and I helped Stence guide it down. As we steered the second one to its resting place, I had to admire the sure economy of his movements. I think now that that day was the first time I realized there were more kinds of intelligence than the one that had made class valedictorians out of Dori and me.

I soon learned the intricacies of feeding fish, scooping moist feed for the smaller ones, shoveling dry for the larger. You could feed trout as fast as you could shovel, but the salmon required more patience—they weren't bottom feeders, so we could feed only as much as they could grab on its way down. And that was how it was with me. I was just beginning to get my legs under me on a few inches of board suspended above several fathoms of cold ocean, a whole new world of sensation and balance, and I had to go slowly, digesting each new thing.

June came in green and misty. Stence had started taking me to his house after work to lift weights with him, and even though I was tall and thin and gawky, I felt myself growing strong, efficient in my movements. During that time between my going to work and Dori graduating, I thought maybe we were going to get lucky, and summer would unspool calmly and placidly, but that was an illusion, or a wish, or maybe a prayer.

☙

Soon it was graduation day at Quoddy High. Rico and I were ecstatic when the principal announced that Dori had won the Hoover Scholarship, the richest prize, worth over ten thousand dollars a year for her four undergrad years. Wellesley, which had been in doubt, was secure. Dad was a no-show, but Mom's sisters were there, Aunt Mim and Aunt Jo, and the uncles, all of whom had driven down from Bangor. They snapped endless photos and applauded long and loud after Dori's valedictory address, which was so full of good advice anyone would've thought she lived in a wise and perfect world.

After the ceremony ended and small groups gathered around each graduate in the cedar-scented gym, both aunts remarked on Dad's absence. It was well known that the entire Callahan family thought Mom had married beneath herself, and none of them had any use for Dad.

Rico said, "Dad doesn't have much to do with us any more. He's real depressed over losing his job."

"He'd have another one by now if he had any gumption," said Aunt Mim, who had never, to the best of my recollection, had an unexpressed thought. "Of course, after that incident, maybe no one will hire him."

"What incident?" Dori and Rico asked simultaneously.

"Just be quiet, Mimsy," Uncle Abel, her husband, said, but that was a concept Aunt Mim had never understood.

She crinkled the tail of her silk scarf and then smoothed it against her ample bosom. "The incident at the paper mill, when that woman—" She got no further. Uncle Abel took her by the elbow and marched her towards the exit. We all looked at Aunt Jo, but she just shrugged and shook her head.

Uncle Maury cleared his throat. "Be best if you just ignore that." That was one bit of advice I didn't plan to take. If Dad lost his job because of something he did, I wanted to know what it was.

☙

From graduation, we moved on to a party at the home of Dori's friends, the Evans twins, Charity and Monica. Dori took me along with her and her boyfriend, Pip Kingsley.

The Evanses lived on a bluff above the ocean at Norton's Head in an ultra-modern house with a living room big enough to hold comfortably the thirty or so partiers there. I was catching up on the past year with some of my old friends when Charity Evans came up to me carrying two plastic glasses of white wine.

She held one out to me. "Mom says it's okay if we drink tonight as long as no hard stuff and everyone has a sober driver. Would you rather have a beer?"

"No, this is fine. Thanks." I knew I was grinning like an idiot while I tried and failed to think of something clever to say.

We stood there for several minutes by the glass wall at the end of the living room, watching the yellow moon that hung just above East Haven, its reflection broken by the waves.

Charity finished her wine, cleared her throat three or four times, and ran her fingers over a large, mottled leaf of some potted plant. At last she said, "Going to the prom?" and I allowed as how I probably was. A peachy blush crept up her cheeks. "I don't usually do this, but I was wondering—would you like to be my date?" I didn't even get my brain around that before she rushed on, "David and I broke up a couple of weeks ago."

"Sure," I managed to get out. "I'd like that."

"That's awesome." She reached up on tiptoe and kissed my cheek. I was too surprised to kiss her back.

It was a great party. I hoped the glow would last until the graduation ball the next night. I wanted to clear my mind of the hassles of my life, so that I could enjoy my date with Charity.

※

I woke up before six the next morning, and what I saw sent my heart and brain racing at top speed for panic land. All four of Captain Asa's feet were paddling as though he were swimming, his eyes were rolled back in his head, and long strings of foam and drool had formed on his skinned-back lips. I'd never seen an epileptic seizure, but I knew that's what it was. It was too early to call the vet, who didn't keep emergency hours, but the second he opened I planned to be on the phone.

Right then Asa started to shake, and his bowels and bladder let go all over my bed. After ten or fifteen minutes, when he came out of it and lay there panting and disoriented in his own waste, I toweled him off with the sheet and laid him on a clean blanket on the floor. I took the dirty laundry and hotfooted it down to the basement before Dad woke up. Once the washer got going, I carried Asa out on the back porch and sat with him until it was time to call Doc Thornton.

Dad was standing in the kitchen doorway when I hung up the phone. "You better not be putting long distance calls on my phone bill."

"I'm not. Asa's sick. He's got to go to the vet."

"You shouldn't have to do that alone." For just a moment he looked like my dad again, the guy who took me fishing and taught me how to grill a steak and turned me into an almost unbeatable cribbage player. "I'll go with you. We'll take the pickup."

"You sure?"

"Some things you don't want to do alone," he said, and I thanked him for that.

Dad drove up route one towards Mayfield while I held Captain Asa on my lap. I was thinking about how awful it would be without him, and at first I didn't notice that Dad had cut the wheel and turned up the Fremont Road. Then he turned again, and we were bucking down a tote road, and Dad wasn't answering my question, "Where are we going?"

He pulled into a clearing and got out. I got out, too, and set Captain Asa on the ground, where he stood blinking in the June sun. When my father grabbed the blue nylon-web leash out of my hand, I was too surprised to resist. He tied Asa to a low tree branch with less than a foot of slack.

It amazes me to this day that I was so slow to catch on. "What are you doing?" I asked, but when I saw him take the Mini-14 from the pickup's gun rack, I shouted, "No. No, you can't!"

Dad thrust the rifle at me, but I put my hands behind my back. "He's your dog. It ain't right, getting the vet to give him a shot. You should do it yourself, you think so much of him."

I was shaking so badly I could hardly speak. "Are you out of your mind? I'm not going to have him put down. I'm going to— to—whatever they can do for him."

"He's old. Sick. He don't want to live anymore. Look at him."

Asa stood with his head hanging down, as if he didn't have enough energy to look up at me. The seizure had taken a lot out of him, but I knew he'd be better tomorrow.

"You shoot my dog," I said, "and you'll be sorry." I didn't know what I meant to do, I just knew that some violence would rise up inside me and take vengeance on my father. I went to Asa and started to untie him.

"Last chance." Dad raised the rifle. I ran towards him, but he side-stepped me and took aim again. The barrel wobbled when he squeezed the trigger. There was a loud crack, and blood poured out of Captain Asa's left shoulder as his front leg went out from under him.

I was thinking, *I can still take him to the vet, they fix dogs that have been shot all the time, it'll be okay.* But before I could take even a few steps towards him, my father fired again, the bullet tearing through Asa's back. His hind legs collapsed, and I knew his spinal cord was severed. He was yowling now, trying to drag himself towards me with his one good front leg, his toenails scabbling in the dirt.

"For God's sake, Dad," I cried, but he didn't seem to hear me. He took a deep, deep breath, swelling his broad chest, and this time the bullet found its mark above the left eye-socket.

For a heartbeat I stood there in disbelief. Then I realized my father was shaking his finger in my face.

"I've tried to make a man out of you," he began, but I didn't let him finish. The blood was pounding in my head, and through a red haze I could see that finger in front of my eyes, that trigger finger. I reached out and snapped it like a dry twig, and before I even knew I was going to do it, I'd made a fist and punched him right in the face so hard I thought my high-school ring was going to be permanently embedded in my finger. He staggered backwards but didn't fall. A cut had opened on his cheekbone, and it looked like in a few hours he'd probably have a beauty of a shiner.

He took out his handkerchief with his unbroken hand and touched it to the wound. I half-expected him to whale the living tar out of me, but he didn't. "I tried to teach you a man's got to do some tough things. You should've done this yourself, but you wouldn't, so I tried to do it clean. You know I got the shakes." I hadn't known that, but I could see the tremor as he mopped his cheek.

"You could've given him one last thing," he went on. There was no way to make him stop. "You could've given him a quick, clean death. You could've done that."

He turned his back on me and walked back to the truck. I wrapped Captain Asa in his blue blanket and carried him against my chest and laid him in the bed of the pickup, then climbed in and took him in my arms again. My father looked out the rear window at me, started the truck, and drove towards home. Later I would ponder his words, would feel guilty that I had been too slow to figure out my father's intentions and spare Captain Asa his final slow suffering. But right then, all I could think was that my father had tricked me and killed my dog, and that a punch in the face and a busted finger didn't come close to evening it up.

Before I went to work that morning, I buried Captain Asa and his favorite ball and Frisbee under the quince bush my mother had planted back before Rico was born. My father and I didn't speak, and I sure didn't plan to break the silence.

∞

Everyone was gone when I got home that afternoon. I figured Rico was still working, since they often kept the processors overtime. Dori had gone to get her hair done and then to a makeup session with her gal pals. I didn't know where Dad was, and I didn't care.

I put Charity's corsage in the fridge, then showered and dressed for the prom, and still no Dad. Dori came in breathless, her blonde hair pulled back and woven with bunches of tiny white dried flowers. Here was my kid sister, looking so grown-up and glamorous it was downright intimidating. I wondered if the same magic had worked itself on Charity, and just the thought was enough to make my hands sweaty and my throat feel like I'd swallowed a grapefruit whole.

The plan was for Dori and Pip, Charity and me, and Charity's twin Monica and her boyfriend Steve to go to the Chart Room for dinner before the dance. "All the summers I've worked here," Dori said, "and this is the first time I've ever had dinner."

We scored a table right by the big window overlooking the dock and the Canadian islands across the bay. The sun was still high, one of those long June evenings as we approached the solstice. Sharp points of light reflected from the ocean and played across the girls' bare, tanned shoulders and pastel prom dresses, and Pip and Steve's white dinner jackets. Charity was easy to talk to, and I relaxed and started having a good time. Captain Asa would've wanted it that way.

That good feeling lasted through dinner, through the grand march of the graduates at the start of the prom, through the dances we danced before our nine-thirty departure to Pip's house for yet another senior party. Any senior who was still at the prom after ten o'clock was considered a hopeless loser.

Pip lived in Bryant's Mills in a 1787 colonial above the meandering river. The summer kitchen and the adjoining woodshed had been set up for the party, and beer and wine coolers were available to those who handed over their car keys to Pip's father and promised not to leave without a sober driver. Technically, the Kingsleys, like the Evanses, were breaking the law, but since it kept the graduates from ramming the camp roads while tanked up on coffee brandy, the cops were willing to let it go.

Or so everyone thought until the blue lights came flashing up the sloping, tree-lined drive. Beer bottles were hastily set down behind chairs, glasses quickly drained, and Mr. Kingsley stormed out the door to meet the cops.

He was back in a couple of minutes and he looked upset. "Cal, could you come out here?"

Charity and I were sunk into one end of an oversized sofa in the summer kitchen, where I'd discovered her lips were a perfect fit for mine. For a minute after Mr. Kingsley spoke, I just sat there, thinking that every time something started to feel right, something else came along to take it away.

The cop was a guy we all called "Snoopy," a beefy, middle-aged sheriff's deputy who lived less than a mile down the road. I knew him because he and my father used to go ice fishing together.

"How you doing, Cal?" he asked when I walked up to him.

"I'm okay."

He took off his County Sheriff's Department baseball cap and mopped at his forehead. "There's been an accident." He looked down at the paving-stone walkway, and I swear I heard him sniffle. "It's your Dad, Cal. He crashed his truck into the ledge at Dudley corner. The people at the Texaco said he didn't even slow down, just ran right through the stop sign and crossed route one and slammed head-on into the rocks. Didn't try to turn or nothing. Accelerator must've stuck. He's a good man, your father. I'm awful sorry about this."

I couldn't speak. I felt like a murderer, every mean thought I'd ever had about my father come home to roost. It didn't even occur to me then to be wondering where he was going so late at night.

"He's alive," Snoopy said, answering the question I hadn't yet asked. "But he's in awful bad shape. Broken bones, a massive head injury, internal injuries. They took him to Mayfield to stabilize him before they airlift him to Bangor. You better tell your sister and get up there."

"What about Rico? Was he home? Does he know?"

"That's a sad thing." Snoopy hitched at his utility belt. "He and Barton Dale were right behind your dad. They saw it all."

It was all evaporating now, the loveliness of the summer night, the kids in their party clothes, the festive rite of passage that was the senior prom. And Charity, lovely Charity, whose breath against my ear had carried the words, "I really like you, Cal. I like you a lot." I felt sad and lost and angry as the beautiful summer I'd dreamed about turned to smoke and faded away.

I went back inside, wishing I could just let Dori stay and enjoy this final party, but I knew I couldn't. Whatever problems Dad had caused or been a part of, he needed us with him now.

What I didn't understand was why my brother was with Barton Dale, a bit of an outlaw who was older than me and had never been Rico's friend.

☙

Rico was standing alone in the emergency room, staring out the double Plexiglas doors of the ambulance entrance, when Dori and I walked in. I could tell Dori was going to hug him, but he kept his back to us and stood passively as she put her arms around him from behind.

"What do you think happened?" I asked him.

"Suicide," Rico said. "He did it on purpose. And it's my fault."

"No," I told him. "My fault. I was the one wished he was dead after he killed my dog. I punched him and busted his finger. I made him so upset he didn't know what he was doing."

"No," Rico said. "He knew what he was doing. I was just trying to help, and I caused everything."

"That's simply not possible," Dori said.

"I called Aunt Mim. Do you know why he lost his job? He didn't get laid off because of downsizing. They'd shut the paper machine down to clear a jam or something, Aunt Mim wasn't too clear on the details, but somehow Dad . . . he keyed the machine back on and there was this woman on their crew, she'd moved over from the chip-and-saw about a month before. Anyway, she—her arm got caught and—and well, she got sucked in, and—"

Rico fell silent, and we waited. "She wasn't that old," he went on, "maybe thirty. And I guess her family was going to sue, and, well, anyway, someone said Dad was drunk, and—I didn't mean to upset him, I just wanted him to know it was okay, no matter what. It was an accident, it could've happened to anyone."

My eyes met Dori's. She looked as amazed as I felt. "You told him you heard this?" she said.

"Yeah. When I got home from work tonight. We had so many fish we didn't finish till almost ten, and I thought it'd be a good time to talk to him about it. To show him we weren't against him, you know? That no matter what he'd done, even killing Asa—no matter what kind of mistakes he'd made, no matter how far apart we were, we're still a family and we love him." That was Rico, always. Like Mom. The peacemaker.

"Go on," Dori said.

"He freaked out. I thought he'd be glad I reached out to him, but—"

Rico hadn't turned from the door during this recitation, but now he faced us and in the cold glare of the fluorescents I could see the lurid, swollen shiner, his cut lip and cheek, his broken nose.

I felt as though I was wrapped in cotton batting, fighting my way through something thick and smothering. I hugged my brother, and he hugged me back and just held on. "It won't happen again," I said. "I swear I won't let it happen again." Then I shut up, realizing that our father might very well not be around to do anything to us ever again.

In a while—I have no idea how long—the emergency room doctor came to tell us that Dad had passed on.

❧

We all slept in the next morning, and over frozen waffles and two pots of coffee we tried to figure out what we needed for funeral arrangements, and how we were going to pay for it. Finally, we called Aunt Jo for help, and then we all retreated. All morning from Rico's room I could hear the straight-ahead thunder of the old-school rock bands he loved, and from the kitchen came the rattle of bowls and pans and the slam of cupboard doors as Dori went into a baking frenzy. I knew that by the time she was done, there'd be a month's supply of bread and rolls and cinnamon buns for the freezer.

I tried to read my favorite novel, *The Three Musketeers*, but I couldn't concentrate. I lay on the bed and stared at the ceiling, and finally I fell asleep. When I woke, it was evening again, and I went out and sat on the back porch and watched the long blue twilight creep across the wide lawn where Captain Asa and I used to play Frisbee. I remembered all those lost summer days, Asa snuggled against me with his head on my thigh, neither of us with the faintest glimmer of what was to come.

I sat there until the stars came out, the Milky Way like glitter dust floating in the deep void of the sky. From the kitchen screen door wafted the yeasty, comforting aroma of baking bread. I lay back against the steps and breathed it in, wishing I could become so light and warm that I could float up among the distant stars, wishing I could forget everything that had happened since my homecoming. I was nineteen years old, and this was my last teenage summer. Looking back, I realize I had expected it to be a carefree time, the last truly carefree time as I stood on the threshold of adult responsibilities.

I gazed at the sky. All those stars and planets, so apparently motionless yet moving to their own rhythms, the great celestial harmonic unseen and unheard. I tried to make myself still, to slow and even out my breathing until I could hear the soft drum of my heart, to empty my mind of all ideas and perceptions and opinions. There were no easy choices, no clear answers. This was what it meant to be an adult, this awful responsibility, this sense of never getting it quite right no matter how hard I tried.

The house was dark and silent by the time I went back in. On the kitchen counter, loaves of bread were lined up with military precision, French baguettes, round loaves of honey graham and anadama, bags of cloverleaf rolls both white and wheat. I marveled at my sister's ability to turn tragedy into productive work, a lesson I never managed to master. All I could ever do was retreat into the abstract, my mind clamoring at top speed until it exhausted itself and I became, as Pink Floyd once put it, comfortably numb.

☙

I went back to work the day after the funeral. On the cage site, I shoveled feed like a robot, the rhythm and speed fixed in muscle memory. All my thoughts were on what was going to become of us. One thing I swore—no matter what, Dori and I were going to college come September. Rico might have to move to Bangor to live with Aunt Jo or Aunt Mim, but that had to be better than his life with Dad had been.

It took two quick gunshots to snap me back to the here-and-now. I turned towards the sound in time to see Stence lowering the shotgun. Beyond him, the torn bodies of two harbor seals bobbed on the swells.

"What are you doing?" I shouted, as the shots that took down Captain Asa played again in my brain. "What the freaking hell are you doing?"

"Orders," Stence said as he stowed the gun in our boat. "They really tear up the nets. The company's lost a lot of fish these past few days, so orders are, shoot them. They're no good for nothing anyway."

I've always enjoyed seeing the playful seals, clown-dogs of the ocean, and killing them for the sake of business seemed all wrong. I'd seen too much killing already this summer, and I just couldn't face any more.

I walked to the skiff, took out the gun and dropped it in the ocean. "I'll send someone for you," I told Stence before I started the engine.

He didn't try to stop me. When I got ashore, I walked to the office and quit. I tried to believe that Dori and Rico and I could survive this summer, damaged maybe but still functioning.

∽

As I remember all this, I'm sitting in our kitchen, and the smell of baking anadama bread fills the air. In the two years since she became Mrs. Callahan Charles Barrett, Charity has learned to bake bread that rivals Dori's. And now, on the threshold of thirty, I have found myself at last in the loss of my big dreams.

Dori, with her consistently perfect 4.0s, is in Manhattan, where, ever the idealist, she works in poverty law. Rico's an architect in Portland. I made it to Harvard Law, wrote for the *Law Review*, and got myself a nice position with a Boston firm.

It took me two years to realize that the law wasn't what I'd thought, wasn't about righting wrongs and seeing justice done. I couldn't do it and have any peace of mind—I needed something cleaner, less hair-splitting, more humane.

That's why I decided to come back to Spruce Island, to buy back the house we had to sell after Dad died. I paid less than we'd sold it for before the housing market collapsed, and I'd lived here less than a week when I ran into Charity, who teaches French and Spanish at Quoddy High. I'm teaching too, these days, history and political science at the Riverton branch of the state university that Dori and I just didn't think was good enough for us all those years ago.

I'm still trying to sort out all the lessons of that time, but I doubt I ever will. I sit here now in the thin February sunshine that streams through the wavy antique glass of the kitchen windows, Silas the beagle's chin resting on my left foot. I think of Rico, and Dad, and Captain Asa, and the terrible things we sometimes do to each other, always in the name of love.

ISLAND SECRETS

EVERY JUNE, DURING MY two-day drive from Pittsburgh to Maine, I live for this moment when at last my tires sing across the iron bridge that connects East Haven to Spruce Island.

This summer will be different. Claudia, my daughter, is staying in Philly, and Jane's husband died in February of a massive stroke. So it will be just the two of us this year, Jane and me, and Summerwind, the gallery we've run for eighteen years, and days spent painting in the white crystalline light of the sea. Time on the island flows in a slow stream; it unfurls smooth and straight as freshly-ironed hair ribbons, no knots, no twists, no creases. Or so it always has, and I have no reason to think that anything, change or absence, will interrupt our summer serenity.

The academy where she teaches in White Plains let out at the end of May, so Jane arrived first this summer; I had to stay at Carnegie-Mellon to teach a summer course through June. There in the moist river-swelter of Pittsburgh, I thought about Jane, all alone in that big old summer cottage through early summer's long blue nights and fog-bound dawns, those hours when memories crowd in and loneliness flourishes.

As I come off the bridge, I look longingly down Shore Road, which leads to my house on the island's wild and windy seaward side. A lingering herbal bath, a snifter of cognac, an applewood fire tempt my road-weary body, but my mind and heart are focused on Jane now. I've never had a long-term relationship with any man, so I'm puzzled by what her loss feels like. And I'm not terribly fond of change, my own or anyone else's, so I hope that she and I can be as we always have been, best friends, confidantes, close as sisters.

I drive down Leavitt Avenue, expecting to see Jane sitting on the verandah sipping a tall gin and tonic and talking to neighbors out on their twilight strolls, as she and Fred used to do on summer evenings. But when I park at the curb, I notice that the ship's lamp above the front door throws its yellow glow on empty wicker chairs.

The front door's locked—something no one does on East Haven. It's when I step off the porch that I notice there are two vehicles in the driveway, and I stop with one foot on the bottom step and one on the brick walk and gawk at an old poptop microbus with Pennsylvania plates. For one long, confusing moment I almost convince myself that my baby Claudia's here, but she drives an old Honda Civic and has this summer's dream internship at the Philadelphia Museum of Art.

Of course Jane knows other people from Pennsylvania, I tell myself. No doubt they and she are on a twilight walk of their own. After all, she isn't expecting me until tomorrow—I'd planned to spend a night with friends in Bennington, but once I reached Vermont I was too eager to complete the journey to Maine.

I swing past our gallery on Bayview Street, not expecting Jane to be there, and she isn't. For the second time this evening, though, I stand slack-jawed as I try to comprehend what I'm seeing. A huge framed oil of what looks like the beach view from my own back porch stands on an easel, and the sheer scale of it dominates the landscape of the gallery's left window. I'd know Jane's pretty pictures anywhere, and her audacity in upstaging the artists we earn money representing leaves me breathless.

Nothing to hinder me now from having that bath, that drink. I continue around the island to my summer home, an old Cape that was once the centerpiece of a two-hundred-year-old saltwater farm. Tim and Marianne, year-round islanders who live in what had been the hired man's house nearby, have already opened my house for me. Split wood and kindling are laid in the sitting room fireplace, and in my bedroom a pitcher filled with white and purple lupine graces the stand beside my four-poster bed. The linen sheets smell of lavender and pure sea air.

I call the number of the college friend Claudia's staying with this summer so that they'll know I've arrived safely, but there's no answer. Then I light a copper tray of candles and pour a cognac and sink into a soothing rosemary bath.

As I soak, I think about Jane. Loneliness has led her to seek being noticed by putting that huge painting in the window, so I'll be gentle with her when I tell her to take it out, and give her lots of extra attention, and everything will be fine this summer.

☙

The next morning, I boil water for tea on the hotplate in the small framing room at the back of our gallery. Then, mug in hand, I wander around, studying each painting, flipping slowly through the matted prints, running my fingers over the few pieces of sculpture. It appears Jane's taken on six new artists without my input, breaking a rule we made when we started Summerwind, to show only artists we agree on. I don't recognize any of these new painters, and I'm not impressed with their picture postcard landscapes, scenes for tourists who want just a pretty Maine scene for their walls. Jane's always been a sucker for the romantic and the sentimental, and I've always expected big ideas or significant themes or technical brilliance. Our combination of tastes is probably what's made Summerwind so successful for all these years.

When I go into the back room to pour another mug of tea, I notice a portfolio propped against the workbench. Another artist wanting to place work, I assume, as I carry it to the window and look inside. A dozen or so unsigned charcoal drawings of nude males demonstrate a fine eye for composition and a bold hand. The lines of the bodies flow confidently and the shading is startlingly dimensional. In one drawing, a fair-haired young Adonis stands in front of a long cheval mirror, while in his reflection his penis has started to spring to life as though aroused by his own perfect form. In another drawing, a young man sits on a caned chair. His head's bent forward, only his forehead and the tip of his nose visible between curtains of dark hair, as he strokes his erect penis. I think of Aubrey Beardsley drawing with the detailed precision of Andrew Wyeth in a seamless and fascinating blend of art and pornography. If we show this artist, Summerwind will be the talk of East Haven, and probably the coast.

Jane likely found these works shocking, but maybe I can convince her to take a chance and represent them. There's no clue to the artist's identity, so I hope Jane will be willing to get in touch.

ଔ

I'm at the back window, watching four people in a sleek, sassy speedboat leave the inner basin way too fast, setting the entire tethered fleet to bouncing, when the three brass temple bells above the front door jingle. Two women come in, the blonde one tall and slim in khakis, a white tee-shirt, and a linen vest, the other shorter, with shoulder-length hair a deep blue-black that perfectly matches the darkest shade in her long batik skirt.

Before I can say, "Good morning, ladies," I have to grab the door-frame to steady myself. For a long moment, I'm absolutely convinced that I've been transported to a parallel universe—how else to explain the woman coming towards me, a doppelganger of someone I know and love now disguised beyond casual recognition?

This is not my friend Jane, who's worn a neat ash-brown bob in one variation or another for over twenty years. The Jane I know thinks that even frosting or streaking her mousy hair would be egregiously fake. This Jane looks as though she's had a close encounter with a bottle of India ink. Her upscale suburban matron look, tidy polo shirts, chinos, and rope-soled espadrilles, is galaxies away from this hippie skirt, tank top, and chunky sandals.

"Emma?" she squeaks, and I say, incredulously, "Jane?" Then we both begin talking at once.

"I wasn't expecting you—"

"You look so—"

"One at a time, you two," says the young woman who's remained standing under the bells at the front door, and my knees almost buckle as I hear that familiar voice.

What has happened to my baby? Gone since I saw her at spring break are the flowing blonde ringlets she's worn since childhood, shorn into a close cap that exposes her delicate lobeless ears and the tender nape of her neck. I know I'm staring in disbelief, speechless, the questions crowding my mouth but unable to make it past my lips. *Why such a severe change? Why here instead of Philly? Why didn't you let me know?*

Claudia comes close and hugs me, a little gingerly, I think. Her face is very pink as she says, "Mummy, I had such a change in plans. I thought I'd surprise you, but I guess it's the other way around."

"Oh, it's a surprise all right," I say. "I thought the internship was your dream job."

Claudia wrinkles her nose, making her look for a moment like my little girl. "It wasn't what I expected, Mummy. I didn't realize it would be so boring."

I shouldn't be this happy over her retreat from independence, but I am. Summer has become normal again, the three of us together as we always have been.

Jane, as always, fills every pause with chatter. "Have you had time to look around, Emma? Aren't the new artists *fabulous*? Such pretty scenes. And I've done *so much* work since—since Fred—um, his, you know. I've *totally* rediscovered painting, I've just improved in *leaps, everyone* says so. Isn't that right, Claudia?"

"She's been working like a demon," Claudia agrees breezily, but my baby doesn't fool me for an instant. She recognizes calendar art just as easily as I do.

"So what do you think, Emma?" Jane persists, but I'm rescued from telling her what I think by the day's first customers. We fall back into our old routines, Claudia at the cash drawer and Jane and I working the floor. What we sell that morning is a mixture of works by Jane's new artists and the ones we've handled for years, and I think, *Maybe Jane's onto something here after all.* Soon a woman comes in and must, absolutely must, have that big painting in the window. I can tell Jane's thrilled as the woman gushes about how wonderful the painting is, and I can't stop grinning as I watch summer's first problem disappear out the door into the back seat of a red Cadillac.

Lunchtime comes, and Claudia walks two doors down for takeout pita sandwiches from Mario's Deli.

I go in the back room to lay out plates and glasses and napkins while Jane finishes a sale. The portfolio of nudes is gone—Jane's probably hidden it so it won't offend Claudia's delicate sensibilities. I have to smile at that. Claudia was more sophisticated at fifteen than Jane will ever be. But not too sophisticated, I hope. I dread even the thought of her falling in love for the first time when I reflect on how she came into my life. I hope she never finds herself as I did then, pregnant and alone.

ଔ

I'm rinsing salad greens when I hear the front screen door snap closed. Claudia. All day I've been looking forward to a good session of girl talk on the back porch while evening bleeds indigo into the washed-out lavender of the eastern sky. In the two hours since I left the gallery, I've repapered her bureau drawers and put a bouquet of daisies in a Sandwich-glass vase on her nightstand and prepared *salade Niçoise* with her favorite Italian tuna in olive oil, everything just the way she likes it. It's an unexpected gift, my daughter spending another season here. I want every day of what will probably be our last full summer together to be absolutely perfect.

"Where's your luggage?" I ask. The flabby leather backpack she's got slung over one shoulder is certainly not the only thing Claudia brought from Philly. She gestures towards the driveway.

"In the bus. Everything I need, everywhere I go."

We stand there in the hall, looking at each other wordlessly. My first thought is, *I hope it's not the poptop's bed that she needs*, but I'm projecting again, I know it. I push that thought away, and realize that what I'm seeing here in front of me is the woman my little girl's about to become. It seems like yesterday that Claudia left home for the first time, my baby in curls and a flowered sundress going off to Philadelphia alone. At spring break, I had no clue that she was going to burst out of her familiar cocoon. Now I have so many questions, but I'm determined to keep things light, to let her tell me what's going on in her own way and her own time.

I can't help prodding things along a little, though. "Looks like you and Jane won the makeover lottery."

"It was time to grow up." Claudia ruffles her cropped hair. "I knew you'd hate seeing my little-girl curls go, Mummy, but it's such a relief not to be all flowery and feminine. I just feel so modern now."

"Well, it suits you. You look good." She does, too, but she's someone else now, someone new, and it's going to take me a while to adjust.

"It was getting out of Pittsburgh, going somewhere where no one knew me. I could reinvent myself, be what I wanted to."

"And Jane?"

Just for a moment, it's as though a shade's come down. "Jane will have to speak for her own self."

We eat dinner on the back porch, the hearty salad and a crusty baguette of French sourdough from the local hearth bakery and a bottle of Pinot Noir. Claudia tells me anecdotes about spring semester in Philly, about how the job she had such hopes for turned out to be dry-as-dust cataloguing, but says nothing about her three weeks with Jane this summer. By the time we both sink back in our Adirondack chairs with the last of the wine, I'm wondering about this uncharacteristic reticence. I decide to try a new angle.

"Were you in on the new artist selections?"

"I told her you wouldn't like them, if that's what you mean." Claudia cups her chin in one hand. "Jane's whole life's changed, you know? So maybe it's best to let her have her way a little."

"I guess," I say. When, how, did my daughter grow so wise, so compassionate? I know I shouldn't feel so left-out, but I do. Damn that course that kept me in Pittsburgh.

Silence grows between my daughter and me as dusk creeps in half-steps across the blue lawn. Heron heading home to their nesting grounds sail in silhouette across the horizon where the sea meets the sky, and off Cartwright Point the bell buoy is tolling. I don't want to feel excluded, or angry, or any of those other negatives that suck the life out of the place and season I love best, so I tell myself, *Stop fretting. Your daughter's here, your gallery sells something for everyone now. It's okay, it's all okay.*

And for about twenty minutes, as we sit in comfortable silence and listen to the whispering tumult of the tide washing against the shingle beach, it is okay.

Then I say, "We should carry your luggage in before it gets much later." I know Claudia won't go to bed until her room is perfectly organized. She's been that way since she was a child, and right now I feel so relaxed and lazy that I know the carry-in will be a chore if we wait any longer.

"Oh, that's okay. I have everything I need tonight right in my backpack." She looks at me, and even in the subdued light of the citronella candles on the white iron stand between us, I can see her cheeks are as pink as the beach roses that cling the slope above the shore.

"I don't know how to tell you this, Mummy, so I'll just say it. Jane's asked me to stay on. She gets real depressed sometimes, and I think she's scared in that big old house all alone. She's always hearing noises and worrying about prowlers. I'm sorry, Mummy. I didn't know what else to do."

"I understand," I say, and I do. But part of me feels as though Jane has stolen my daughter, and I'm annoyed at how needy my best friend's become.

A little north of east, moonrise spreads its orange glow across the sea. I look at my daughter's upturned face, and realize that so many things about this summer have become as unknowable as the moon she gazes at.

❧

The next day, Jane, as I expected, goes vague when I ask about the nudes. An artist left them, she can't remember who, but it was only for her professional opinion on them, not for showing. I manage not to say sharp things about professional opinions from high-school art teachers, but I do feel stonewalled.

"So tell me about this new look," I say while we're eating chicken Caesar salads from Mario's Deli. Claudia's taken off for the afternoon with Barbara Boudry, a year-round islander and a summer friend since they were twelve. The gallery's empty right now and it seems like a good time to have summer's first real talk with Jane. "I can't believe you colored your hair, after all the hard times you've given me about staying as blonde as I was when I was young. But I love your new clothes."

Jane shrugs and looks out the window for a long moment. She runs one French-manicured thumb and index finger down a lock of hair. "I . . . I feel like my *whole life's* changed. Like without Fred, I've turned into somebody else. And—and first I just kind of *forgot* to get my hair trimmed, and then I got a couple of compliments on it, and . . . and then *Claudia* came and, well, you have to agree it *suits* her, and . . . " She shifts in her chair and shrugs again.

"It does suit Claudia," I say. "This suits you, too. You look good. You really do."

She focuses her gaze on the tiled floor, and her glossy hair tumbles forward so that I can't see her face. "Thanks." She's quiet for a few heartbeats before she adds, "And I've decided—I'm not going along any more."

Not going along with what? "I don't know what you mean."

She looks up at me, her face honestly puzzled. "Neither do I," she says. "Neither do I."

☙

The days drift by, but it's not our usual summer, as placid as the tide pools on the shore below my house. Like the restless green waters of the Bay of Fundy, Claudia or Jane now surges close to me and our former unguarded intimacy, now drifts away again, but there is never a day when all three of us are perfectly in sync, the way we used to be.

I tell myself that of course being widowed is a long adjustment, and of course I can share my daughter with my best friend, even though turned-down dinner invitations make it plain that Jane doesn't need me. I tell myself it's only natural for Claudia to spend free time with her friends instead of her mother as she begins to establish her adult life. I tell myself that after my busy life in Pittsburgh, a solitary summer is just fine. I don't believe a word of any of this, but I keep reminding myself all the same.

By the time high summer comes to East Haven, I've settled into my new routine. I work on my oils, and garden, and walk on the beach between the cliffs and the white-capped sea. I still feel as though Claudia and Jane have secrets I'm not privy to, but I can't even imagine what they might be.

☙

Jane's out on some mysterious errand the afternoon a young man in his mid-to-late twenties comes into the gallery carrying a manila envelope. He has one of those faces that catches the eye and keeps it focused, some play of light along a perfectly-angled jaw, some trick of perspective that makes it seem an endless distance to the back of his eyes. It's hard to draw and even harder to describe. I don't know why, but what crosses my mind is what a handsome couple he and Claudia would make. But there's something about him, some bad-boy hint of danger in the lift of his eyebrow and the set of his shoulders, that makes me think twice. What I hope for for Claudia is someone steady and kind.

"I'm looking for Jane Thomas," he says.

"She'll be back in an hour or so, if you'd like to come back. Or perhaps I could assist you?"

"Alex Marshall." His handshake is warm and firm and held just a few heartbeats too long.

"Emma." I feel breathless, and just a little embarrassed for such a reaction. "Emma Williams."

"If you'd give her this." He proffers the envelope. "I wasn't sure which paintings she might be interested in, so I took photos of all of them."

Oh, Jane, I think. *When were you going to tell me about this?*

"I'll see that she gets them." I'm careful to keep my voice casual, because there's no need for a stranger to know that all is not perfect here at Summerwind. It was one thing for Jane to acquire works when I wasn't here, but this is a slap in my face, nothing less.

I watch him cross Bayview Street with an athletic, balls-of-the-feet stride and drive away in a battered old Land Rover before I stick the "Back in 15 Minutes" sign in the door glass. Then I go into the back room and lift the flap on the unsealed envelope. Inside it are twelve plastic sleeves, each holding a photo of a painting.

I move to a window to catch the afternoon light. The first photo makes me catch my breath—it's "Fog and Lighthouse," a watercolor of the sparkplug lighthouse in the Narrows. The artist, Haskell Whitney, is a New York watercolorist who was affiliated with East Haven's art school in the decades between the World Wars. My heart's fluttering by the time I examine the last photo. Truly, this is a find. Whitney, a stylistic heir of Winslow Homer, is just now on the cusp of a revival.

I have to hand it to Jane—she finally got one right. But why didn't she tell me about this deal that hasn't yet gone down?

When she returns, I hand her the envelope and say, "Alex Marshall left this for you." Then I go in the back room and put the kettle on.

It's not five minutes until she comes in. "You *looked* at these, didn't you?" She's annoyed, and that annoys me.

I keep my cool, though, as I stir honey into my tea. "I didn't see your name on the envelope. What did you expect me to do? Just let you keep on making the decisions without even consulting me?" There. I've said it.

"That envelope could've been something *personal*. Papers or—something."

"Nonsense. He told me it was photos, and I knew you wouldn't be buying paintings for yourself. You've done enough on your own this summer. From now on, it's back to agreeing before we do anything."

Jane hunches her shoulders, and stares out the window at the sail-dotted channel. At last she says, "I was *all alone* here. Of *all* the summers for you not to be here for me, *this* was the *worst*. I had to do *something*, or go out of my mind. I had to feel like—like—like I *mattered*. Oh, *why* didn't you just tell them you couldn't stay past spring semester? And then I did that *beautiful* painting from your porch, and I was so *proud* of it, and it looked *so* nice in the window, and—and—" She sips lemon tea, then slams her favorite Monet mug down with what I'm sure is enough force to shatter it, but doesn't. Tea sloshes across the round oak table. "You *hated* it, didn't you? You couldn't *wait* to get it out of here."

I run every one of my twenty-two sterling bangles up my arm one by one, then slide them each back down again. "I thought the point was to sell. What are we doing here, otherwise?"

"I . . . I just wanted it on *display*."

"So you should've told me. But it didn't belong in the window if it wasn't for sale."

"No, I don't mean it wasn't for sale, I just . . . "

She looks like she's on the edge of tears, and I'm suddenly angry, and I'm not sure exactly why. The paintings, the theft of my daughter, the incredible sucking neediness of Jane without Fred, the way I've been relegated to the periphery of our lives this summer—it all combines into a supernova of white heat, and I hear myself saying, "Just wanted to hang it here and show it off, as if your work is on a par with—with Haskell Whitney, for example."

Now she's crying, big deep air-gulping sobs, and now she's throwing the Monet mug in the sink so hard it does fly into a thousand pieces. And now she's running out the front door, and I have a moment's panic that she's going to run straight into the side of Merritt Blakeley's BMW, but he swerves wide and Jane stands there, boohooing with her face in her hands as if there's no tomorrow. I think what a spectacle she's making of herself here on busy Bayview Street, but as I go out the door to lead her back she dashes into her car and drives away.

I wait ten minutes before I call her house, but she doesn't answer. Then a young couple in backpacks and tie-dyed tee-shirts comes in, and more customers follow, and when the gallery's empty again I'm surprised that almost two hours have flown by.

I'm in the back room washing the tea things when the phone rings. Alex Marshall. "I gave Jane the photos," I tell him. "But she's left for the day. Perhaps you can reach her at home."

He takes down her number. "I wanted to invite the two of you over to see the Whitneys. Say, seven o'clock?" I get directions to his house, and he tells me he's calling Jane as soon as we hang up.

I'm not thrilled about the way this is going, but I do want to land those Whitneys. Maybe it will be better if Jane and I next meet on neutral ground with a third party present.

⋄

Jane doesn't call, and I don't either. I assume that Alex Marshall has reached her, and at six-thirty I tuck a red silk shirt into my jeans and slip my feet into my best pair of sandals. My grandfather, as well-dressed a man as I've ever seen, always said you could tell a lot about people by the quality of their shoes, and I'm thinking about Alex Marshall in the gallery this afternoon, impeccable in pressed khakis and Mephisto walking shoes. I want to look good, and I don't know why.

The Marshall family's summer home, a much gabled, porched, and turreted Queen Anne, is only a block from Jane's. At the north end of the house, a flagstone walk passes through a shade garden gone wild, huge sprays of ferns, hosta in every variety of leaf, sweet and creamy lilies-of-the-valley. Grosbeaks twittering in a weathered concrete birdbath take flight at the sound of my footsteps.

Although it's been an age since I've picked up my watercolor brushes, I'm seized with a sudden urge to paint in that fluid medium again, something soft-edged and impressionistic, deep mysterious foliage and the bright jewels of birds.

Barefoot, wearing only an unbuttoned madras shirt and baggy khaki shorts slung low on his narrow hips, Alex himself answers the oak-and-stained-glass door. His wavy hair's wet, and a few water droplets glisten in it. For a moment, I wish I were twenty-five years old again myself.

"Welcome, Emma," he says as we start down a hall papered in sage-green damask and hung on both sides with double rows of what have to be Haskell Whitney watercolors, mounted in his signature style, natural linen mat and driftwood-grey frame. Alex leads me into the library, where the golden-oak bookcases are half-filled with well-read books and half with a variety of old and new *objets d'art*. Celadon jardinières of blooming tuberous begonias flank the black marble fireplace.

We start to speak at the same instant. I let him go first.

"I never did reach Jane." His left eyebrow lifts. "Probably out on a date," he says, and before those words even penetrate my brain, he goes on, "No reason you and I can't finalize this deal anyway."

Jane, out on a date? I'm aware that I'm staring at him slack jawed with some idiotic dumbfounded expression on my face, but I just can't manage to pick my chin up enough to close my mouth. He's tactful enough not to let on that he notices.

"Would you like a glass of wine before we negotiate? I uncorked a very nice Merlot." I accept the faceted crystal glass he fills, and we raise our glasses. "To art and commerce," he says. "May they share a long and happy relationship. And to summer friends—may we become such."

In front of the fireplace, we touch glasses, and I can't help myself. I have to ask, even though I shouldn't involve a stranger. "What do you mean, Jane's probably out on a date?"

He looks directly into my eyes and does not look away. "Your best friend and partner, I assumed you knew. About her and my uncle."

"Your uncle?" *Who's his uncle? Do I know him? Where did Jane meet him? And why hasn't she told me?* But I don't ask Alex any of this. I just stare back at him.

"It used to be a few-times-a-summer thing, but then this year, since her husband died—Are you okay? You look like you're going to faint." He takes my arm and guides me to the sofa, and I sit down.

"I had no idea," I say, but I can't hear myself above the thunder of blood in my temples. I concentrate on breathing evenly. One thought pierces my brain like a shard of crystal. *Does Claudia know? If she does, why didn't she tell me?*

"He's quite the rogue." Alex refills our glasses, then sits in a chair opposite me. "My grandparents put him on remittance, as they called it. They gave him a share of Mulgrave Island—" He gestures towards the eastern end of East Haven. "—and after that he wasn't allowed on Marshall property here or in New York or in Florida. Ever."

I knew Mulgrave, a small island off towards Canada with three or four summer houses on it, all Marshall holdings, apparently. "Where'd they meet, your uncle and Jane?"

"Some committee about the Blake's Island Light."

I remember those *Save the Lighthouse* meetings. That must've been four or five years ago. Jane has been having a summer affair for all this time, and I never knew. It's hard to believe, but for some reason I don't doubt what Alex has told me.

We look at each other across the polished oak floor. I have to come back to earth from this news of Jane and from the way Alex Marshall's frank gaze is making me feel. "You have a lot of Whitneys. Tell me why you're selling."

"He's my grandfather. My mother's father. And in his will he left it that four paintings would be released from his Private Trust every year. To keep his name out there, you see. He was a genius at creating demand."

"Seems to be working. Two major retrospectives this year."

Alex looks down at the floor for a moment, the palm of one hand rubbing his bare chest just at the breastbone. "I really miss him," he says, but I can't say anything comforting. I'm concentrating on not noticing his perfect skin, his smooth chest and the narrow trail of dark hair that begins just below his navel and disappears behind the waistband of his low-slung, baggy shorts.

I know Whitney died about ten years before, well into his nineties, and I know he painted until the end. That means that since he died, probably forty paintings have been added to his available body of work. Despite our being one of only two galleries on East Haven, none of these paintings have come our way—nor can I recall seeing any at the Purple Door Gallery, either.

"Why Summerwind?" I ask.

"Uncle Sean told Jane about them, about how his brother—my dad—had married into the family and there were these paintings, and she called me. Mother and I figured maybe it was time to do something local."

He fills our glasses for the third time, and we carry them as we stroll the upstairs and downstairs halls and survey the paintings. From the twelve possibles, I choose four—three seascapes, two of them of local lighthouses, and a landscape of a view of the mainland. Then I spy a still life, terra cotta tubs of coral geraniums blooming in shafts of sunlight that strike through a dark-green wooden lattice.

"I didn't know Haskell Whitney did still-lifes," I say. What I'm thinking is, *I could buy this if it isn't part of the gallery deal.*

Alex says, "He did them for my grandmother. A series of them. This one's actually from the back porch here."

I step close to examine the work in detail. "I'd love to have this one for my personal collection. If you ever decide to sell it, please give me first refusal."

Alex looks at me, at the painting, at me again. He tugs his left earlobe. "I might be persuaded. Let's see how things go."

We return to the library and talk prices, outright sale versus contingency. By the time we're close to agreement, the Merlot is gone, and I feel as exhausted as if I'd played three sets of tennis. I've held serve, though.

Alex reaches across the library table and circles my wrist with long, tanned fingers. The heel of his hand rests on the back of mine. I sit very still. "You are one tough negotiator." He winks at me. "I should've stuck with Jane—I could've had my way with her."

I know he means in bargaining, but his words make me think of Jane's affair, and I wonder again why she hasn't trusted me with this knowledge. It isn't as if I was a fan of Fred's—I tolerated him, but that was all. I can't dwell on Jane now, though, when this deal's just about closed.

"You're a sharp bargainer yourself." I stare at Alex's hand.

Before he takes it away, he says, "Your pulse is racing. You like the hunt, don't you?"

"I like that still-life. I can't wait to find out if you're going to sell it to me."

"I'll think about it tonight. When I deliver these tomorrow, you'll know."

He releases my wrist. The evening air strikes my skin with a little chill.

I drive home with the windows down. The sharp smell of salt and seaweed is strong on the easy breeze. I feel as though I'm on fire, and I can't believe a guy who's years younger than I am can get me this bothered.

At home, I sit on the back porch. The taffeta backwash of the ebbing tide is a soothing sound, and from a nearby tree or my own rooftop the lament of a mourning dove bubbles softly through the quiet night. I think about Jane, and realize she's almost as far from me now as the icy shimmer of the stars. But mostly I think about Alex Marshall, the next-generation version of those beautiful, long-haired boys of the Jersey shore of my youth, one of whom—but which one?—was Claudia's father.

○₹

At noontime the next day, I'm still psyching myself up to talk to Jane about the Whitneys when Alex Marshall comes in carrying a stack of paintings wrapped in brown paper.

"What's *this*?" Jane says.

Alex sets the stack on the table where we keep the cash drawer, then lifts off the top package and hands it to me. "Here's your geraniums." He winks, and I want to shout, *Yay!* but I don't because of Jane. He looks at her and says, "Couldn't reach you last night, so Emma and I went ahead."

"You did this *without* me? Alex, this was *my* deal."

"I thought it was Summerwind's deal. And I'll tell you, I could've done better with you, because Emma's one tough negotiator. But it all came out okay in the end."

"And you sold her *another* painting? I thought it was four a year."

Alex smiles his heartbreaker smile. "This one was from private stock, not the Trust." He shakes hands with me, then sticks out his hand to Jane, who glares at it. "A pleasure doing business with you ladies."

"How *could* you?" Jane says after the door clicks shut. "How could you *interfere*?"

Her words make my head feel like a balloon that's about to burst, but I manage to keep my voice level anyway. "Summerwind's my business, too. I don't think I'm interfering."

"Well," she says, "I *disagree*." It infuriates me that she refuses to recognize my place in all this. I feel myself losing my composure.

"Look, Alex tried to call you, and I assumed he'd reached you until I actually got to his house and found out about Uncle Sean." I could bite my tongue off, because that isn't something I want to put into play, not now.

Jane pales to the color of gesso. "Alex told you?"

"Well, yes. I had no idea you and Fred weren't—"

Jane starts sobbing. She dabs at her eyes with her knuckles, and between sobs and hiccups she says, "I *never* loved Fred. But *you* had *Claudia* about the time I met him, and I was *all alone* and he kept coming around. I just can't *bear* to be alone."

"Why didn't you tell me?"

"I *knew* you wouldn't approve, not when Fred was alive, and not now, either. You *always* liked Fred, didn't you? Admit it. You *wanted* him."

"Never," I say. "Never."

Jane wipes tears, then narrows her eyes, and I know things are about to turn really ugly. "Oh, come on. Of course you wanted Fred. You were *such* a *whore* back then. You would've gone for *anyone*."

I clench my fists, willing myself not to slap her. I have to get out of here. Claudia's probably at home right now, sunbathing on our back lawn, her habit on sunny days off. I need to find out if she was in on Jane's secret, and why she let me find this out from a total stranger. I grab my purse, and out the door I go.

Claudia's bus sits in my driveway—good. I'm heading down the hall when through the screened back door I hear the droning, dreamy music she favors. She must have my old boom box out there.

I stop with my hand on the door latch and stare, even though I know I should turn away.

Barbara, a small, dark girl, lies with my daughter on a cabbage rose comforter on the sunny lawn. Both are topless, and they're sharing a kiss as lingering and passionate as any I shared with those long-lost summer boys of my youth.

The voyeur scene has never been for me, but here I stand, caught in a web of disbelief and curiosity, no more able to stop staring than I am to soar like the herring gulls wheeling overhead. Claudia and Barbara push down each other's bikini bottoms, and I summon every bit of will and turn my eyes away.

I can't stay home, and I can't return to Summerwind. My life is a shambles, and I have nowhere to go, no one to confide in. It seems like a perfect afternoon to get smashingly drunk.

Whatever I wanted to talk to Claudia about has evaporated now. She's gone beyond me, far, far beyond my experiences and expectations. I think about her plan at the end of July to go on the road with Barbara. This is not just two friends sharing an adventure. This is love.

The Quarterdeck seems the best choice of our local pubs—not a place where the summer colony gathers, but a quiet spot frequented by tourists and day-trippers. I take a window table overlooking the marina, and order a Tanqueray and tonic. It goes down easy, its crisp cold a pleasant bite, so I order another.

§

I've just started on that second drink when I hear a voice say, "May I join you, Miss Emma Williams?" I look up to see Alex Marshall standing there, in his hand a straight-up martini with a twist. I do hate to drink alone, so I tell him that certainly he may join me.

He does, and I realize that without the Whitney paintings as common ground, I have nothing to say to him.

"This doesn't seem to be your kind of place," he says.

"Nor yours."

"I saw your car outside, so I decided to check it out."

"I've never been here before either," I tell him, and it's all I can do to keep from spilling it all, Jane, Claudia, everything. "I needed a drink. It's been a stressful day."

He nods, but doesn't say anything. We begin to chat about inconsequential things, and when the waitress comes he orders me a third drink.

I really should go home. Claudia and Barbara have probably gone back to Jane's, since my sunny backyard is apparently the only thing that draws my daughter to my side of the island. I really don't want Claudia to see me in this state of mind. What I need is a long soak and a good night's sleep.

"You think you should drive?" he says. He walks me to his Land Rover instead. "Your car will be okay here—or are you one of those people who worry about gossip?"

I shake my head and wave one arm in a sweeping gesture. "Let the rumors begin." Alex boosts me up into the passenger seat, and with the part of my brain that's still functioning normally, I think about how unusual and pleasant it is to be taken care of.

We travel up Bayview Street. The afternoon sun strobes between downtown's three-story buildings and through the leafy elms and makes me feel dizzy and disoriented. I surprise myself by suddenly bursting into tears.

"It's such a mess," I say as I blot my cheeks with the palms of my hands.

Alex drums his fingers on the steering wheel as we sit at the stop sign at the intersection where the south end of Bayview Street splits to Shore Road to the east and the road to the mainland to the west.

"I'm a good listener, if you want to talk," he says. "In fact, how about having dinner with me? I know this place called Stone Shore Farm, an hour down the coast, very private, very good. You can tell me all your troubles on the way, if it'll help."

What will people think, a distraught forty-year-old woman out with a man obviously still in his twenties? But since when have I cared what people think? I have no one else this summer, so why not share my misery with the only person who'll even listen?

"Emma?" Alex says, and I realize that we're still sitting at the stop sign.

"It sounds lovely." I want to pour out my heart about Claudia and Jane, but now this feels almost like a date, and that makes me shy.

We drive down route one, and I can't help it, I start to tell him about the part of Jane's reaction to the Whitney paintings that he didn't see, and the hateful things she said about me. I even tell him about finding Claudia and Barbara in a passionate embrace.

"Claudia," he says. "My brother's friends thought she was really a free spirit when that whole thing with the drawings started, but then to find out she likes girls—"

"What drawing thing?" But then it hits me like an eighteen-wheeler. The portfolio. It was Claudia's artful charcoal work. I'd've recognized it if I hadn't been focused on the daring subject matter.

Alex pushes his hair back from his face. "I'm sorry. I shouldn't have said that. I thought you knew."

"Just tell me, okay? Tell me everything." As if this day hasn't already had enough surprises.

"You sure?" When I nod, he says, "My little brother Cameron was in on it. He said his friends Chaz and Laurence both went for it, so he went along but it wasn't as much fun as he thought it'd be. He said it felt, well, in his words, like getting all hot for nothing."

"Go on."

"It was a joke at first, I guess. There was a party at the Houghtons'. Claudia and Barbara were there, and Laurence, Chaz's cousin from Rhode Island, was trying to get the girls to go out with them—Laurence and Chaz—and Claudia says she'd like to draw Laurence because he has a really strong face. So he says, I might agree if you'll do a nude of me—just teasing, Cam thought at the time. But, well, one thing led to another, I guess, and the next weekend I hear they were at—they were—well, I guess you could call it life drawing with extras, if you know what I mean."

"I know what you mean." I try to concentrate on the rapid beating of my heart, slowing it, calming it, but one of those drawings takes over my brain. One of the young men was lying on a rose print comforter—Claudia's sunbathing comforter, the very one she and Barbara were sharing earlier today. *She used my house*, I think, but I find I've spoken aloud when Alex says, "I know."

"Everyone knows everything, except me." *No*, I tell myself. *Don't whine.*

"At least it isn't like they had an orgy afterward. You know, it was just posing, just fooling around. A few—portraits and that was it."

"I can't handle any more surprises. Please tell me there aren't any more surprises."

I start to cry again, and Alex reaches across the space between us in the front seat and grabs my hand in a firm grasp. "No more surprises." I squeeze his hand and hold on and think about how long it's been since someone gave me a hand, literally or metaphorically. It's ridiculous to feel this grateful, but I do.

He releases my hand so he can turn the Land Rover down a long gravel drive flanked by low stone walls with balsam firs growing thickly behind them. Our destination is a cedar-shingled Cape much like my own.

When he opens the vehicle's door and helps me down, I'm glad to find I've recovered my equilibrium. We're ushered into a small dining room, one of several, cozy with firelight and fine Georgian antiques. The food is as tasty as I've ever had, spinach salad crisp and cool with Portobello mushrooms and tangy dressing, airy crab crepes under a blanket of subtle curry sauce, decadently rich sherry trifle.

After we eat, we sit in the porch rockers and watch sunset glow like hardwood embers in the clouds. By the time twilight smudges the sky, we've sunk into a peaceful stillness broken only by the whisper of tide against shingle and the intermittent raucous gossip of seabirds at some nearby rookery. Lamplight falls through the nine-over-six windows and glazes the lawn with golden rectangles.

I feel calm now, calm and fragile, as though one more surprise will shatter me like a goblet hurled into a fireplace. This afternoon has burned away all my expectations; all illusions of an orderly life, of knowing the people within that life down to the level of total honesty, are only that—illusions.

The last of the diners are leaving now, and we leave, too. When I catch the heel of my sandal on a brick in the walk, Alex is there to steady me, and lets me lean for just a moment against his chest.

Halfway home, he turns down a side road over which we lurch for several minutes to a wild expanse of ledgy beach. We sit on a big flat rock and watch the moon rise golden with reflected fire across the black mysterious sea.

"Let's have dessert again." From a German-silver case he produces a joint rolled smooth and straight as a soda straw. By the time it's half-gone, I feel sixteen again. When Alex soul-kisses me until I feel it down to my toes, I almost believe I am young again, back on the Jersey shore, back in a perfect dream.

"I guess all that talk about the nudes got me going," he says. I don't say anything, but I know what he means. When I separate what happened from my daughter's part in it, it gets me going, too, a little bit—or maybe it just reminds me of how long it's been since anyone held me.

Only for a moment, when he slides inside me hard and eager as only a young man can be, do I think, *I'm too old, too responsible, for casual sex with a near stranger.* I push that thought firmly from my mind. I look up into his face, the bright planes and mysterious shadows of it in the golden moonlight, his eyes focused on me as though we are the only two people in the universe, and for one manic moment I wish I could keep him mine forever. But I know how impossible that is, and I let it go.

Soon we catch the rhythm of the stars and rock together until we sail away.

଺

The rest of the summer is a season of changes, closures, and new beginnings. The day after our fight, a note from Jane, delivered by Claudia, is the way I find out that she's leaving Summerwind. Her lawyer will be in touch about selling her half. I hear from Claudia, who returns to our summer home, that Jane has given up her job in White Plains and intends to live with Uncle Sean on Mulgrave, but within a few weeks that falls through, and she returns to White Plains after all. She doesn't call to say good-bye, and it appears our long friendship is over.

I understand that my daughter and my friend had entered into a pact of silence: Claudia's drawings, Jane's affair. It's a sad little exercise in blackmail—if you tell on me, I'll tell on you. And to what purpose?

I tell Claudia I know about the nude drawings, but I don't ask any questions. She volunteers that she used our house, and that it was in the aftermath of those hot young men's bodies that she and

Barbara consummated their relationship for the first time. I tell her the important thing is to have someone to love who loves her back, and I release her to it.

Finally, I get a brief letter from Jane. It's been almost a month since the last day I saw her at Summerwind, the longest silence of our friendship. She didn't get her job back, so she's enrolled in an MFA program at NYU. I call her.

Alex and I come together in secret for the rest of the summer, and it's bittersweet to realize that for me, sex will never be this free and exciting again. For one last summer I have recovered my youth, and I know I'll forever miss the way Alex says my name when he enters me, his tenderness, the green-apple smell of his hair. By the time August comes around, I've stopped wondering if anyone knows about us—I don't care, I've had enough of secrets.

Except for one, and it's a secret I can't keep much longer now as the first chill breezes of winter set in. When my second daughter is born next April, I shall call her Danielle Alexandra, and in the fullness of time I'll tell her about the summer she was conceived, and the handsome young father she'll know only as a family friend. I'll tell her how sometimes the stars align and disrupt our gravity, the stars or maybe the longings of our most secret hearts.

ಬಂಡ

RELENTLESS TIDE

SQUINTING INTO THE AUGUST sun, Jared Parker scans the horizon as the *Wayfarer*, eighty feet of steel-hulled trawler, knifes eastward through Big Musquan Bay. He's about to start setting trawl when Lemuel Sharpe hollers, "Jared, get in here! Quick!" from the wheelhouse.

Grey-faced and gasping, Jared's father lies on his back, his feet splayed beneath the boat's wheel. The spilled mug of tea soaks his navy pullover and tan canvas pants. Unattended, the boat begins a slow turn to port while Lem, Pop's oldest friend, slides his folded plaid wool shirt beneath Pop's head. As Lem carefully straightens his arthritic back, Jared captures the mug with one hand, steadies the wheel with the other. "I'll take it," Lem says, and steps around Pop to the helm.

"What happened?" Jared asks in a wobbly voice. He sinks to his knees, pats Pop's shoulder.

"Heart attack's my guess," Lem says.

The words punch Jared in the gut, hard, knocking all the wind out of him. The old man's seldom sick, and then only an occasional cold or sore throat. Unsure of what he's supposed to be listening for, Jared leans forward and presses his ear to his father's chest. He can't hear anything through the layers of sweater and shirt, but he feels the hitch as Pop fights for each breath. "What in hell do we do now, way out here?" It's half a shout, half a cry.

"Get back fast as we can, I reckon." Lem keys the mike and calls the Coast Guard.

The radio crackles, and a Coastie's voice assures them an ambulance will be waiting at the breakwater. Search and Rescue can't come— their forty-four-footer is down off Markham Harbor, where a lobster boat's on fire.

Lem hangs up the mic. Jared pulls off his Bundy Marine cap and runs the back of his wrist up his forehead and over his close-cropped red hair. He says a quick prayer. *Please, let him hold on.*

Pop groans, clutches feebly at his chest, but keeps breathing. Almost seventy years old, he's hard and unyielding as Maine granite, knows everything about holding fast.

"Thank Providence we weren't farther out," Lem says. Jared only nods. "He's a fighter," Lem says.

Jared swallows hard, grips Pop's right wrist. "I know. I know he is." What will become of them if something happens to Pop? Just thinking about all that responsibility—the house, the boat, the business—sends Jared's own heart lurching.

Ten minutes crawls like an hour, fifteen like two. Jared grits his teeth, gives Pop's wrist one more squeeze, then stands up and paces the deck to work off some of the frantic energy that's making his head and heart pound.

Off the starboard bow, he spies a sleek black speedboat slapping over the swells, straight towards them. It slows and runs alongside, matching the *Wayfarer's* speed, and Jared catches his breath when he sees the skipper's black eye patch. Allan Woodsome is just about the last person he'd expect to see today—or any day, for that matter. Woodsome's shouting something, and Jared leans out over the rail to hear.

"Heard you over the radio. I can get your dad ashore a lot quicker than you can."

Jared looks over his shoulder at Pop's ashen face, knowing he'll feel like Judas no matter which choice he makes. Though one of the flinty old man's sworn enemies, Woodsome's still the best chance Pop's got right now.

They lower him down in a sling of seine, and Woodsome tenderly settles him into the arc of cushioned seats in the stern. *It'll be okay,* Jared tells himself. *Pop won't be angry afterwards.*

"You coming with us?"

Jared runs his index finger up and down the sharp, freckled bridge of his nose. He tells himself that Lem isn't too used up to dock the *Wayfarer* alone, but that's a damn lie. Moving Pop has taken everything Lem's got. "You get going," Jared says. "I got to bring the boat home." Woodsome reaches for the throttle, and Jared leans over the rail again. "Just one thing. Why you doing this for him?"

Woodsome looks up, his one eye flashing. "This ain't for him. For you, neither. This is for Robbie." He cuts a wide turn and roars away. The *Wayfarer* continues her course towards home, and Jared thinks about Robbie, his long-lost brother, and the part Woodsome played in his disappearance almost thirty years before.

☙

Jared races home, but Mom's not there. She monitors their radio, and must've already found someone to take her to the hospital half an hour away. It's the last place Jared wants to go, with its untouchable antiseptic surfaces and complicated gadgetry and Pop sick and helpless.

On his way off-island, he gasses up the truck and buys a can of Mountain Dew. What he really wants is a beer, but Mom doesn't hold with drinking alcohol. As he drives across the causeway connecting Spruce Island to the mainland and turns up route one, he realizes he never thought this day would come. He's thirty-seven years old, and Mom and Pop and the *Wayfarer* have been his whole life—no wife and children, no serious girlfriends, no hobbies, no real friends. His sister Mattie got out, went to college on a scholarship, teaches school in Indiana, of all places, far from the ocean. Jared stayed, to please Pop.

In ICU, his mother stands outside the curtained cubicle, eyes closed, head bowed in silent prayer. For the first time, Jared notices how old she is, the copper faded from her hair, hands twisted with arthritis from years in the cold and damp of the sardine factories. "Mamma," he says. He hasn't called her that since he was maybe six years old. "Mom, is he . . . "

"Holding on." She slides her wedding rings around her finger. "I haven't seen him since they brought him up from the emergency room. They're still . . . " She pauses. ". . . working on him." Jared doesn't like the sound of that—as though Pop's an engine with a stuck carburetor or broken timing chain.

A brisk, rumpled nurse pushes the curtain aside. She carries a tray of needles and tubing, and there's one small, dark spot of blood on her rose-colored tunic. "You can go in now, Missus Parker." Shesmiles what's probably meant to be a reassuring smile, but it doesn't reassure Jared.

Propped up by pillows on either side, Pop seems smaller, more transparent. IV bags drip mysterious fluids. The oxygen mask fogs and clears with with his labored breathing. Beneath his iron-grey hair, his face is pale as paper. Green lines ping across a video screen, tracing a jagged pattern over and over and over. "He's sedated," the nurse tells them. "But he knows you're here." She touches Pop's ankle through the white waffle-weave blanket. "Robert, here's your family."

Jared thinks, *She should have some respect and call him Mister Parker.*

Mom sits in the one chair, rests a hand on Pop's. Jared moves to the window, stares down at the parched lawn where one tenacious birch sapling rattles its thirsty leaves. He hates Pop being here, and he hates feeling disloyal for wanting to be somewhere, anywhere, else.

Soon, the nurse is back—So sorry, hospital policy, ten-minute visits each hour, mustn't tire our patient. She directs them to the lobby, because there's no waiting room in ICU, and they walk down the hall like dutiful children, neither of them daring to demand more time with Pop. Jared feels guilty relief at being freed from that sad, white space where Pop seems to be slowly sinking into nothingness.

They sit on a slippery plastic double seat in the lobby, and Jared asks, "Did you call Mattie?"

"She's flying in to Bangor in the morning, getting a rental car." The way Mom flattens her lips together makes him think she wants to say more. She doesn't.

He flips through a six-month-old issue of *Outdoor Life* without registering even one page of it. "I don't know what to do about the boat. Where can Lem find a crew on such short notice?" Pop and Lem and Jared have run the *Wayfarer* for almost twenty years, have it down to a science, but no other three men could manage it.

Mom pats his hand. "I think you should still go. Mattie'll be here, and you can come up in the evenings. I don't know if Medicare covers everything or not. This all must be terribly expensive." She pauses, pushes the sleeves of her cardigan up her freckled forearms. "Let's try and keep things as normal as possible."

Normal? What's normal any more? Everything is rudderless now, drifting into uncertainty the way a boat might drift into storm-chop on a foggy sea. But if Mom wants him to fish, well, this isn't the time to refuse and upset her. "Maybe I can get the Weeks brothers out," he says.

Mom nods. "It's what Pop would want." Jared holds that thought as he walks to the pay phone.

☙

Since their boat, the *Lady Starr*, is laid up after grounding out on Nancy Ledge, David and Larry Weeks are willing to help Jared out. Lem, however, is a different story. "Taking the wife to see her sister up in Gouldsboro." He pauses, sneezes. "Been thinking, ain't none of us knows how much time's left."

Jared hangs up the phone and wonders if Lem's trying to tell him he should stay ashore with Pop. But Mom wants him to fish, so now he's got to find a fourth. He sits back down with her. "Who can we get?"

Mom doesn't hesitate. "Allan Woodsome." Jared's jaw drops, and she goes on, "Close your mouth, son. It's not that bad a solution."

"No. No way Pop would have Woodsome on the *Wayfarer.*"

"Some things has got to be put behind us." Mom taps him on the arm with every word.

"Pop says—" Jared begins, but she shakes her head slowly. "We've always—" he tries again, but she cuts her gaze away from him and looks into her purse.

"Is Spruce Island a local call?" Once Mom gets set on something, that's it, no matter what. Jared prays Woodsome will say no.

He watches her cross the lobby to the pay phone, where she talks briefly, and then he watches her come back again. "It's done," she says. "Allan will go."

☙

When he thinks about Allan Woodsome, Jared's reminded of the winter he was seven, back at the beginning of the 'Seventies. It seems so long ago now that the century's turned, a memory so detailed it could have been etched with acid.

His big brother Robbie, nineteen then, stormed into the house one February afternoon like a northeaster, trailing snow from the hems of his bell-bottoms across the freshly-waxed kitchen floor. He dropped the mail on the table, then strode to the woodstove. As Jared and Mom and Mattie, who was twelve, watched, Robbie levered off a lid and held an envelope above the leaping orange flames. The bottom edge turned black and curled up, and he dropped the whole thing into the fire.

Jared couldn't figure it out. The letters Mom got always made her happy, but Robbie looked beyond mad.

"Bad news?" Mattie asked.

Robbie turned towards her fast, and his shaggy dark hair slapped against his cheeks. "Shut up."

"You watch your mouth, son. Don't you be talking to your sister like that." Pop, just back from scalloping, stood in the doorway between woodshed and kitchen.

"Sorry," Robbie mumbled.

Pop pulled off his fish boots and put on his moccasins. "Get anything done with the truck today?"

Robbie hooked one foot through a rung, pulled a chair from the table and sat down. "The truck's beyond me." He picked up the deck of cards from the blue and white oilcloth and shuffled. "I was going to take it to Daggett's, but Allan's father says that transmission place over the river is better. Got an appointment tomorrow."

Pop sat down and put matchstick pegs in the board as Robbie dealt for cribbage. "What's this world coming to? Have to go to Canada these days to get an American truck fixed. 'Tain't right."

"Yeah, I know," Robbie said. "But it's the way it is."

Early the next afternoon, a blizzard closed school and drove the entire scallop fleet back to port. "Ain't Robbie back from Canada yet?" Mattie asked as she padded across the kitchen in her stocking feet. "I got decimal division to do."

"Not yet." Mom picked up the chopping knife, began dicing salt pork for chowder. "They left at nine. You'd think the truck would be done by now."

Pop, already settled into his rocker in front of the woodstove, drank two cups of tea while Mom finished the chowder. Mattie kept reciting lines from Robert Frost's "Stopping By Woods on a Snowy Evening" and checking her English book to see if she'd gotten it right, until Mom said, "Could you do that in the living room?" Jared listened for the truck as he pushed his Matchbox racers around the kitchen floor. The phone rang, and Mom talked a few minutes to Allan's mother, saying that no, she hadn't heard from the boys yet. The Regulator clock above the kitchen table ticked away an hour as the chowder aged on the back of the woodstove. At last, headlights flashed across the blue gingham curtains.

"Thank God," Mom said, and dashed through the kitchen door to the woodshed. Jared followed. The heavy storm door creaked open, letting in a big swirl of snow. But it wasn't Robbie—it was Allan Woodsome, alone.

"Here's the keys and the receipt, Missus Parker." He bent close to Mom's ear and whispered something Jared couldn't make out.

"No." Mom folded her arms and shook her head. "No. He would've told me."

"He couldn't," Allan murmured as Pop came into the woodshed, mug in hand and Mattie right behind him. "Got to run," Allan said. "I'm sure Mother's worried."

He started out the door, but Pop grasped one shoulder of his parka and pulled him back. "Where's my son?" Allan looked at Mom and then at the floor. "Where's Robbie, Allan?" Pop's voice was tight, as if he was both scared and mad.

"Let him go," Mom said. "We'll talk without the little ones around."

Pop said, "You answer me, boy."

"I left him in Canada. That letter yesterday—Robbie says he ain't getting caught in the draft."

Pop drew back his hard, salt-cracked fist, and Jared heard a squishy, crunching sound as the punch landed on Allan's nose.

Mom reached out her hand between them, her work-worn fingers spread wide. "Robert, don't. Allan, I'm so, so sorry."

Mattie grabbed Jared by the arm. "Come on. This is grownup stuff." Jared shook her off.

"By Tophet, I'll bring him back," Pop said. "No son of mine's going to be a shirker and run off to Canada."

"You won't find him." Allan sounded like he had a bad cold as he fingered the squashed bridge of his nose. "He got on a bus this morning. Hundreds of miles away by now. He's not coming back."

"Not ever?" Jared's voice squeaked out around the lump in his throat. What would make Robbie leave them forever, especially without saying good-bye?

Pop's shoulders slumped, but only for a moment. He drew himself up, his bushy eyebrows coming together like two black caterpillars. "I can find him. There are ways. Now you get your sorry butt off my property."

"His nose—" Mom began, but Allan said, "It's all right, Missus Parker. It'll be fine." He went out, and pushed the plank storm door shut behind him with a gentle click.

Mom shooed Jared and Mattie into the kitchen as Pop stood staring at the door. "We can talk about this later," she whispered. "Your father's too upset right now." Mattie nodded, so Jared did, too. With Pop in a rage, all you could do was stay out of his way.

Mom cleared Robbie's place from the table and served the chowder. Pop buttered a slab of homemade bread. His sharp face looked even sharper, skin stretched tight over the bones. "We got two fine kids," he said. "Two fine kids. Don't nobody mention that shirker's name in this house ever again." His voice cracked just a little on "ever again."

No one spoke for the rest of the meal. Mattie opened the latest issue of *American Girl* magazine, and neither Mom nor Pop told her it was rude to read at table. Jared fished his Matchbox Stingray out of his pocket and drove circles around his chowder bowl. The silence bore down like a heavy weight.

After the supper dishes were done, Jared heard Mom's slow footsteps echo up the back stairs. The quick patter of Mattie's feet followed. Jared knew they'd lie on Mom and Pop's big bed and talk softly together. He used to be allowed to join them, but once he started school Pop said he had to stop hanging around with the women.

Pop sat in his rocker before the woodstove and sucked on his pipe until the smell of Cavendish tobacco filled the air. Jared arranged his Matchbox racers in two lines and began smashing the cars together, and all at once he knew. The Saturday before, Robbie and Allan had gone ice-fishing and wouldn't take him. Jared had told his friend Mickey he hoped Robbie fell through the ice and never come back. Mickey must've told his mother, and she wrote that letter that Robbie burned.

Jared shoved the mess of tiny cars under the table and crawled in after them to the safe cave made by the overhanging oilcloth. "I'm sorry, Robbie," he whispered. "Please come back. I didn't mean it." He stayed under the table for a long time. Tears rolled down his face, but he didn't dare make a sound. Pop would strap him and tell him crying was sissy stuff.

Above the creak of Pop's rocker and the crackle of the woodstove fire, he thought he could hear his mother and Mattie sobbing in the bedroom. But maybe it was only the wind in the eaves.

ଔ

The sky and sea are early-dawn silver when Jared watches Allan Woodsome descend the ladder and step aboard the *Wayfarer*. David Weeks is inspecting the trawl and Larry's dipsticking the oil, so it seems like the right time to get things straight.

"I just want you to know," Jared begins, "I don't think this is a good idea."

"Your mother more-or-less said that last night." Woodsome lights a cigarette, flicks the match over the rail. "Look, I know you're like your old man—you'll hold a grudge from a shout down to a whisper, and then you'll keep holding it long after the echo's gone. That's you. But your mother asked me to do this for her, and what kind of shit would I be if I said no?"

"The kind that helped my brother run away." Jared is probably more stunned than Woodsome at hearing that pop out of his mouth. He looks up at the breakwater that rises twenty feet above them now at dead low tide. Topside are three old-timers, who all turn away when Jared glances at them. He's certain they're watching this meeting with great curiosity.

Woodsome gazes upward, too. "That's your father's opinion. Get this straight. Robbie did what he had to do, without encouragement. And so did I—I helped my best friend. And then I went to Nam, and Nam took half my sight and all of my peace of mind, tore me up so bad I can't even wear a glass eye. Instead, I have to look like a fucking pirate. If anyone's earned the right to despise a draft-dodger, it's me." He pauses, and the look he gives Jared cuts to the bone. "Robbie did the only thing he could do, and it took guts, more than you can ever imagine. You have no idea what a choice like that costs."

Jared isn't sure what to say. He picks a couple of pieces of lint off the sleeve of his sweater. "You do your job and I'll do mine, and things will go okay."

"I'm on this boat, I'm giving a hundred per cent," Woodsome says. Jared nods and heads for the wheelhouse.

He sets a course for the distant Hubbles, the outermost islands in Big Musquan Bay, tall and shimmering in the thick, moist air. It seems strange, being at the helm instead of out on deck tending the trawl, stranger still running the *Wayfarer* with a completely different crew. He grew up with the Weeks brothers, has always been friendly with them, especially Larry, but Pop will be furious if he finds out Allan Woodsome is walking the *Wayfarer's* deck. Still, Jared tells himself, it's what Mom wants. Sometimes he figures she's like the vice-president, in charge when the president's laid up, and because of that he's right to do as she wishes.

There's only one cure for all this noise in his head—work. Jared studies the fish finder, but the depth lines across the screen remind him of those monitors in ICU. It's not right, all this responsibility. Lem should be in charge of the boat now, he's had so much more experience. Pop's told Jared what to do his entire life, and he's always done it, the good son.

A cloudy form appears on the screen, and they swing into action. The trawl pays out with a rattle of tackle and spreads like a dark shadow in the sunlit sea. Jared holds the course as the net fills, and his crew winches it on board. Pogy flash silver in the hard, bright light as they spill into the hold.

☙

The sky's orange with sunset when Jared turns the boat towards home. The catch is good, but now it dawns on him they'll have to split the take after expenses among four, not three.

They tie up to the Swope Marine wharf, and Jared climbs the ladder. Unlike their herring cousins, pogy go for fertilizer, except the scales, which by some secret process are turned into pearlessence, the stuff that gives nail polish its frosty gleam. Percy Swope, Swope Marine's owner, quotes Jared a price several dollars a hogshead below what he was paying Pop. Swope's probably guessed that Jared can't dicker like Pop, who could bargain the birds out of the trees, and it's obvious the old weasel intends to take full advantage.

"It's the market." Swope shoves his hands in his pockets and rocks back on his heels. "I got a business to run here, just like you do."

Jared's still pondering this when Woodsome comes topside and bends close to his ear. "We heard his price. Sorry to be eavesdropping, but, well—you know." Jared nods. "It ain't right. The brothers say you can do better at SeaPride."

Jared calculates. It'll take twenty minutes to get around the island. Then, if SeaPride's buying, they'll have to negotiate, unload, settle up, get back to port—the list goes on. He'll be late getting to the hospital, and Mom will worry. But he can call and leave a message that they're going to be late getting in, then surprise her at the hospital with the good news that he's managing as well as Pop would. Her expectations drag at him like a long anchor chain.

"Let's do it," he says, and they cast off lines.

ଔ

Mom and Mattie are sitting in the hospital lobby when Jared arrives, and he's relieved to see his sister hasn't changed in the two years since he last saw her. Her face is serene as ever, and her hair, black as Pop's once was, has only a few threads of grey. And it looks like she's finally found a man—a thin, fiftyish fellow with a shaved head shares the settee with her. He looks strangely like her as couples sometimes do, the shape of his nose, the cut of his mouth below the bushy silver mustache. But as Jared walks towards them, he notices something else: the man's left ring finger cut off at the top knuckle. Jared remembers a finger like that, its first joint severed in the winch on the *Martha Matilda*. He stops and stands in the middle of the lobby, unsure what to do. He wants to talk to Mattie but not to Robbie, not until Pop says it's okay.

Mattie crosses the space between them, throws her arms around Jared. "I'm so glad to see you." She steps back and takes his hand and leads him to his brother. "See who I brought," she says.

Jared nods stiffly. It's the best he can do. "Has Pop seen him?"

Robbie and Mattie glance at each other, and Mattie murmurs, "Told you so."

Robbie shakes his head, and the gold hoop in his left ear catches the light. None of the men Jared knows wear earrings, and he can't imagine the kind of man who does. His brother might just as well have been hiding in another galaxy all these years as in another country.

Jared wavers between curiosity and loyalty, but as always, loyalty wins. "Has Pop seen him?" he says again.

Mom looks down at her hands and shakes her head. "No. Your father ain't been much awake today. I think he's real sedated."

Robbie drapes his arm across the back of the settee. "Pop will understand, once I talk to him. I know he will."

Jared doesn't think so.

No one speaks as uncomfortable seconds creep by. Mattie touches Robbie's wrist. "Let's see if the coffee shop's still open." Together they disappear down the hall.

"So," Jared says.

Mom doesn't look at him. "Except for my red hair and freckles, you've always been the spit of Pop." She runs two fingers up and down a seam on her purse. "Don't make the same mistake he did, Jared. Don't shut out your family because their choices aren't the ones you'd make."

Jared doesn't want to hear this. "How'd Mattie find him?"

The expression in Mom's hazel eyes is as tough as Pop's. "We didn't find him. He wasn't ever lost."

Jared feels cold fingers marching down his spine. "Maybe you better tell me what you're talking about."

Mom sighs. "That spring after Robbie went away, Allan came over before he left for basic and gave me Robbie's address. We've been in touch ever since."

"And Pop never once got the mail before you, in thirty years? Come on." Jared picks at a hangnail.

"I took a box at the Bryant's Mills P.O. I'd mail a letter one Monday, and he'd mail one from Toronto the next. So, every other Monday, I'd go to Bryant's Mills."

"No. That's not possible. You never had a car."

"Ada Woodsome would take me, or once in a while old Mrs. Tully." Jared's amazed to see Mom almost smile. "When the fish factory was running, we used to save all our breaks that day and run up on our lunch hour. But when them long-distance phonecard things came out, I got one and we'd talk instead. While you and Pop were fishing."

Jared stares at her. For thirty years she's been false to Pop, and that's just too wrong for words. "You've been living a lie."

Mom folds her arms and looks straight at him. "Maybe so. Do you think that's better or worse than living with a heart full of hate?"

◌

Jared thinks about Mom sneaking away from the factory, and suddenly a memory clicks on like a movie in his head, something he hasn't thought about in more than twenty-five years. He was eleven, and Pop had agreed to take him fishing. In those days they still ran the *Martha Matilda*, a thirty-eight foot Novy boat rigged for scalloping. Pop and Lem were spending the summer, the off-season, handlining for haddock off Yellow Rock.

They'd been on the fishing grounds maybe four hours that July day when Jared drove a fish hook through the meaty pad below his left thumb. It happened fast—one minute he was removing a haddock from his jigs, and the next he was clutching his wrist and trying not to scream.

While Jared bit down on Pop's leather belt, Lem worked the hook through enough to cut the barb off and pull the rest back out. But the double puncture bled and bled and bled, even when Lem clamped a handkerchief over it and pulled Jared's arm above his head. "Must've nicked a blood vessel," Lem said. "Better get him ashore." Pop hauled the rest of their lines and turned the boat for home.

They tied up hastily at the slip, and Pop and Lem hurried Jared, dizzy and stumbling, up the ramp. All three of them came to a dead stop at the empty space on the breakwater. Pop said, "Somebody stole my damn truck."

"Everyone knows you leave the keys under the floor mats," Lem said. "Let's get the boy seen to. You can worry about that later."

After Doctor Cassidy stopped the bleeding and did Jared's hand up with smelly salve and gauze and adhesive tape, Lem and Pop went to tie up the *Martha Matilda* in her usual place while Jared sat on Lem's tailgate. He was still feeling woozy, and at first it didn't register that Pop's truck was pulling into its parking space with Mom behind the wheel. With her was another lady in a factory apron. Jared jumped up, yelling, "Mom! Mom!"

A frightened look passed across her face as she walked towards him. "What happened to your hand?" she asked breathlessly, and then, "Where's Pop?"

"I got a fishhook in it. And Pop's coming right behind you."

Mom took a deep breath, and turned around. "Robert! How did it happen?"

Pop glanced from Mom to the truck and back to Mom again, and when he spoke, his pinched, white lips barely moved. "You stole my truck. What were you thinking?"

Mom spoke lightly and evenly. "I was thinking, it's a rare thing for me to need that truck, but it is mine, too, you know. As your wife. And you weren't using it."

"You took it without telling me. Where'd you go?"

Mom tucked a strand of red hair back into her factory hairnet. "Missus Neely had to go to Bryant's Mills to feed her sister's cats while she's away, and her car wouldn't start. The poor things couldn't go hungry. Seven of them, Robert."

"You're lucky I had Jared to take care of, 'cause otherwise I would've called the police."

"The police would realize it was a misunderstanding. No harm done."

The one o'clock whistle blew and Mom walked back to the factory, and so far as Jared knew, the incident was never mentioned again.

∽

For several days, Pop continues to drift. Jared comes to the hospital late, sits on the opposite side of the lobby from the rest of them and ignores the greetings sent his way. It isn't just Robbie he's mad at. It's Mom, too, for being faithless to Pop for so long. And it's Mattie, who'd apparently been visiting back and forth with Robbie since college. And it's whichever president gave amnesty to a pack of draft dodgers and allowed Robbie to come home again. Mom and

Mattie and Robbie, in league against him and Pop all these years. Jared doesn't know whether he's more hurt or mad to have a family that's such a pack of sneaking backstabbers.

Every day he hopes Pop will be awake enough to talk, so he can say how wrong he thinks it is that Robbie's come back. Pop should know at least one member of the family is on his side.

Then one evening a nurse meets Jared the second he walks through the door of ICU. "Thank goodness you're here. He's alert tonight, but he won't see your mother or brother or sister." Jared feels as though he's let Pop down by not arriving earlier. He goes into the cubicle, where Pop's sitting up in bed eating a dish of radioactive-looking green Jell-O.

"Hello, son." Pop's voice sounds different because they've taken away his dentures.

Jared fights the urge to throw himself on the bed and hug Pop hard, though he and Pop haven't hugged since he was maybe eight years old. "It's damn rotten what Mom and Mattie have done to you. I ain't speaking to them, neither."

Pop nods. "How's you and Lem doing on the boat?"

"Lem's in Gouldsboro. The Weeks boys are helping out." He feels like Mom, lying by not mentioning Woodsome. "We're doing good. Price is up."

Pop nods. "Credit to you, boy. Never would've thought you could get more out of Swope than I could."

Jared grins. "He's a sharp one, ain't he? Couldn't do a thing with him. We're selling to SeaPride."

Pop coughs, flecks of green Jell-O all over the white covers. "You're taking my catch to Hacker Mitchell?"

"I—" Jared begins, but Pop's bunched jaw and red cheeks silence him.

The old man makes fists, beats the mattress. Blood backwashes into one of his IV's. He's trying to shout, but his voice comes out a reedy whine. "I ain't spoke to Hacker Mitchell nigh on fifty years. You let that old bastard get one up on me? Don't seem right, a man's whole family turning against him."

"Pop, I didn't know. I'm sorry." What had he let Allan Woodsome talk him into?

Pop punches the call button ferociously, and the nurse comes running and whisks the curtain shut.

Jared shuffles down the corridor to the lobby. He wants to howl, and his chest hurts from keeping all the sound inside. Now he's tarred with the same brush as the rest of them.

Mom gets up when she sees him, and so does Mattie. "Has—has something happened?" Mattie asks, and he realizes they think Pop must be—must have . . .

"He told me to get out."

Mom puts her hands over her mouth. Mattie touches his arm. "I'm sorry, Jared. I know how hard you try to not disappoint him."

Jared wipes his eyes with the heels of his palms. On the other side of the lobby, Robbie sits and watches across a space that seems wide as the Bay of Fundy.

༄

The *Lady Starr's* back in business so Jared loses the Weeks brothers, but Lem's ready to work again. Jared tells him the whole story as the *Wayfarer* slices the green late-August sea on the way to the pogy grounds. "What a tough old bird," Lem says. "Holds a grudge tight as a barnacle. Him and Hacker fell out over a wager on the lobster boat races down Jonesport way. Your pop said they was betting even money and Hacker said it was three-to-one odds. Your pop refused to pay up. That's the whole of it."

"That's it?" Jared tries to make sense of a feud that's as old as Mom and Pop's marriage, older than him or Mattie or even Robbie. It doesn't seem possible to stay mad that long.

Lem adjusts a knob on the fish finder. "Him and I had a set-to once. So trivial I don't even recollect what about. Round about the time Robbie went, it was. He put me off the boat, said don't come back. 'Course I just showed up anyway. First day, wouldn't let me aboard, scalloped short-handed and the sternman threatened to quit. Second day, he had to take me but wouldn't pay me." Lem scratches one armpit and chuckles.

"I didn't know you two ever passed a cross word."

"Land, yes. Third day, I told him, Take me back regular, or I'm spreading it around the fleet that your boy skedaddled to Canada. 'Cause he'd put out that Robbie'd gone down south to work the

Gulf shrimpers. Things got back to normal pretty quick after that." Lem dips snuff. "Don't suppose you got any leverage like that?"

"No," Jared says.

"Then I guess you got to hope you wear him down."

Wear him down, Jared thinks. *There isn't enough time in eternity to wear Pop down.*

ᛒ

They're just finishing a lunch of deviled ham sandwiches when the call comes from the Coast Guard. Pop's taken a turn for the worse and Mom wants Jared to come quick. Lem and Allan drop him at the breakwater and head for SeaPride with the catch, and Jared races to the hospital.

Time's running out now for him and Pop to mend fences. Jared's prayers are usually a shorthand he knows God will understand—*Please, Lord, help me*—but this time he feels he has to be more specific. *Please, Lord, let Pop live, or at least let him forgive me before You take him home.*

There's no one in the lobby when Jared walks in, so he hurries to ICU. The curtain's drawn across Pop's cubicle, and a woman in green scrubs and a white lab coat stands talking to Mom and Mattie and Robbie. Mom and Mattie are crying. Robbie's staring at the floor, chewing one side of his mustache. Mattie runs to Jared and hugs him. He wants to pull away, but doesn't. "He's gone," she says. "Gone."

Jared feels as though someone has driven a knife into his spine at the base of his neck. His legs go so weak, he's afraid they're going to collapse. His fingers lose their grip on the truck keys, which rattle to the floor. Robbie picks them up, and Jared takes them without touching his brother's skin.

"Did Pop—did he mention me?" It's all he'll have to hold on to, Pop's forgiveness at the end.

"He wouldn't speak to any of us." Mattie goes to Mom, puts an arm around her shoulders. "We'd come in, he'd turn his face away. Oh, Jared, what he's put Mom through these past two weeks. It isn't right. She devoted her whole life to him, and look at the way he leaves her."

This, Jared thinks, *is how it feels when your heart finally breaks. This cold, squeezing feeling in your chest and head. This utter emptiness.*

ISLAND SECRETS

☙

Pop hated any kind of hoopla, wanted nothing more than his ashes scattered at sea, so there's no funeral. Lem's the one who says, "Essex Island Point on an outgoing tide. He'd haunt us forever if he ended up in East Haven."

Now Jared, Mom, Mattie, and Robbie stand quietly on the deck of the *Wayfarer* with Lem at the helm. It's a grey day, the sky almost pearl behind the long dark streaks of cloud, the water dull as graphite. There must be a storm offshore somewhere, because seabirds—gulls and terns and shags—are sailing landward. But here all is calm, just the flat tidal wavelets and a fitful briny breeze.

Mattie's twisting her fingers in her long black hair the way she did when she was a kid. "I tried hard to be a good son," Jared tells her. He's tried more than once to talk to Mom about this, but she just pats his shoulder and says, "And you were." It's not enough.

Mattie strokes his cheek. "You are. But Pop was angry his whole life, never saw the good in anyone or anything. Mom's the one who saved this family. I mean—" She grasps Jared's chin, and he can tell she's as set on what she believes as Pop ever was. "Just learn the lesson, Jared. Don't be like him. Let us be a family again."

For the first time in his life, Jared feels as though he might be seasick. But maybe this nauseated, disoriented feeling isn't seasickness—maybe it's the vertigo of having everything he's always held on to stripped away, as though there's no more gravity, no more sea below and sky above, no order. He fixes on Essex Island, across dark water cold as Pop's anger, and feels anew the paralysis that always came when Pop's expectations ran contrary to what the whisper in his heart told him was right.

"Make peace with our brother," Mattie says softly, and Jared knows he must, and knows also that he doesn't know how to begin. Across the deck, Robbie's talking with Mom, who holds the urn that contains Pop's ashes. Essex Island Point looms ahead, a grassy field above the raw grey cliffs that rise out of the ebbing sea. Jared feels something loosen in his chest. Even if he can't find the words, he can still put out his hand to his brother.

He crosses the deck. Robbie ignores the outstretched hand and grabs Jared in a hug, tentative at first, but growing stronger. Jared pats his brother's back awkwardly, then takes a deep breath and holds on tight.

When they step back from each other, Jared clears his throat, pauses, then shrugs. Robbie winks at him. "It's okay, little brother. We're okay."

Jared nods and says, "I missed you," and hearing himself, he realizes it's true.

Suddenly the world seems wider, limitless. Out towards the Eastern Passage, the corrugations of the sea swells are echoed in the mackerel sky. The sun is distant and dim. Jared holds onto Mattie in the tight circle of their brother's arms. It's Mom who scatters Pop's ashes on the restless tide that carries them away.

ಸಿಂಡ

QUARRY SECRETS

THIS SUMMER'S BEEN WAY hotter than normal for Maine. Lakes and ponds and wells are drying up from lack of rain, and up at the old quarry, all kinds of things are being exposed, things that no one wants to think about. Generations of kids swam in the quarry before they built the public pool over in Mayfield, but this summer only Christine and I still prefer the quarry to the chemical tingle of pool water. It seems so much less pristine now that rusty old car parts and the skeletons of dead dogs and cats lie revealed on the pink granite ledges. And something else, too.

Four junior-high boys made the discovery. I was sketching in my favorite oak, high above the quarry, when they came up the western path, bitching about missing the rec bus to Mayfield. I didn't pay them much mind until I heard one of them say, "What's that?" in a weird shaky voice. I thought maybe they'd found the horse that went missing from Braxton Farm a couple of months ago, although getting a horse up that steep and twisty path seems impossible. Then another kid said, "Holy crud, that looks like a hand," and I understood. They found Harley Dunlap. I knew it was just a matter of time.

ೞ

The TV news says that Harley Dunlap, upcoming student body president and point guard for the Quoddy High Mariners, died from diving into shallow water and striking his head on the rocks. I could tell them different, but what's done is done and there's no point in stirring it all up again. I don't care about Harley Dunlap's reputation, but I don't want to hurt Christine.

QUARRY SECRETS

We're the quirky, arty girls at Quoddy High, Christine and me. The cool kids like Harley Dunlap look down on us the same way they look down on the geeks and goths and granolas. They laugh at our thrift-shop retro wear and our poetry in the school lit-mag and our ukeleles. We act like we don't care, and I truly don't. But after Christine's parents divorced last winter and she decided she couldn't go on living without a boyfriend to love her, she did start to mope about being an outsider. That was one element in the collision that created this summer's perfect storm.

☙

They haven't hauled granite out of the quarry for almost a hundred years. The hardwood forest grows thick now on all sides of it at the far west end of Spruce Island, perfect cover for anyone up to no good. It's a hike from town—a mile or so to the gate off Remsen Road and then another half-mile to the western path that winds and climbs among the trees. I like to come by the eastern path, which is shorter but steeper and more overgrown, and I thought I was the only one who knew it until the day that Harley Dunlap died.

We're a week past Fourth of July when the second thing happens. Christine and I are sitting on the rocks at the quarry strumming our ukuleles when all of a sudden she says, "Do you ever want to just strip naked and stand in the sun?" I'm speechless, wondering if she's lost her mind. I can't imagine putting my skinny, awkward body on display, even if it's only for the trees and birds and deer.

"I'm going to do it," Christine says. She stands up, pulls off the top of her swimsuit, and steps out of the bottom. Her arms spread wide, her nipples hardening in the breeze, she says, "Come on, Lizzie. Be brave."

"Not me." I get up, cross the ledges and grab the rope that hangs from my tree. It takes me less than a minute to reach my branch. I sit there gazing towards the horizon through the lobed leaves. To the south, the bay glitters hard and green in the sun. To the west, on the mainland, the forested slopes of Carver's Mountain rise to a bald grey summit. Everything is hot and still, the only sound the lazy droning of bees.

Then I hear something else, a sound like small pebbles sliding. I look down at the quarry. Christine stands there like a naked statue.

Nothing is moving, not on the water, not in the trees. It's possible-unstable ground has caused a little landslide, but I'm suddenly wary. I make my way down from the tree and grab her arm. "Get dressed. Let's get out of here." She must see something in my face, because after a split-second hesitation she reaches for her clothes.

We're halfway down the western path when she says, "What's going on?"

"I don't know. I heard something."

"So?"

"So, what if someone saw you?"

"Hey," she says. "Slow down."

I do, but not much. "Think about it. Just because we didn't see anyone—"

"Stop being paranoid." She halts and sits on a big boulder. "You're jealous."

I mean to keep walking, but this stops me.

Her chin comes up and she gives me a hard look I've never seen before. "You wish you had the guts to get naked. Admit it."

"Wrong." I turn away and keep going down the path.

By the time we reach the gate at Remsen Road, she's crying. Her mood swings are starting to give me whiplash. "I'm sorry, Lizzie," she wails. "I'm so sorry." Then it all spills out. Her father is getting married again. Her mother is sliding into another depression. She has to find someone to love her. "I'm just as cool as they are," she says, lifting her chin again. She slats away tears with both hands. "Even though I'm not a cheerleader."

Then I get it. Over the Fourth, according to local gossip, the cheerleaders had a skinny-dipping party at someone's camp. The boys heard about it and got someone's dad's telescope and had a good time watching them from further down the lake. I remember Christine saying how cool and brave and sophisticated those girls were. I thought they were a bunch of stupid exhibitionists.

I don't know what it feels like when divorce rips a family apart. But I do know that trying to fit in somewhere else by being something you're not is a useless, pointless game. And sometimes a tragic one.

The next morning when I get out of the shower, I find a text from Christine.

Can't C U 2day. TG2BT. TBL.

"Too good to be true." I wonder what it means. Has her father changed his mind about getting remarried? Is the family coming back together? It seems unlikely. This isn't a fairy tale.

With nothing else to do, I put my sketchbook and oil pastels in my backpack and hike to the quarry. Up the tree I go, and for some reason I'm not sure of, I pull the rope up after me. Fireweed is in bloom off towards the bay, a vast magenta field of it below the high cloudless sky. I get out my sketchbook and start to work.

It's not long before Christine shows up. I wonder what happened to her plans. She sits on the ledge almost directly below me, but something stops me from calling her name. I wait to see what happens next, and it's something so unexpected I almost fall off my branch. Harley Dunlap comes out of the woods and sits beside her. Hoping they don't look up, I grip my sketchbook and breathe real slow and quiet.

"I was so surprised you called," Christine says. "And happy."

"Yeah," says Harley Dunlap. He leans towards her, lays her down, and kisses her. For what seems like several minutes they grind against each other. I know I should look away, but it would feel like turning my back on a rattlesnake. His hand slides up under her pink tank-top. When she flinches, he takes his lips away from hers and says, "Come on, baby."

"I . . ." says Christine, and stops. "I like you," she says. "I really do. But—"

He laughs. Who would think a laugh could sound so cruel? "Then let's have a good time. You know you want to, or you wouldn't run around up here naked."

Christine gasps. Harley Dunlap rips her pants down. She starts to scream as he forces himself into her, and he puts one hand over her mouth. My sketchbook and backpack go flying out of the tree as I lower the rope and slide down it. I don't even notice the burn as my palms are rubbed raw.

I know what to do. I pick up a big, jagged chunk of pink granite and drive it into the back of Harley Dunlap's skull as hard as

I can. I have to bite my lip as the rough rock digs into my hands. He stops in mid-stroke and half-looks over his shoulder. I let him have it right in the temple. When he tries to get up, he falls over backwards, his shorts below his hips, and hits the water with a tremendous splash.

Christine is rocking back and forth, sobbing. I gather her into my arms and hold her tight while I wait for Harley Dunlap to come back up. He doesn't. "Come on," I say. "Let's get you to the hospital." I take out my phone, but she grabs my arm so hard it hurts.

"No. Don't tell anyone."

"But he *raped* you."

"Please. Don't tell. It's too embarrassing."

"It's not your fault."

"Yes it is." She's crying so hard I can barely make out the words.

"He's an asshole," I say, but I'm beginning to understand that if I do make her go to the doctor or the cops, she'll deny everything.

"If I don't tell, maybe people won't believe him."

She thinks he's still alive. Shock or denial, it doesn't matter. I try to say *I killed Harley Dunlap*. But I can't.

I find my backpack and sketchbook. My pastels are scattered who knows where. Taking Christine's hand, I lead her down the path. By the time we get to her house, she's calm as can be. Too calm. Almost as calm as I am.

∽

That night, a photo appears on my phone from someone named Corey Remsen. It's Christine, naked at the quarry. It takes me a while to figure it out. Corey. Remsen. Quarry. Remsen Road. The sound of falling pebbles. Someone had been watching us, and yesterday he hit the jackpot. But not Harley Dunlap, unless he's sending photos from the beyond.

I call Christine. No answer. I call her landline, and it rings for a long time before her mother picks up. "Christine's gone," she says. I ask her what she means, and she says, "I don't know. She left a note she was going to her father's. But he's in Mexico on his ... his *honeymoon.*" She spits out the word as though it's acid, and hangs up.

∽

It's been over·a month and a half now, and today they found Harley Dunlap's body. I hope that when school starts next week—

without Christine, who's living with her father in the other end of Maine—everyone's forgotten about that photo. I know it was sent all over town because even the outsider kids like me were talking about it on Facebook.

I am the only one who knows the true story, and I intend for it to stay that way. I have always been able to keep a secret.

I don't swim at the quarry any more. Instead I go there and sit in my oak, reflecting on how the choices we make, out of hope or desperation or plain carelessness, can destroy the very thing we're trying to create. And it seems like nothing, not friendship, not love, is ever strong enough to stop the destruction.

ঝCষ

ISLAND TO ISLAND

LUCAS CASTILE STRETCHES his long arms over his head and props his feet on the veranda railing. The veranda runs along the back of the old foursquare farmhouse his grandparents had bought for a summer home back when his father was just a toddler. As he did yesterday, the first day in over a decade of waking up in this house, Lucas spends some time studying every detail of the ever-changing view of land and sea. It's a scene he paid little attention to in the long summers of childhood and one he seldom thought about in the years of college and work when East Haven was too far to travel on the occasional weekends when he could get away from Manhattan.

Before him lies the sloping lawn that gives way to beach roses and grey ledges and beyond them the unceasing ocean. On either side, wildflower meadow and birch and spruce stretch to the lands of his unseen neighbors to the south and north. Complete privacy. After a dozen years spent entirely in the City, all the open space and wide sky feel more than a little strange. Yesterday, he wondered if he'd made the right decision in coming to East Haven, if it were truly the last resort he thought it was when he walked out of divorce court. Today he feels as though since nothing else has worked out right, it's as good a place to be as any and he needs to make his peace with it.

He remembers what his college sweetheart Pippa once said in the deep ravines of Manhattan. "Lucas, I need more sky. I need to see the sky from horizon to horizon. I'm feeling way too constricted here." Sky, that little strip of blue between the buildings on either side. It was something he, life-long dweller of the streets of the East Village, never thought about. He thinks he might now be starting to understand what she meant, if not yet how she felt.

Lucas sips his vanilla chai and tells himself he needs to think about what comes next, not about that ancient history. For most of his thirty-four years, he was pretty sure he knew what came next, but the past is gone now and somehow, it seems to have taken with it the future.

His brother Barry comes out the back door and sits on the railing beside his feet. "How you doing?"

"I'm okay."

Barry nods, but says, "I'm not so sure you are. Let's do something today. Maybe bike around the island after lunch?"

"Maybe."

He knows Barry's trying to be the wise and good older brother. To give him room and at the same time give him support. It's a balancing act and, given a choice, not the way either of them would have wanted this summer to unfold.

☙

Lucas remembers how poleaxed he felt four months ago when his divorce lawyer told him that Louisa was going after the bakery.

"She can have everything else," he said that day. "The apartment, the furniture, the car, I don't care. But the bakery's mine. I built it from nothing. She wasn't even in my life then. She had no hand in it at all."

"Didn't she put up the money for the renovations three years ago?" His lawyer tapped his pen on the yellow legal pad.

"Her father's money. Not hers." But Lucas could see the problem, and because Louisa had the best lawyer that Daddy's money could buy, he knew he had no chance of holding on.

He'd opened little bakery in the East Village the summer he graduated from New York University. He'd gotten into baking bread with his grandmother while he was still in junior high and had been making artisan breads in his apartment for some of his professors and friends since his freshman year of college. By the time he graduated, he had gallery representation for his watercolors, but that was not going to pay the bills. Unless he wanted to teach, which he didn't, he didn't see much he could do with his shiny new art degree. But his hobby had potential; having his hands on yeast dough all day in his own little shop seemed like a good way to make a living while still having time for painting. So he began, and his professors and friends spread the word, and within a year he was on his way, busier in his hole-in-the-wall bakery in the East Village than he had ever dared to imagine.

Then came Louisa. And now, ten years later, she's gone, and so is everything he worked so hard for.

"You want to check out the new bakery?" Barry says that afternoon. They've pedaled their bikes to the south end of Shore Road where it loops onto Bayview Street, and now they're coming into the downtown.

"I am kind of curious," Lucas tells him.

They lock their bicycles in the library bike rack and amble down the island's main drag. It's mid-July and the season is in full swing, throngs of tourists and day-trippers and resident summer folk. Lucas remembers the East Haven of his childhood, a quiet place for families who'd been spending summers here for generations and very few tourists.

Barry says the Bayside Bakery opened a couple weeks earlier in time for the Fourth of July crowd. Lucas likes the looks of the raspberry croissants, so he orders one with a cup of lemon and ginger tea. On the deck that overlooks the harbor where most of the summer colony's motor yachts and sailboats are moored, he eats the croissant and samples a morsel of Barry's blueberry scone. Both are excellent. Lucas sips his tea and thinks it would have been fun to be the one to open a little bakery here on East Haven.

༄

They're walking back towards the library for their bikes, but Lucas is thinking about his lost bakery instead of watching where he's going. He's about to crash into one of the iron lamp-posts that line Bayview Street when someone—not Barry—grabs his arm and brings him to a halt.

"Careful, there," he hears, and then, "*Luke?*"

Barry says, "Henry Braxton, you old devil!" and Lucas looks up to find himself face-to-face with the past, a friend from back in the endless East Haven summers of childhood when the three of them played on the same Little League team. Even as a kid, Henry had an arm that terrified all but the most composed batters. A star pitcher at Quoddy High, he'd been scouted by several colleges but turned them all down to stay on the family farm, a decision Lucas and Barry found incomprehensible at the time. Lucas still doesn't understand it.

Henry tips his straw cowboy hat to a couple of middle-aged women passing by and says to Barry, "I had no idea your little brother was here this summer." Then, "How you been, Luke?"

Lucas runs his hand through his auburn hair. He wants to tell the social lie, but it's impossible to say he's fine with any conviction. "I'm getting by," he says.

Henry looks at him as though he's as easy to read as the top line on an eye chart. "You look like you could use a change of scene and some country cooking. Let me see what Joline's got going on tomorrow and if she can throw a dinner party for you two. Did you know she started a microbrewery last winter?"

"I didn't," Barry says. "That's pretty cool."

Lucas adds, "That is cool. Good for her."

He remembers someone named Joline from when they were kids, a small, fierce girl with long, wild brown hair. He never would have put her with easy-going Henry, and wonders if it's the same girl.

☙

"I've got some editing to finish up," Barry says when they get home from their ride, before ascending the stairs to his third-floor office.

"It's so hot, I think I'll just chop up a Cobb salad for dinner," Lucas tells him. "Come down when you're hungry."

After he finishes making the salad and a cruet of red-wine vinaigrette, Lucas goes out to the veranda with East Haven's weekly newspaper, *The Island Sentinel*, but it stays folded on his lap. He thinks about opposites. Joline and Henry seem as unmatched as he and Louisa were, and yet they've apparently made a go of it, if the pride in Henry's voice when he announced the microbrewery is any indication. Barry's the one who found someone about whom everyone said, "Made for each other." His husband Charles would be here now, but Charles' father is dying of cancer so he went back to New Orleans for the summer. Barry and Charles FaceTime every day, and that's when Lucas feels the most lonely.

Louisa. He thinks he might have finally figured out what she saw in him: someone whose gentleness would allow her ambitions and her father's money to take them where she wanted to go without much pushback. He's long known what he saw in her: one of those beautiful and charming girls who normally never gave him a second glance. They liked enough of the same things—classic foreign films, chamber music, and exploring used-book stores—that he hoped it would all work out. He spent their engagement period and the first few years of marriage feeling absurdly grateful that someone like her, a privileged girl from the Upper West Side, would love someone like him, a child of the East Village counterculture.

But then it all began to change. First, it was the gallery. Why, she kept asking, was he letting someone else represent his work when he could open his own gallery in the recently-vacated storefront next to the bakery? He tried to explain that he had neither the contacts, the reputation, nor the energy to run a gallery, that a second business would take his attention away from painting and baking. He should have seen the first glimmer of what was to come when, after weeks of him quietly and reasonably resisting her every argument, she said, "Okay, Lucas. I'll let you win this round. But don't expect to win them all."

She did win the next round, pushing him to renovate his bakery's funky-cool decor and providing some of Daddy's money to do so. Two years later, though, he surprised both himself and her by balking at opening a second bakery farther uptown. He didn't want to divide his attention, to have to cede the process and the product to someone else, someone at a separate location who might not feel the same dedication to quality that he himself felt.

"Do this," she said. "Do it or I'll have to take it into my own hands." He thought she was bluffing. After all, what did she know about baking bread or running a bakery? But it wasn't a new location she was taking into her own hands. Oh, no. Instead, he found himself served with divorce papers in his bakery in front of God and everyone.

He has to stop thinking about this because it's giving him a headache. He sighs, unfolds the newspaper, and starts reading the letters to the editor. It amazes him what people get worked up about in small towns.

ଔ

Late the next afternoon, Lucas and Barry are in the vintage Toyota Land Cruiser that since their childhood has been the family's East Haven summer vehicle, headed to Henry and Joline's for dinner. The farm is on the mainland in Bryant's Mills, off route one on the Ironworks Road with the Little Wapatquan River marking one edge of the property. A sign graces the lawn in the arc of the long circular driveway, lettering incised deeply into the dark-stained wood and highlighted with yellow paint: *Braxton Farm. We Grow What's Good For You. Established 1897*. Under that, suspended by short chains, is a matching smaller sign: *Ironworks Microbrewery*.

Barry turns the Land Cruiser into the driveway. Lucas wonders how many generations of Braxtons have farmed this land. He was able to hold onto his business for only twelve years, but here is a family that's kept the enterprise going for well over a century. Maybe Henry turned down college and a possible career in pro baseball because so much family history was at stake. Lucas marvels at how a farm kid from the rural coast of Maine had such clarity at the age of eighteen.

Joline, a thin woman who still has the wild, wavy brown hair she had when they were kids, turns from the cast-iron skillet where chicken is frying. "Welcome, guys," she says. "It's been a long time."

"Too long." Lucas holds out a paper sack containing two loaves of whole-wheat *pain au levain*. "Here. Fresh from the oven."

"Thank you." She takes the bag and places it on the cutting board near the black cast-iron sink Lucas remembers from childhood visits to the farm, then reaches into the refrigerator. "And here's something I made," she says, handing Lucas and Barry each a green bottle with a white ceramic spring-top. "My new doppelbock. First batch." Waving a hand towards the sack of bread, she goes on, "Isn't it interesting, Lucas, that you and I can take the same ingredients—grains and yeasts—and turn them into two such different foods? Bread and beer. The staffs of life, you could say."

Barry says, "Good observation."

Lucas agrees, trying to grasp a sudden thought that floats just out of reach.

Dinner is deliciously hearty, the kind Lucas seldom indulges in—country-fried chicken, potato salad, fresh garden peas with dairy butter, and homemade mustard pickles, all of it from right there on Braxton Farm. By the time raspberry cobbler and hand-churned vanilla ice cream are set before him, Lucas is thinking a low-key life on the coast of Maine might be just the thing to help him get his bearings. Barry, who with Charles spends three seasons of the year in Loreauville, a tiny Louisiana village on Bayou Teche, has made the adjustment from big-city bustle to quiet small town. Maybe he can, too. As a text-book editor, Barry can telecommute from anywhere, but that's an advantage that Lucas knows he will not have, and if he's going to stay on East Haven, he's going to have to find work. It's hard to not wish the Bayside Bakery didn't exist.

☙

Lucas wakes up the next morning and realizes that something—maybe either three days on East Haven or relaxing with friends at the farm—has driven the constant monkey-chatter from his brain. It was a ten-year daily presence that always seemed to be saying in Louisa's voice, *More-more-more* and *Not-good-enough-not-not-not*. The sun is streaming in yellow ribbons through the open four-paned windows as a soft, salt-laced breeze wafts in. The quiet, the absolute quiet, is a wonderful thing.

After setting some focaccia dough to proof, Lucas goes out on the veranda with a cup of chai. For the first time since Louisa set the divorce in motion, he feels the urge to paint. He goes up to his room and gets paints and brushes and a block of watercolor paper and begins an impressionistic watercolor of the veranda view towards the southeast, thin birches white against the evergreens and all the Queen Anne's lace in white flower in the wide meadow down to the sun-sparkled high tide. He feels serene. He hasn't felt this way in a long, long time.

☙

Lying in bed that night with moonlight through the half-closed wooden venetians laying stripes of silver on the wall, Lucas is seized by an idea and realizes it's the one that was floating just out of reach at the farm. Joline operates her microbrewery out of her and Henry's house. Why can't he do the same with baking bread?

He's noticed that at the Bayside Bakery there's an abundance of pastries, and even hand-dipped chocolates, but no yeast breads. He can't keep drifting, using up his financial reserves, slender though they are now that Louisa's lawyer is done with him. And there are only two things he knows how to do well. He might as well jump into both of them.

The next morning, he calls Summerwind, the gallery that Barry recommends partly because the owner, Emma Williams, lives next door beyond the trees. After sending her some digital images of his watercolors, he makes a phone call to the East Haven town office. There he learns that home occupations aren't heavily regulated, as long as he doesn't put up a flashy sign and detract from the ambiance of the neighborhood. He's amused that the voice at the other end of the line actually uses that word, *ambiance*, as though Shore Road were some sort of high-end restaurant rather than a simple country byway. Apparently, one could open an opium den on East Haven, as long as everything was tasteful and pretty and didn't impact the scenery.

Laptop on the kitchen table and phone in hand, Lucas spends a few hours contacting suppliers for organic flour and yeast, professional-quality bread pans and bowls, and a vendor who'll print his new logo—which he doesn't yet have—on brown paper bread bags.

Coming up with a name and the concept for his logo is harder. He can no longer use the bakery name that had to be given up to Louisa, Panis Angelicus, the bread of angels. Mulling over a variety of names as he takes a break in late afternoon on the back veranda, he's frustrated that none feel right. Then his attention wanders to a bald eagle flying overhead, and he thinks of his newfound freedom, and his new start here on the eastern side of the bay's easternmost island where the rising sun greets the entire country at certain times of the year. It comes to him then: New Beginnings Bread. It probably wouldn't survive even a first assignment in Marketing 101, but he likes it. Sketch pad in hand, he comes up with his logo: the rayed sun rising over the sea and an island shaped like a boule of bread with an eagle soaring above it.

The next day, he turns in his sole-proprietorship paperwork at the town office. From a sign printer in nearby Mayfield, he orders a sign featuring the new logo. He places an ad in *The Island Sentinel*. And then he waits. Either it will come together and be successful or it won't, but in the interval, Lucas thinks positive thoughts and finds that he's feeling the way he did when he first opened Panis Angelicus, as though he's doing something that's good for his soul as well as his bank account.

∽

Two weeks go by. Slowly, slowly, word is spreading, and the orders come in, a trickle at first and then one day, he finds himself wondering when he's going to have time to fill all the orders and still paint. Since Summerwind has agreed to take him on, he has to make that work as well. He realizes he might have gotten lazy—he was busier than this in the City, but the slower pace on this island makes it harder to kick things into high gear.

Early one evening after their work is done, he and Barry are throwing a frisbee back and forth on the front lawn. A silver Lincoln SUV comes slowly down Shore Road and then turns into the driveway. He doesn't recognize it, and neither does Barry.

The woman who comes across the yard is tall and thin with large eyes, a long nose, and a head of short, spiky white hair. The whole effect reminds Lucas of a giant wading bird.

"I'm Margaret Standish." She nods towards Barry and sticks out her hand to Lucas. He grasps and shakes it. She has a firm, no-nonsense grip.

"Happy to meet you," he says, and waits.

She looks him up and down with a wry expression. "You don't know who I am, do you?"

Lucas searches his brain for a memory of her extraordinary appearance and comes up empty. "No, ma'am." Barry shrugs and shakes his head.

"Well, that's probably because when you two visit my place, I'm always in the back." She pauses for a beat and adds, "Baking."

For a moment, Lucas can't think of a word to say. Knowing the Bayside Bakery did not sell yeast bread, he never considered that he might still be treading on its toes.

"Well," he says at last. "I love your raspberry croissants. The best anywhere, even Manhattan."

"Thank you." She gazes straight into his eyes. "Look. I'm not here to give you a hard time. Quite the contrary. I think we can help each other."

Over a pitcher of iced tea on the back veranda, Lucas discovers that Meg Standish loves to make pastries, but considers yeast bread a major chore that takes too much energy and attention. But a small local supply, top quality as some of her customers have told her his is, delivered to her door, that would be just the ticket.

"I'm trying to develop my own brand here," he tells her.

"And that's fine. Actually, that's what I want, too. I already sell 'Harborside Chocolates by Paula Devane,' and I can also sell 'New Beginnings Bread by Lucas Castile'."

Lucas has to admit that sounds pretty good.

"Here's how I see it," Meg says. "I don't expect you to stop selling retail. There are people who like the excuse to drive or bike around the island, but there are also people who love your bread but don't like having to order ahead and then drive out here."

"I get it," he says. "But I can only do so much, and I'm kind of reaching a tipping point already. This isn't a commercial kitchen. And the bread is hand-made. No machines."

Meg says, "Some of your customers would buy from me. In fact, some suggested that I team up with you As I said, they don't want the ordering and the coming out here, they want one stop for pastries and bread. You will make a little less per loaf, but it'll be a steady income, not up and down with the seasons. My clientele comes from as far away as Mayfield and Riverton."

It comes down to the details. He tells her the two kinds of bread he makes each day, and that he doesn't plan to deviate from that schedule. They work out prices. As they shake hands to seal their new partnership, Lucas tries to remember how he kept up with the demand at Panis Angelicus.

☙

Back from a Sunday-afternoon bike ride a few days later, Barry goes upstairs to take a shower and Lucas checks the landline's answering machine and caller ID. There are no messages, but there is a call from a New York area code. He doesn't recognize the number, but doesn't think it's Manhattan. *If it's not important enough to leave a message*, he tells himself, *it's not important enough for a callback.*

He makes a cup of chai and goes out to sit on the veranda. He's reached the point where he's made his peace with being on East Haven instead of home in the city and now he can enjoy the view and the sun and the breeze without thinking about Louisa or how he got it all so wrong. He might even be happy. He's doing what he loves, and with his business taking off, he's going to go ahead with something he's always dreamed of, something he could never have done in crowded Manhattan: a traditional stone beehive oven in the back yard. He already has the drawings and a stonemason to do the job. He's thinking of adding a wood-fired brick oven in the kitchen as well, but that's for next year, or the next.

The phone rings, and he goes into the house and glances at the caller ID. New York again. "Hello," he says. "Lucas here."

"Hello, Lucas," says a voice he hasn't heard for over a decade, since before Louisa. "It's Pippa Maslin."

Pippa. His breath catches in his chest. "I—" he says. "I—how are you?"

"I'm good. I'm really good." She pauses, and he hears her take a deep breath. "I have something to tell you, Lucas. Something I should have told you years ago. But back then I decided I was never going to tell you."

"I don't understand."

Instead of saying whatever it is, she says, "I'm only telling you now because I heard you and your wife got divorced."

"You heard about that?"

"Yes. I ran into Tom the other day, and he told me you and your wife got divorced and she got your bakery and you went to your childhood summer home in Maine."

Tom, one of Lucas's college apartment-mates. Lucas had messaged him with the landline number before leaving the City, since Barry had said that the local cell phone service was spotty. He's suddenly absurdly glad he did.

Pippa went on, "I'm just going to say this straight out, Lucas. You have a son. He's eleven years old."

Lucas almost drops the phone. "Me? A son? Our son?" So many questions flood his brain, it's like a dam bursting, but all he ends up asking is, "What's his name, Pippa?"

"His name's Riley. He's a great kid. Look, Lucas, when we broke up, I didn't know. I didn't find out I was pregnant until after I went back to White Lake. I kept hoping you'd call and say you'd changed your mind, but you didn't."

"I was waiting, too," he tells her, "hoping you'd come back."

"If I had, I never would have known if we were together because you loved me or because it was your duty. Because of Riley."

"It's not too late. And I don't say this because of Riley, I say it because I've never stopped loving you, Pippa. I would treasure a chance to get back together, the way things were meant to be. I hope you want that, too."

"Oh, Lucas." She doesn't say anything else for a long moment. He can hear her breathing.

"Come to Maine. It'll be great." His mind is already spinning pictures of picnics and beach hikes and bike rides and visits with Henry's family at the farm.

Pippa says, "I can't, Lucas. I'm married."

"Married." He feels as though with one word all the life and hope have been sucked out of his body.

"Yes, last year. I love him and he loves Riley and me. I've never stopped loving you, either, Lucas, but it's not in a romantic way now, it's like a cherished old friend. And I know I should have told you and Riley about each other before I married Jeremy, but I didn't want your toxic wife anywhere near my son. Our son. But now that she's gone, I would like Riley to get to know his father. Riley doesn't know about you yet, and if you don't want to meet him, I won't ever tell him. But I hope you want to."

"Of course I want to. And I'm glad you're happy," he adds, and means it with his whole heart.

"We're planning a trip to Nova Scotia, and—well, we thought we could stop by on the way, give you and Riley a chance to meet, to spend a little time together. Would you want to do that? No pressure, just if you want to."

"Yes. Oh, yes."

Pippa says, "I'm so glad. Look, can you book us a bed-and-breakfast on your island for Friday night?"

"Stay here. Please. The house is huge, and my brother will be so happy to know he has a nephew."

Lucas wipes his eyes on the tail of his t-shirt. He has a son. He has a son, and the road ahead has taken another sudden turn.

௸

He met Pippa when they were both sophomores at NYU. She was an art major, too, and people said they looked like brother and sister, both tall and lanky with auburn hair, hers a curly pre-Raphaelite cloud. She was from upstate, a tiny hamlet called White Lake near where the Woodstock festival had been held, and for Lucas she was a country breeze in the canyons of Manhattan. They were inseparable. She even liked to help him make bread.

They graduated and he opened the bakery, and she took a job teaching art at a private academy. He could see it all ahead of them, the bakery downstairs, the little apartment upstairs until perhaps they needed more room for their future children.

But then in February Pippa became sad and withdrawn, until on a chilly and miserable March afternoon she came home and said, "Lucas, I gave my notice at school. If I don't get back to the country, something terrible is going to happen. I'm sorry I didn't discuss it with you, but today it all overwhelmed me and I just did it. I think it was a panic attack. Come to White Lake. We'll bake bread and paint and breathe the good fresh air."

How could he leave? The East Village was his lifelong home. His bakery, not quite a year old by then, was successful. His watercolors that the gallery handled were street scenes and cityscapes, the subjects he was becoming known for. How could he ever find the courage to cast it all aside and start over in the quiet countryside that bore no resemblance to home? The City was in his blood, as the country was in hers. Maybe this was her way of saying she wanted something different than what he could offer.

Now he knows that while he was sitting in Manhattan hoping that she would change her mind, she was sitting in White Lake, waiting for him to do the same. And when that didn't happen and Louisa came into his life, he was just lonely enough to be flattered by her attention, lonely enough to marry her on the rebound when his heart still belonged to Pippa.

It suddenly occurs to him that maybe that was also a factor in the failure of his marriage. He wonders how he could ever have been so blind, so stupid.

☙

Whatever awkwardness Lucas is anticipating on seeing Pippa again does not materialize. He shows Riley and Pippa and Jeremy their rooms and then takes them down the path to the beach, where they settle on the rock ledges and look at the sun glinting on the incoming tide.

Riley is tall for eleven, as Lucas himself was. He has Pippa's almond-shaped hazel eyes and pale translucent skin, and the first hints of Lucas' own adult bone structure, an arched nose and strong jaw. His hair is Lucas' shade of auburn and the curly texture of Pippa's.

"What do you think?" Lucas says as they watch a couple of seals frolicking in the waves and a sailboat drifting across the horizon.

Riley says, "It's different from Bethel. I kinda like it." He looks hard at Lucas and adds, "Mom told me you're my real father."

"That's right," Lucas says, not daring to look at Pippa for assurance but not daring to leave the remark unanswered, either.

Riley nods. "We kind of look like each other, I guess."

Lucas nods, too. "I think we do."

Pippa says to Riley, "Are you okay?"

"Yeah. He seems like a cool dude."

"Oh, he is," Pippa says, smiling now. "A very cool dude."

☙

Pippa and her husband Jeremy Sykes have an organic farm in Bethel, New York, so Lucas calls Henry and suggests getting together.

"Perfect timing," Henry says. "I was going to call you anyway. A bunch of friends are coming over around five to play some music and have dinner and sample some of Joline's new home brews. You'll remember some of these guys from when we were kids."

Riley and Pippa and Jeremy take a tour of the island with Barry and eat lunch while Lucas finishes up the day's baking.

Late that afternoon, he packs up the five loaves of bread he reserved for the dinner and they all climb into the old Land Cruiser and head out, Barry driving, Pippa in front, Lucas and Riley and Jeremy in the back.

"What are you going to do in Nova Scotia?" Lucas asks.

"I want to drive around the Cabot Trail," Jeremy says.

Pippa adds, "I want to see where the Acadians came from."

Riley says, "Can't we stay here a few days and hang out with Lucas and Barry?"

"We'll talk about that tonight," Pippa says.

Riley bumps Lucas in the ribs with his elbow and whispers, "That means yes."

Whatever happens, Lucas finally believes it'll be okay. All the false starts and stupid choices and missed connections no longer matter. He gives Riley a thumbs-up, then turns his face to the breeze through the open window as they cruise across the causeway, heading towards the music jam and the future that lies beyond it.

LEAVING WAPATQUAN

NONE OF THEM REALIZE IT. In truth, I am just realizing it myself, now that we've gathered on the dock for an unobstructed view of the sunset from our Adirondack chairs. They—my boys, Clarence and Pauly, and their wives—are no doubt seeing this evening, this ritual, as simply one in a long chain of last summer evenings here at the lake. But I know better.

They will continue to come to this Maine lake-house as Carmichaels have for three generations. They are, after all, only in their sixties. But I turned eighty-eight last month, and every year both the trip to Lake Wapatquan and my rambles around its woods and fields and shore become more difficult.

Gloria, Clarence's wife, has already arranged a blanket for a chair cushion. I sit, and Pauly grasps my ankles and lifts my feet to the footstool even though I don't need his help. I am, as everyone likes to tell me, very healthy for my age—"for my age," what a qualifier!

The younger generations—my grandchildren and their children—have already gone back to Boston and New Haven and Atlanta. It is just the five of us now, the boys and their wives and me, and we are all long past needing to fill every silence with idle chatter. Stuffed to the gills with grilled rib-eyes and fire-roasted potatoes and buttery corn on the cob, and the blueberry cobbler for which Gloria is justly famous with the MIT English department, we sit with our separate end-of-summer thoughts.

I lean back and try to quiet my mind. The sinking sun is sending long, rosy rays through the dark spruces above Roark's Point, rays that lie with geometric straightness on the lake's glassy surface now that the breeze has died. A pair of bald eagles break free of the trees, sailing in widening circles against the apricot sky and lavender puffs of cloud. At the far end of the lake, a loon's eerie laugh rises. I try to take in every detail. I need to. I must not forget any of it. Not since Paris have I had a summer without these sunsets.

I've just closed my eyes to fix it all in memory when Joyce, Pauly's wife, breaks our companionable silence. "How many summers have you come here, Momma Giselle?"

My eyes fly open. Stephen and I liked Joyce immediately when Pauly brought her home. It would be hard not to be charmed by her Savannah-belle manners and warmth. Less charming is her disconcerting way of verbalizing other people's thoughts.

"Longer than we've been alive." Clarence runs a hand through his white-blond hair, a boyish habit he's never let go of. "What is it, sixty-five?"

"Sixty-six," I say. "Sixty-six summers." Memory's door to past summers is opening. It's exactly what I've been trying to avoid. I seek a change of subject. "Listen."

Youthful voices are raised in argument about "borrowing" a neighbor's canoe. We listen.

Pauly says, "It's so weird how you can hear conversations from clear across the lake but not from next door."

"It's an acoustic-geographic anomaly." We all look at Clarence, wondering where that came from.

Pauly laughs. "Don't try to sound like your scientific buddies. You're an English prof, remember?"

Joyce slaps Pauly on the knee. "Be nice."

Gloria says, "It's like the old party lines on the telephone. No secrets."

That gets me thinking about the past again. The conversations that float on this ancient lake. The arguments that lie like shoals beneath it. Does everything circle endlessly back? Time feels fragile now, as though the membrane between the past and present has worn thin. Could I slip through it and hear a Passamaquoddy mother crooning a lullaby or telling her children the legends of Koluskap? Or see an early settler woman pegging the wash on the line? Could

I reach through time and grasp the sticky hands of my tanned and sun-bleached young boys eating watermelon on this very dock? Or slide into the cool linen sheets where my naked husband waits for me to finish brushing my hair? Stephen. Oh, Stephen.

I sit silent, trapped in my memories. Stephen showing me all his childhood haunts. Making love in the tall grass with daisies and red clover waving around us. Clarence and Pauly, teenagers with their first sailboat. Clarence and Gloria's firstborn, waterbaby Teddy, learning to swim before he could even walk. All my grandchildren, Teddy and Alex, P.J. and Poppy and Lulu, and their children, all part of this summer place. These summer memories. I am eighty-eight years old, and life has been a wonder.

The sun has dipped behind the hill now, leaving only a faint golden glow through the trees. Indigo is creeping down the sky, smudging the tops of the clouds with charcoal. I close my eyes and breathe deep. This scent of lake water and piney woods. The aroma of summer.

I had planned to tell Clarence and Gloria my decision during tomorrow's trip back to Boston, but suddenly it seems better to say it once to all of them. "I'm not coming back next summer. It's too—" My voice fails me. I feel on the verge of tears, and now I'm wondering why I thought I could live without Wapataquan summers.

For what seems a long, long time, no one speaks.

Then Joyce says, "You might could feel different when next summer comes."

"Or I might be dead or in a nursing home. No guarantees."

Pauly says, "Don't talk like that, Mama."

Clarence says, "It won't be summer without you."

Joyce swirls what's left of her lemonade. "It's been hard enough without Poppa Stephen."

"Don't," I tell her. "Don't talk about Stephen."

Darkness is falling fast now. Behind us, a barn owl hoots softly. A cheshire-cat smile of a moon rocks on a wisp of pale cloud. Tomorrow at this time, I'll be home in Back Bay. This blanket of shimmering stars will be a faded remnant, only the brightest able to compete with the city's streetlights and headlights. Like memories—only those of greatest magnitude persist.

I slip my arms into the sleeves of my cardigan. Gloria asks, "Are you cold, Mama Giselle? Do you want to go in?"

I lean on her arm going up the stairs from the dock, and again up the stairs to the second floor of the house. "Go back out," I tell her. "I'll be fine."

My bedroom overlooking the lake, the master bedroom the boys have insisted I keep, has gathered the heat of the day. In my nightgown and robe, I open one of the tall windows and sit in the Boston rocker where eons ago I nursed and sang to my boys. As I rock, I realize I can hear them talking on the dock.

"So sad," Gloria's saying. "You're right, Joyce, it hasn't been the same without Papa Stephen. And without either of them—I can't imagine it."

"If only she could've stopped him," says Joyce.

"No," Clarence tells her. "There was no stopping Papa once he made up his mind."

Pauly says, "That's the truth."

"Drowning." Joyce's voice again. "So avoidable. So awful. If only we could've forbidden him to go swimming."

"Like forbidding a dog to wag its tail," Clarence says.

I hear the quaver in his voice and feel it in my heart. Better a stuffy room than this conversation on the rising breeze. I close the window and get into bed.

☙

I wake early, thinking about Stephen. I am the only one who knows. They think they know, but they don't. I have considered telling Clarence, but always stopped short of it. He doesn't need the questions that would nag him, doesn't need to wonder if there was something he could've done. There wasn't.

Stephen didn't drown because he couldn't swim as far as Roark's Point. He could. He didn't drown because exertion brought on a heart attack or a stroke. It didn't.

Stephen drowned because he had decided it was his time to go. He had chosen not to have the surgery, the chemo, the radiation, all those things that prolong the life but not the living. He knew the cancer was in his lung and in his brain. Of course he chose to leave on his own terms. That was Stephen.

LEAVING WAPATQUAN

The morning he came out on the porch in his baggy swim trunks, I understood what lay ahead. Everyone else was at the salmon festival on East Haven. We were alone. He held me for a long time. I tried not to weep, but I could feel the film of tears sliding between my cheek and the curve of his neck. "I love you," he said. "I will always love you." Then he tottered slowly down the dock and stepped into the lake.

He was going to swim to Roark's Point and then as far around the lake as his strength and breath would carry him. I wanted to watch until he was out of sight, but that went against the plan. Instead, I lay on our bed for the agreed-upon half hour, wondering if there were any chance he'd change his mind. He didn't, of course.

I was calmer than I had believed I could be when I made the calls to 911 and then to Clarence's cell phone. Calm when our boys and the ambulance and the state police divers arrived. Still calm when at last the undertaker came to take Stephen's body away. *It's what he wanted*, I kept telling myself. Like nearly everything else in his life, it went according to plan.

This last morning, no one is up yet except me. I pad down the stairs in robe and slippers, pour a glass of tomato juice, and step outside. The rising sun forms a golden mist above the lake, and birds I've never learned the names of are calling from the trees. Monarchs flit among the milkweed beside the well house. I cannot bear to think I'll never feel this peace again.

"Stephen," I say, and he is here.

He is always here, in a way he never is in Boston.

I go back into the house and slowly, quietly, up the stairs. I find my old bathing suit and put it on, then go down the dock and swim to the float. I try to measure the distance to Roark's Point. It is not far, but I am no longer a strong swimmer.

The sun is full up now. It's hot on my back and shoulders as I sit dangling my feet in the water. I feel them calling me, Stephen and Lake Wapatquan.

I slide into the water and start to swim.

SEA CHANGE

GEORDIE WALLACE PARKED HIS old Ford pickup on the Spruce Island breakwater and climbed out into salt air acrid with blue smoke from the failing carburetor. Out towards the Eastern Passage, a thin yellow line lit the horizon—no red sky, no sailor's warning. If he were lucky, both the truck and the January weather would hold, and the catch would be good, and Karen, his wife, wouldn't have any reason to push him to find work ashore. Not today at least, and today was all Geordie could manage now. One day at a time, like those guys who went to AA were always saying.

In the grey half-light of dawn, the ocean wore the dull sheen of a sheet of lead. Geordie's winchman, Kenny Sabatis, was already on board the *Starwind*, his perpetual red beret looking wildly out of place with his orange survival suit, his shoulder-length straight black hair lifting in the chill five-knot breeze. Kenny was Passamaquoddy, part of the Wabanaki nation. His people had been fishing the Bay of Fundy back before history was written down.

Little bigger than a twelve-year-old, Charley Lindahl came down the breakwater ladder after Geordie, wearing his shy half-smile and stretching to reach from rung to rung. Last to arrive was Stu Pooler, the other sternman, who still had the quick, athletic stride of the basketball star he'd been back at Quoddy High. Stu was their strongman, able to steer with one hand the heavy drag full of scallops.

While Kenny made sure the winch was lubed and oiled and in perfect running order, the cable wound smooth and tight around the spool, Charley and Stu checked the heavy drag. Over six feet wide, it looked like a sack made of linked inch-and-a-half iron rings, open at the top to scoop up the scallops. Two locked iron bars opened at the bottom to drop the scallops on the shucking table at the stern of the boat.

Everything squared away and in working order, they cast off lines, maneuvered out of the row of tethered boats and headed for the scallop beds. Every day, the *Starwind III* was the first boat out, a tradition that went back to Geordie's grandfather aboard the original *Starwind*. But unlike the old days, competition was fierce now, the big draggers coming in from the westward early in the season, harvesting more in a day than the local boys could in a week. Destroying the fishery, destroying the sense of community that kept the Spruce Island fleet alive, giving Karen just one more reason for wanting Geordie to find a different future.

They spent the morning dragging at the mouth of Little Musquan Bay, running between the red and green channel markers through eddying plumes of sea smoke. Then it was time to shut down for lunch, time to relax for a few minutes and jaw.

Stu finished half a bologna sandwich in two bites. "Well, Geordie, guess there ain't no easy way to tell you. Tomorrow's my last day."

Geordie's tea splashed over the leg of his survival suit. He and Kenny and Stu had started out together on Geordie's father's boat, the *Starwind II*. For almost twenty years, it had been their life's work, scalloping in the winter, purse-seining in long-gone summers before the herring started to run out, setting trawl for groundfish the summers since.

Kenny said, "You're leaving the *Starwind*? Why?"

"Woolen mill's hiring." Stu pulled off his Red Sox cap and ran a chapped hand over his blonde crewcut. "It'd be steady. Insurance. Paid vacations."

Charley began, "But Stu—"

"But nothing. Fishing's near run out." Stu stared doggedly at his black rubber fish boots. In his stubborn refusal to meet their eyes, the shakiness of his decision seemed plain. Would anything Geordie could say make Stu change his mind? Would anything keep him on the *Starwind*, keep the crew, arguably the fleet's best, intact?

"You'll be miserable in that factory." Geordie poured more tea from his thermos. "Indoors all day, summer as well as winter. Mark my words."

Stu's big freckled face quivered for a moment, but then he set his bulldog chin. "This ain't for me. It's for Wanda and the kids. Ain't right, keeping them without."

Charley and Kenny nodded. Geordie, too, knew what Stu meant. The pants and sweatshirts handed down to his son, Scotty, from his sister's kids. The patient, unheeded explanations of why expensive game consoles and video games weren't going to appear under the Christmas tree. The worries about something on the boat breaking down, or the furnace quitting, or the truck needing major repairs.

None of that mattered, though. Scotty was going to learn that some things were more important than money. He wasn't going to have to be a paid slave in a dead-end job. He'd be able to work on his own terms, even if the family business was, admittedly, banquet some seasons and starvation others. He would get by, and be richer for it.

"We've had good years," Geordie said. "Plenty of them."

Stu looked from the shore to Geordie and back again. "Some. But not lately. Not enough."

Geordie wrapped both hands around his heavy ironstone mug, but that didn't warm them. He was cold now from something besides the chill, damp air. "Any time you want to come back. Any time."

"Don't offer me that." Stu turned his head to follow the flight of a pair of sea ducks overhead. "I don't want to have that choice. I don't ever want to have that choice."

༺༻

That night, Geordie fidgeted until the blankets came loose at the foot of the bed as he stared wide-eyed into the darkness.

The Wallaces of Spruce Island had followed the sea for over a hundred and fifty years, and they'd follow it for a hundred and fifty more if it were up to him. He wasn't going to be the one to break tradition. But with Stu gone and a new sternman—if he could even find one—who might quickly become part of the crew but only slowly part of the team, everything was going to be harder. No more four old friends able to work wordlessly, anticipating each other's movements, meshing like the gearwheels of Kenny's winch. It was all going to be different now, and change meant uncertainty, and uncertainty wasn't productive or comfortable, not at all.

Geordie fell into restless sleep, and then the dream came. At first, he was on the *Starwind*, cutting across a glassy sea at full flood tide on Little Musquan Bay. It was summertime, the air against his bare arms as hot and dry as a desert. Although the season closed at the end of March, he was scalloping, alone, running the helm and the winch and the shucking table simultaneously, under a sunset that had set the whole western sky glowing orange as fireplace coals.

He bent over the winch and put it in neutral so the drag would freefall to the ocean floor. When he looked up from the winch, though, everything had changed. The hiss of water against the *Starwind*'s hull was drowned out in a horrible metallic clacking. The boat disappeared, and above Geordie towered a complicated machine, its many parts moving in a weird and contradictory random unison. Arms lifted and slammed down. Jaws opened and closed. A web of threads ran everywhere, feeding giant spools. As he watched, unable to move a single, paralyzed muscle, one of the threads snapped and its end snaked out and wrapped around his arm. Other threads broke and wound around him, tight as a cocoon. He was tethered to the machine so tightly there'd be no escaping till the end of time—if then.

Barely able to breathe, he struggled against his bonds, and woke, rolled in the blankets. Karen was tugging at them, saying, "Geordie, I'm cold." Once the covers were straightened, she fell back to sleep immediately, but Geordie lay there while his heart hammered and he gulped down breath in ragged gasps.

Wind howled in the tall old chimneys. Snow skittered against the window glass. At last, the alarm clock read four-thirty. He padded downstairs in his underwear, shivering in the drafts. In the kitchen, he flipped on the CB radio and listened to the boatmen's chatter. No one was chancing it. So much for Stu's last day, he thought as he climbed the stairs and fell back into bed, and at last into exhausted dreamless sleep.

⁂

When he woke again, the Saturday smell of blueberry muffins baking teased his nose as he groped for his old plaid robe in the drafty bedroom. In the kitchen, he poured a cup of tea from the old brown betty teapot and stood at the kitchen window. Beyond the glass, the whirling snow was coming so hard and fast that he couldn't even see the bay.

Karen, her golden hair swinging free to the belt of her pink fleece housecoat, pulled a pan from the oven and flipped the muffins into a towel-lined bowl. "I love these storm days. Just like when we were kids. I still pretend we're going to be snowed in until spring. Do you think we'd survive?"

She slipped one arm around Geordie's waist, rested her head against his chest. Geordie held her close. "We'll always survive," he said. He hadn't told her about Stu yet. She'd ask questions, sensible questions, like where would he find another sternman, one who wasn't a dub, and what would happen if he couldn't find anyone at all? Lying awake last night, he'd run through every name in town, and there wasn't anyone experienced who wasn't already on a boat. But he didn't want to tell her that. She'd point out that running the *Starwind* with three would be next to impossible. Only one boat in the fleet was managing it, and that was the *Five Sisters*. His only answer for that was that her crew, like his own, had logged a lot of time together, and if they could do it, so could he and Kenny and Charley. Of course, if he told her that, she'd point out that the sternman on the *Five Sisters,* Tony Readfield, was built like a linebacker, and say Charley's size was against him when it came to managing the drag.

Karen was the practical one, for sure, and had the ability to do what needed doing regardless of whether she wanted to or not. Geordie, the wisher and dreamer, both loved and feared that in her.

He decided to keep quiet about Stu a while longer. He didn't want to wreck their snow day together. He didn't want to bring the storm inside. "Breakfast ready?" was all he said.

"Yeah." They smooched and stepped apart.

In the TV room, Scotty lay on his belly on the floor, his chin in his hand as he read a *National Geographic* borrowed from the school library. "Breakfast, son," Geordie said, and Scotty, with a sigh, shut the magazine. No reading at the table, that was a family rule.

"Mom, I need a bag like onions come in. For school." Scotty scattered sugar over his oatmeal. Karen said she thought there was one in the pantry.

"What are you working on?" Geordie asked. Sometimes he couldn't figure out where Scotty had come from. He had the lean Wallace build, the cleft chin and unruly brown hair, and he had Karen's eyes, but if not for his looks and Karen's absolute faithfulness, Geordie could've wondered whose son he was, this quiet, serious, straight-A seventh-grader who'd never shown the least interest in fishing.

"It's a for science. Danny and I are making an aquaculture site."

"An aquaculture site?" Just the word was enough to set Geordie off. Those big cage sites, encroaching on the scalloping grounds, polluting the sea floor with salmon waste and uneaten food. But he clamped down on his tongue, because Karen was already darting him warning glances.

"Mister Chipman says it's the future of harvesting the sea," Scotty said. "He says commercial fishing's almost done with."

Geordie poured more tea, the pot's spout rattling against the rim of his mug. Karen was still narrowing her eyes at him, pale green eyes, ice green, the color of seawater churned up in propwash, and he made a mental note not to look at her again until the conversation was over. "Did Mister Chipman happen to say why?"

Geordie sat open-mouthed as his son came back with an answer that would've made one of those meddling fishery experts proud. "We're doing a unit on marine biology." Scotty sat up straight, as though he were making a presentation to the public. "We went to Trumbull's Head on a field trip and counted green crabs. They're an invasive species that eat the baby clams, so the clam beds won't come back. A lot of the finfish went since the canneries can't dump their fish waste back in the ocean any more, because they used to feed on it. Plus, the fish and the scallops have been over harvested, and the urchin draggers are tearing up the scallop beds and disturbing their life cycle. So if people want to eat fish and shellfish, they'll have to grow them themselves."

Well, Geordie thought, *haven't you turned out to be a regular little parrot*. He couldn't disagree with the theories, though. Clams, scallops, herring, haddock, what Scotty's teacher had taught him was likely true. It was aquaculture, their crazy solution, that was the real problem.

"Fish ain't cows, son." Geordie steadfastly refused to look at Karen. "And aquaculture ain't fishing. It's farming, tied to one spot just like on land. And who knows what they use for feed, what we end up eating when we eat farmed fish. It ain't right. It dirties up the bay, and it takes our fishing grounds."

"It gives people jobs, too," Scotty came back. "Fish is healthy food and more people are eating it and more people have jobs. So it's good."

"It's not good." Geordie felt his heart hammering. How could his own son take sides against him? "It's destroying our way of life, generations of fishermen. How can you listen to that bullsh—I mean, that claptrap? Don't believe everything you hear in school."

"Geordie." Karen buttered half a muffin with such force it crumbled in her hand. "He loves to learn. Don't destroy that for him. And we're all snowed in together here. Let's have a good day."

"Oh, sure," Geordie said, his earlier decision forgotten. "Stu's leaving the *Starwind*, Scotty's teachers are turning him against the family business, and you expect me to have a good day?" He smacked his forehead with the palm of his hand. Now his mouth had really gotten ahead of his brain.

Karen pounced like a mousing cat. "Stu's leaving the boat? When? Why? Why didn't you tell me?"

You know why I didn't tell you, he thought. What he said was, "He's going to the woolen mill. He thinks he'll be better off there."

Karen squared her placemat with the edge of the table. "Well, maybe he will be. At least it's steady, a paycheck you can count on. And health insurance. That's something."

"That mill could fold up tomorrow. Nothing's guaranteed."

"It's good to learn new skills." Karen drew a spiral in her oatmeal with her spoon and gave the edge of the bowl a sharp rap. "Things are changing, whether you're willing to admit it or not."

"Don't talk about that welding thing." Geordie stared at her, determined not to be the first to look away. "I don't want to hear that, not now."

SEA CHANGE

"I just think we should look ahead, not back." He could tell when she wanted to say more, the way her lips opened and closed a couple times and then pressed together as she shook her head. She turned away and carried her dishes to the sink.

Geordie poured another cup of tea and headed for the TV room. As he went through the door, he heard Scotty say softly, "Mom, why would Mister Chipman lie?"

❡

The blizzard continued the next day, Sunday. Scotty's school project wasn't mentioned, and neither was Stu. Through the rooms of their old Cape Cod house, Geordie and Karen passed without speaking, until at last it was late evening and Scotty was in bed and they were alone with their pile of unspoken words between them.

A re-run of *French Kiss* was on TV. It was one of Karen's favorite movies, but Geordie had no patience with love as the movies presented it, foolish obstacles and then happily ever after. Real life was so much harder, messier, so many compromises, so many choices you just didn't know how to make. You had that time at first when love was going to solve every problem and the person you loved was going to be fascinating and kind and generous forever. But reality always set in hard, and you ended up at cross-purposes and couldn't even talk about it. And then you started to drift apart, each bobbing on your own currents, mindless as cork.

After the movie, Geordie knew only one way of making up. "Let me brush your hair," he offered. It was an old ritual, and something about it—maybe the quiet, smooth rhythm of the brushing itself—was often able to calm them down enough to listen to each other and hear what wasn't said.

She got her brush and sat on the old kitchen stool that had its turned wooden legs wired together. For five minutes, Geordie brushed her hair the way she'd taught him, clearing tangles from the ends first, brushing just the bottom few inches of her waist-length hair, then moving higher, and so on.

He was brushing downward from between her shoulder blades when she said, "I've been wanting to tell you since yesterday. I have a chance to go to college. The bank will pay my tuition, and I can get a promotion if I earn my degree in accounting."

Geordie concentrated on untangling a strand of hair without pulling. The bank job was new, something she'd started back in the fall now that Scotty was old enough to stay by himself after school. Karen was convinced they needed two incomes, wanted to put something away for Scotty to go to college. He hadn't objected to her plans, because he knew they could use the extra money, but he hadn't figured the job would change her the way it had, making her at once both happier and more discontented, and ambitious to a degree he never would've suspected. Gone were the days of clearly defined roles, of Karen waiting for him when he came home, of freshly baked pies and the house perfectly organized.

He didn't want to hold her back, he really didn't, he told himself, but the first worlds out of his mouth told a different story. "Riverton is forty miles each way. The truck's too old for it."

She flinched as the brush hit a tangle. "Marla McHenry's driving. Don't worry about the truck."

"I don't know," Geordie said. Would Karen with a degree still want to be a fisherman's wife? She could be independent then, could do whatever she wanted, and he could easily be left behind. When she'd started dreaming out loud about being an accountant, he'd thought it was just talk. He should've known better.

"It'll be fine," she told him. "You'll see. Scotty deserves better than we had. College, books, nice clothes. A trip to Disneyworld."

"I've taken care of this family for a long time now. I've done my best. And now that's not good enough."

Karen reached back and caught his hand as the brush swept smoothly now from the crown of her head to her waist. "Charley's wife works at the IGA. Kenny's wife works at the tribal office. I work at the bank. It's the way it is now. Families need two incomes to make ends meet. It's not personal." She slipped off the stool, put her arms around his waist and rested her head against his chest. "It's not a contest. I've always helped. I always will."

"I know." He'd watched her struggle through three difficult pregnancies to produce Scotty, had seen her bent over her books many midnights, studying for her G.E.D. even after he'd given up trying to get his, had seen her hands sliced and salt-burned from summers of packing sardines. He knew that even though she looked as pale and fragile as a princess, she was just as strong and even more tenacious than he.

☙

Monday was cutting cold, the brilliant sunlight hard-edged as it struck across the heaving, steely sea. Without Stu, the high-bowed Novy boat seemed big and empty. Charley, small but wiry, struggled to handle the loaded drag alone. And even though he was the fastest scallop shucker in the fleet, at lunchtime they stayed shut down while Geordie and Kenny helped him catch up. It was their custom to return the shells to the scallop beds, something they'd always done without knowing exactly why. Now they were coming back from Little Musquan, where the scallops were particularly large and sweet, with a catch that should guarantee a nice profit for the day.

They'd just made Clement Point when Geordie, through the salt-spray-encrusted windshield of the wheelhouse, saw a blue-hulled dragger making slow headway from the direction of Red Island. "Kenny," he called, "get in here," but as always, Kenny was on the spot before he finished getting the words out.

"What's up?"

Geordie pointed. "That the *Markari*?" Abner Dunbar's boat, named for his son and daughter.

Kenny took up the binoculars, tried to look through the salt-spattered windshield but then went out on deck. "It is," he said when he returned. "Looks like she's lost her drag. And she's wallowing pretty bad."

Geordie changed course, and headed for the *Markari*. It was always something out here, no matter how squared away you thought you were. The cold and the salt air were hard on equipment. If you saw someone in trouble, no matter what you were doing, even if you'd found a bed of scallops in twenty-four karat gold shells, you went and helped the disabled boat. It was the only way.

Ten minutes later the *Starwind* hove to beside the *Markari*. "You need a hand?" Kenny called after Geordie cut the throttle.

Mark Dunbar, Abner's son and winchman, cupped his hands around his mouth. "Lost our drag up on the far side of Red Island. Had a following sea and shipped some water, and you know that bilge pump Pop can never get working right."

Geordie and Kenny and Charley all nodded. It happened sometimes, the drag hooking onto something, the stern of the boat sinking down with the pressure enough to let a wave wash in, the pump sticking and the water sitting there in the bilges, making you slow and heavy.

A squat, round man like a barrel on legs, Abner came out of the wheelhouse and joined his son and the sternmen on deck. Abner had been there for Geordie from the git-go, when Geordie's father was swept off the deck of the *Starwind II* by a rogue wave in heavy seas, and Geordie, at seventeen, was left with a boat to run and no real knowledge of the business end of fishing. The second day of his first scallop season without his father, his winch motor had died, and it was Abner who repaired it. Three years later, Geordie's drag had hooked a ledge off Suffolk Neck and almost tore the transom off the boat, and Abner had lent him the money for repairs. Last summer, when dogfish tore up the *Starwind's* tub trawl, Abner spent several long evenings in Geordie's barn helping them repair it.

"Had that drag two weeks," Abner said. "Brand new. Hadn't even finished paying Grant for welding it."

Charley whistled through his teeth and shook his red head. "Honest to Pete. We might just as well sit in the shower and tear up hundred dollar bills as try and keep the fleet going."

"You're right about that," Abner agreed. "I was talking to Stan a little while ago." Stan, Abner's brother, was the local seafood buyer. "Price is down over a dollar on the Boston market today."

A dollar a pound, gone like the morning fog. Their profit margin was already too slim to absorb it.

"Still got your old drag?" Kenny asked. "You can run that."

"Sold it." Abner shrugged. "We're done for the season. Bank'll laugh me right out the door if I try to borrow any more money."

"You help yourself to the drag in my barn," Geordie said. "Skids are a little balky, is why I put it up, but you can manage it at least till you get a diver down and see if yours is salvageable." He sighed, then caught one side of his mustache between his lip and lower teeth. Everything was so hard, and those boys from the westward were out there, waiting for the local fleet to fail.

Abner picked up the drag the next day. A week passed, and the market price rose a bit, and the fleet was shut down for only a day, when a forty-knot Arctic wind howled out of the northeast. Then came a morning soft and sunny with the promise of a January thaw.

Kenny was oiling the winch gears. "Heard they're doing real good up past the Falls."

"That's 'cause the big draggers can't get up there," Charley said. He coughed, a sound like a rusty file rasped across steel.

"You okay?" Geordie said.

"Just a little bronchitis. Not bad."

Rumor had it right. The catch was very good. "One more pass," Kenny called. "Then we better shut down and help shuck."

Geordie swung the wheel. The boat came about, and Kenny dropped the drag.

Suddenly, Geordie was thrown forward, almost bumping his head on the windshield as he heard Kenny yell, "Watch it!" Falls Island hung in one place beyond the *Novy's* bow, and that was wrong, all wrong.

They were caught, caught good. Terrified the *Starwind's* stern would swamp, Geordie slacked the throttle as her bow rose.

"Cable release is jammed," Kenny shouted. "Reverse, quick!" Geordie reached again for the throttle. Then he turned and saw the cable snap. The boom flew forward, hissing through the briny air, barely missing Kenny's head. In a foolish move, he reached to subdue its wild swing, but missed. The boom struck the rear edge of the wheelhouse roof, then arced back towards the shucking table. Kenny raced to the *Starwind's* stern.

"I've got it," Charley shouted, but then there was a loud, ominous thud. He cried out as the boom bounced twice and came to rest.

"No!" Kenny tore off his knitted muffler and wrapped it around the mass of mangled bone and flesh and rubberized brown glove that had been Charley's right hand. He pressed hard on the wrist, the pulse point, but still some blood leaked through. Charley keeled over like a sheared mast, and Kenny bent with him, still holding fast.

Geordie's throat had closed up so tight he could barely talk to the Coast Guard on the radio. His heart was banging like an engine with a bad connecting rod. *Don't panic*, he told himself. More than anything else, it was panic that was deadly on the water.

Down through the Falls they came. Past the red nun buoy that marked the Howell's Point ledge. Past Trumbull's Head. It seemed to take forever, not the forty minutes that Geordie's watch ticked away. Through it all, Kenny knelt on the deck and kept a white-knuckled grip on Charley's right wrist.

At the breakwater, after the ambulance had taken Charley away, Geordie and Kenny stayed at the slip and shucked the rest of the scallops. Kenny wiped his shucking knife on his pants leg. "What in hell did we latch onto that far upriver? Ain't no chance of getting that drag back. You know Lambson ain't gonna dive up there because of the current."

Geordie said a silent thanks that Kenny was talking about something besides Charley's injury. "I know. It's bad timing, for sure."

"It doesn't seem right to ask Abner for that drag back. On the other hand, it is yours. And you have responsibilities."

Geordie rubbed his forehead under his navy watch cap. He knew what Kenny was really saying, that they depended on scalloping to get them through the winter, and if they couldn't scallop, there was no money coming in, not only for him and the boat, but for the crew, too. "I don't feel right, asking for it back, after all Abner's done for us. Maybe they'll recover his and it'll be fixable."

Kenny moved a full scallop bucket and replaced it with an empty one. "Didn't you hear? Lambson dove for Abner's drag. It was all stove to pieces, tangled right up around an old mooring anchor."

Geordie looked at the buckets of shells that would never get back to the beds. "Then I don't know what to do. I don't know." He wasn't sure if he meant right then, or for the rest of the winter, or the rest of his life. They shucked in silence for another ten or fifteen minutes.

As though no time had passed at all, Kenny said, "We'll get another drag. Eventually. But Charley—he ain't gonna grow another hand."

Geordie felt his heart hammering in his throat. "Best shucker in the fleet, and what's he got left? What's he got to show for it? Nothing. Absolutely nothing." If Stu had been there, quick and strong, this never would've happened. If they'd had a second sternman at all, this never would've happened. He'd tried to take care of everything, the crew and the boat, but this was a major mistake, Charley's injury all his fault, even if the accident itself had been unavoidable. He should've packed it in for this season when Stu quit.

They finished shucking in silence, and sluiced Charley's blood from the deck.

ଔ

Soon after Geordie reached home, Scotty came in, lugging in the big square of plywood that held his and Danny's aquaculture model. "We got an A on our project, and—" He stopped and looked at the clock on the mantel. "Dad, why are you home already?"

"The boat broke down." No need to go into the awful, gory details, although Scotty was standing there obviously waiting to hear more. "Go do your homework or something. Dad's got stuff to think about."

His son went upstairs, and Geordie sat in his favorite rocking chair and sipped his tea, staring out the window towards the bay. The old Wallace homestead was on a tall cliff overlooking the channel and the island of East Haven, but with the spectacular view came the high winds of winter poking icy fingers into every breach. *An old albatross of a house*, his grandmother used to say.

Geordie swirled his tea and listened to the dull diesel whine as the draggers one by one made for the breakwater with the day's catch. Being on the water was more than his job, it was his life, salt sea, salt blood. He didn't want to exchange the roll of the deck for the stable surfaces of the landsman's world. He didn't want to be the Wallace who came ashore, the first son not to fish since his many-times-great grandfather fresh from Scotland set out for the Grand Banks cod-fishing grounds in the 1840's. The *Starwind III* would die, tied at the breakwater instead of running with the waves slapping against her dark green hull. Oil would gunk up the engines. Barnacles would foul the strakes. Winch gears would seize. Man and boat would slowly go to dust and rust.

ଔ

It was almost six, full January darkness, when Marla's headlights lit the yard. Geordie's head ached from trying to find a way to keep doing the only thing he wanted to do. No way around it, he was out of business for this season, no drag, no sternman. Sitting home and waiting for the seasons to turn wasn't an option—he had to be doing something, had to be earning his share, for there was no way they could get along on just Karen's salary. He could do any job on a dragger, but no one had an opening, and anyway, could he stand being the hired hand when he'd been master of his own boat for so long? He didn't think so.

The other option was to get a land job. He could follow Stu to the woolen mill, but he hated machines and he hated being indoors all day. Quoddy SeaFarms would be better. He could join the enemy, work on a cage site, find out what was really up with aquaculture beyond what the fishermen said. But that didn't feel right. His little voice was telling him not to do that, and if there was one thing Geordie knew, it was not to ignore his instincts. So why hadn't he listened when his little voice had asked him if he really thought going out with one sternman was a good idea? Probably because he had a point to prove with Karen, and that overrode all his common sense.

There's one more thing, he told himself. *I got one more choice, and damn it, it might be the only one.* There was money to help displaced workers train for another job, and if he did as Karen wanted, took the welding course at the technical college in Mayfield, the state would pay his way and pay him a small amount, too. Without having to choose between school or fishing, the welding course didn't seem like such a bad idea. True, Karen would win the single biggest battle of their marriage, but she wasn't one to make him eat that every day.

Three hours of hard thinking, and the solution was the one that had been there all along, the one he'd fought so hard. *You just never know where life will take you,* he thought as he heard the back door close.

"You okay?" Karen put a gallon jug in the refrigerator and slipped out of her parka. "They were talking about it at Abbott's when I stopped to get milk."

"It was rough." Geordie raked his fingers through the side of his beard.

"Abner was there, too. Said he doesn't feel right about using your old drag, under the circumstances."

"No. I wouldn't think of taking it back. I lent it to him till he got another, and I'm not going back on my word."

"Abner's helped you a lot, over the years."

"Yes. Yes, he has." Geordie ran his thumb around the rim of his mug.

Karen bent her head, and a curtain of blonde hair swung forward. She tucked it behind her ears. "I don't want you to think I'm trying to get you to stay ashore. But there might be a message in this."

"I know. I been mulling this over, while I was waiting for you. No drag, no sternman. I guess it's time to try something new."

She was silent for a long moment. At last she said, "It's not either-or. I know you can't stop fishing, no matter how you feel right now."

He wanted to hold her close, to make everything go away even for a little while, but he'd done too much thinking on this long afternoon. Things had to be said.

"I'm gonna ask Kenny if he wants to take that welding course with me. We'd be just about done when ground-fishing starts. Keep us going through the slack spells, a little business on the side. Help the fleet, too. I guess this month's proved there's always a market for scallop drags."

"It sounds fine," she said. He could tell by the way she opened and then closed her mouth that she was trying hard to let him reach these conclusions by himself.

"And when we do get back to fishing, Charley could man the helm or run the winch on the days one of us had to be ashore welding. They'll give him a hook or something so he can use that arm, won't they? It'd help all of us, I guess, taking that course."

"That's what it's all about."

"I hope I can do it. I hope I'm not too stupid."

Her fingers traced his cheek. "You're not the least bit stupid. Of course, you'll have to study. You never liked that much."

"I'm pretty good at doing what has to be done, though. Don't you think?"

"You can manage. Why do you think I married you? I knew you'd never let me down. Even when things have to change and you don't want them to."

Just don't let them change too much, he thought as she hugged him tight. For the first time since Stu gave notice, Geordie felt as though there was hope. "I won't let you down, Karen," he said. *And I won't let you down either,* he whispered, hoping that they could hear him, all those generations of Wallace fishermen out there somewhere beyond the wind and stars.

ಸಂ

BORDERLINE

SO HERE I AM, THE JUNE BEFORE my senior year, and we've got it all mapped out, Scooter Marantz and Bimbo Dexter and I, ready to run my practically-antique '66 VW microbus up and down the coast from Ventura to Oceanside, almost three months of seeking that perfect wave. It's going to be a totally bitchin summer, the last one before the real world crashes in, and *we* are going to live every second of it.

Or so I think, until the parents tell me they're going to Italy for a couple months to celebrate their twenty-fifth wedding anniversary. I can't hang with my tech-head big bro, Kurt, because he's off to Hawaii, the lucky dog, to upgrade some tourist bureau's web servers, and he absolutely will not take me with him, which rots. What I'd give to ride that big Hawaiian surf! So all of a sudden my plans are in ashes, cold as yesterday's barbecue, and I'm *this close* to being packed off to the farmstands and orange groves of Bakersfield when Gram Nesbitt breaks her hip.

Don't get me wrong, I'm not *glad* Gram broke her hip, nothing like that. But things do start looking up again when my Harlow grandparents in Boston agree to take me to their summer place on a Maine island called East Haven. I hear that Maine has, like, twenty-five hundred miles of coastline, so excuse me for thinking there must be surfable waves there somewhere.

∽

Buddy Dexter, Bimbo's dad, is the one who taught us to surf. We were twelve then, wound-up little grommets, but Buddy had that

Zen thing going, patient as Buddha himself. When he was young and first rode a longboard, soul surfing, being one with the wave for the pure pleasure of it and not for competition, was how most everyone looked at it.

Shaped for Buddy's dad by the greatest board maker of them all, Hobie Alter, Buddy's board was pristine white, a skinny green stripe and a wider blue one on each side of the redwood stringer. The best, but nothing flashy, and not a corporate decal in sight. Scooter and Bimbo dissed Buddy behind his back, not for his skill, but for his clean devotion to the waves. They wanted to be our generation's Kelly Slater, loved dreaming about money and babes and video games with their own names on them. I just wanted to be like Buddy Dexter, in a pure zone and feeling that ocean magic.

Four years later, Buddy had to hang up his wettie, because in one of life's supreme ironies he was diagnosed with MS. I inherited his Hobie longboard, and don't think it didn't immediately become my prized possession. Scooter and Bimbo were ripping with the best of the shortboard riders, getting air like the skate-punks do, but for me, surfing was still a dance with several tons of peaking water. Carving a line across the face of the wave, catching the lightning.

ஐ

Nonnie and Papa meet my flight from LAX, and even though they never do that my-haven't-you-grown-up schtick, we still have to give each other the once over. I'm always afraid, since I usually only see them at Christmas, that they'll have gotten old on me, but they haven't yet. They actually look pretty cool for grandparents, in spite of their upscale-suburban, east-coast style. Papa's got a head full of wavy silver hair and the only pencil-thin mustache I know in real life, and his carefully-faded denim shirt matches his eyes. Nonnie still has that debutante thing going even though she's got to be crowding seventy, perfect posture and blonde bobbed hair and a whole wristful of gold chains and diamond tennis bracelets. If they think I look like a freak with my undercut red hair, parrot-print aloha shirt, baggy cargo shorts, and flipflops, they're too polite to say so.

Their car's a red Saab convertible with Massachusetts plates. I stow my bags in the trunk, and stretch out in the backseat. As we wind on up the coast, the towns get smaller and smaller and shabbier, too, and I get more and more alarmed because there isn't a real beach in sight, not one. Plenty of rocky shores and looming, jutting ledges, so many pebbles they must've rained down from Heaven, but a decent beach, sand like brown sugar? Only in my wildest dreams.

"You didn't eat on the plane, did you?" my grandmother asks, and I tell her no, just some mixed nuts and a power bar I brought from home. Can't trust that yucky airline food. "That's good," she says, "because there's a little restaurant not far from here where we always stop to get a lunch."

Overlooking a small cove, the Pine Cone Diner is a log cabin, paneled in weathered barn boards and hung with watercolor seascapes. Papa recommends the haddock tacos, so I go for that, and he's right on. The French fries look suspiciously like they were cut by hand. A breeze comes in through the screened windows, evergreen woods mixed with salt, a way nicer smell than LA. The air's so clear it's like even the sunlight's been scrubbed.

Then it's back on the road, and finally, two steps from forever, we turn off the main highway. After a causeway and another town, we come around a curve, where spanning a stretch of choppy green water is the old-fashioned iron bridge to East Haven. It's low water, and I see rocky shore and mucky old clam flats. I can't get over how far out the tide goes here, like someone pulled a bathtub plug in the freaking ocean, and I think, *Okay, when all this water comes rushing back in*, then *we should have some surf.* And since this is supposed to be some kind of summer resort, maybe there's even a real beach here somewhere, possibly on the outer side of the island.

"How cold's the water?" I ask.

Papa glances at me over his shoulder. "About fifty-two in the summer. And there's no surf, it that's what you're asking."

"I saw photos on the Internet. I looked it up. Higgins Beach. Cape Elizabeth. Scarborough."

Nonnie shakes her head. "You'd be closer to those places visiting us in Boston than you are up here. That's southern Maine."

In two days the freight people will be arriving with my board, and there's no surf? I check out East Haven's main drag as it slides past, five blocks of red brick three-stories, the street hugging the shore, and the only thing that gives me any hope at all are the two dudes with skateboards under their arms. Sometimes, you have to ride 'em like you find 'em, and I guess this is going to be one of those times. Kurt doesn't leave for Hawaii for another week, so I make a mental note to have him overnight me the old skateboard that was everything to me before Buddy Dexter taught me to surf.

Past downtown, we come into a neighborhood of grand late-Victorian summer cottages. Papa turns into one built in the shingle style—I know this because I'm planning to be an architect—all gables and dormers and deep verandahs. Out the back door, the wide yard goes right down to the ocean. Tall, white-blooming hedges run down both sides, and everywhere, my grandmother's passion: flower beds in white and complementary peaches and purples. My room's huge and airy with golden oak furniture and a view of the bay, and I tell myself I've definitely seen worse digs—until I remember it's not surfable here. But I know those mental fidgets never solve anything, they're just energy vampires.

౸

Next morning, while Nonnie and Papa are doing their geezer version of tai chi among the flower gardens, I ambulate on downtown to scope out the scene. There are all kinds of tourists on the streets, and wall-to-wall cars, but I don't see any skaters. I'm starting to think that even in Bakersfield I'd've had my microbus and could've made it to the beach at least a few times, but here I'm only a few dozen feet from an ocean that doesn't even know the meaning of surf. I check out a pocket-sized park, with a brick path through the middle and stairs with grindable iron railings leading down to the pink granite seawall. It has possibilities, but then I see the sign: "No skateboards, skates, or scooters allowed."

I'm on my way home when I meet a kid carrying a board. He's twelve, thirteen max, trying way too hard with stick-on tattoos and hair peroxided to dry straw, but hey, whatever. I ask him where the scene is, and he tells me it's in Dudley, a town just north of here, which is a bitch for all the skate-rats too young to drive.

"How come there's no park on the island?"

He gives me this look like I'm incredibly obtuse. "It's totally stupid. The tourists don't like us, so it was decided to hide the park over on Spruce Island, 'cept they couldn't find a piece of land. So they put it in Dudley instead." I ask if it's any good, and he tells me not bad, a nice fast half-pipe and a couple of ramps, not fancy but better than nothing.

When I get back to Nonnie and Papa's, I ask where Dudley is. "It's where we turned off route one yesterday." Papa picks up a stamp with a pair of tweezers, looks at it through a magnifying glass, and adds it to one of the piles in front of him. He's got dozens of leather-bound albums back in Boston, and once he told me he started collecting when he was twelve. Maybe that's the kind of hobby to have. I mean, what are the chances I'll still be able to surf fifty years from now?

I explain about the skate park, and then I take a deep breath and ask if I can borrow the Saab, but they tell me no. Nonnie, though, as always, comes through for me. "He could take the beach wagon."

The beach wagon. That sounds intriguing.

Papa examines another stamp. "He'll have to promise not to exceed the speed limit."

"It doesn't go fast anyway," Nonnie says with a little flip of her hand, and I have one of those *uh-oh* moments, because, as any dude can tell you, by your wheels you are known.

೧೦

The beach wagon's actually pretty tubular, a robin's-egg blue 1953 Ford station wagon, which Nonnie and Papa bought with the house. They use it for tailgate picnics and rides on summer evenings, and not much else. It's cherry, 14,723 actual miles, and I just know it'll go faster than they think it will.

After FedEx delivers my skateboard, I follow Papa's directions west to the mainland. Just beyond the turn onto route one, I see the half-pipe and a couple of ramps, surrounded on three sides by evergreens.

Two girls sit on the hood of a rust-bucket Camaro, and even though they hide it when I drive up and park about ten feet away, I'm pretty sure they're smoking a joint. One of the girls is small, with pulled-back hair dyed even redder than mine naturally is, and a tank top that enhances the kind of chestal area my buddy Bimbo admires. The other girl's tall, slender but strong-looking, with thick, purple-streaked black hair past her waist. She's styling, too, in black shorts halfway up her thighs, a purple lace tee-shirt over a black sports bra, and black Doc Martens with purple socks. "Ain't seen you around here before," says the redhead when I walk by, "or your funky car, either."

The tall girl just looks at me, and I eyeball her from behind my ultra-dark Oakley shades.

"I'm visiting," I say. "Just got here a couple days ago."

"You gonna do some tricks for us?"

I don't say anything, I just saunter over to the half-pipe, very casual. It's got a good, fast pitch, and I fly back and forth a few times, then nosestall, hanging on the pipe's lip. As long as I keep it simple, I probably won't embarrass myself too badly, so I roll up the other side and get enough air for a three-sixty with a frontside grab. Then I do it again. It's all coming back to me now, my old moves still there in muscle memory, and I pull off a bunch of tricks before I feel like stopping. When I do, the girls look at me as though I just beamed in from Planet Zork.

The redhead shouts, "Come here," so I walk over to the car. She's taking a joint out of an Altoids tin and, well, I don't mind if I do, because I haven't had any doobage since I left California.

The girls move apart and I sit between them, all of us leaning back against the windshield. The redhead's Lainie, the quiet one, Kat. The breeze is just strong enough to make it hard to light the joint, but at last Lainie gets it going and passes it to me. I take a hit that's not too big to be polite and hand it to Kat. Our fingers brush, and as I look into her eyes, big and deep and grey as the ocean on a cloudy day, I'm immediately caught in the undertow.

As usual, I can't think of anything brilliant to say. "Is Kat short for Kathleen or Kathryn?"

"Neither." She reaches across me and gives the joint to her friend. "Lainie's the only one calls me Kat. My name's Kateri. Kateri Dellis."

"That's a great name. Different. With rhythm."

"It's Passamaquoddy." Lainie looks at me as though she's waiting for a reaction. Kateri studies the sky.

I'm confused. "Passa... what? What's that?"

"Pass-a-ma-quod-dy," Lainie says. "Native American. Indian."

"Don't say Indian," Kateri tells her.

Lainie elbows me in the ribs. "Kat wants to learn to skateboard. None of the bozos around here will teach a girl. Not even the guys on the rez."

"The rez?"

"The reservation," Lainie says.

Kateri says, "Never mind that. Will you teach me?"

"You need sneakers," I tell her.

"I can go barefoot for now. Please?" She's already taking off her Docs.

I set the board down. She stands on it goofy-footed, her right foot forward, but I don't try to correct her. Everyone has a natural stance. Hands out at her sides like she's balanced on a train rail, she starts off easy, rolling down the ramp, barely wobbling. When she feels comfortable with that, she wants to try the half-pipe. I'm dubious, but she shoves off anyway, rolling back and forth a little higher each time, looking pretty steady.

"Hey," she says from two-thirds up one side, "this is really great," and that's all it takes to forget what she's doing. It's a hard wipe-out, and she sits there with her eyes closed and her hands clenched. Lainie runs to her, and so do I, even though I hate being rushed into the "Are you okay?" thing myself. Tears are dripping off Kateri's chin onto her purple lace top, but she doesn't make a sound.

There's a map of road rash down the side of her left leg from shorts to ankle. After straightening out her knee real carefully, she wipes her cheeks with a handful of hair. We help her up, and she limps to the Camaro. Lainie tells me to follow them, so I do, driving across the causeway to the fishing village of Spruce Island that lies between Dudley and East Haven. I can't figure out why summer people haven't snapped up all this shorefront, like they have on East Haven.

We end up at Lainie's, a small house nowhere near the ocean. No one's home. In the bathroom, Kateri pours a quarter-bottle of peroxide over her leg, while I admire her delicate toes with their accent of pale blue nail polish. Lainie gets tweezers and tries to pick splinters out of Kateri's palm without much success. "Let Zach try," Kateri says, and I'm determined to do a good job. Otherwise the hand-holding part will be over way too soon.

⊱

Scooter's the one who gets all the girls. Bimbo's immature and not too bright, isn't above saying, "Nice lungs," or some other dumb anatomical comment. Scooter's *da man*, a smooth talker, has that tanned surfer-dude thing down pat, turns on the charm and they're his forever, or at least until he moves on to the next one, which he does with great frequency. Bimbo's there to pick up the leftovers, and I'm on the sidelines, always, the philosopher rumored to be celibate, but that's not by choice, it's because I couldn't get laid even at a swinger's convention. The ladies just don't dig me—I'm too tall, too skinny, I have red hair and the ghost complexion that goes with it. And I'm a soul surfer, which is so far from cool it's not even on the map.

Just once, Scooter tried to help me out. He met Julie, but in order to go out with her, he had to find a date for her friend Ramona. Usually, it was Bimbo who got the call, but he was visiting his cousins in Palo Alto, so Scooter called on me to help him out.

"This may be your best chance, Zach," Scooter said. "She's a woman with experience, if you know what I mean."

I knew what he meant. Maybe I was going to get lucky.

Towards the end of the evening, we ended up at the beach in the microbus. Scooter and Julie apparently didn't care if we were there or not while they were getting it on, but I did, so I suggested we walk down the beach. We walked a little ways before Ramona apparently figured there was no need to be coy. She peeled down my baggies right there on the beach and started giving me my first hand job. I managed to keep it together for a while, but I was so excited about finally getting to do the wild thing that I came just before I entered the golden gates. Let me tell you, a girl puts max effort into the prelim and then doesn't get to the main event, unhappy doesn't even begin to describe her. As for a guy's reputation with the ladies, well, let's just say word travels *that* network like a chaparral brushfire.

⊱

Thursday, two days later, I'm up early doing tai chi with Nonnie and Papa in the backyard. There's nothing here to stay up late for, no movie theater, no parties, so I'm getting in the groove of going to bed at midnight and waking up at seven. The tai chi thing is good, not like surfing, but I like the discipline of it all, the paradox of controlled movements that free the mind.

So I'm following Nonnie and Papa's moves, breathing in the smell of ocean and French lilacs. The sun's climbing over the angled roofs of the house, sunrise peach and amethyst already bleached from the powder-blue sky. Bridal wreath—Nonnie's teaching me about gardens, says an architect needs to make the acquaintance of green and growing things—has turned the hedges to six-foot-high summer snowdrifts, making this yard so private that only boaters or Spruce Islanders with telescopes could ever see us.

Wind chimes—big bamboo temple ones, small tinkly brass ones, and all sizes and pitches in between—swing from the lower branches of the two old oaks. If I close my eyes and get in that meditative state, the smells and sounds and the cool breeze could almost convince me I'm in some secret Zen garden. It's the closest I've felt to nirvana since my last ride on Buddy Dexter's longboard, now over a week ago.

I'm totally in the zone when I hear a voice say, "Zach?" I open my eyes, and standing there on the path that comes down the north side of the house are Kateri and Lainie. I can't tell if the slightly-pinched look on Kateri's face is embarrassment or nervousness, but she lets Lainie lead the way into the backyard. The three of us stand there, suddenly clueless about what to say to each other. Nonnie and Papa watch, and I know Nonnie would be over here in a second if Papa wasn't holding her hand.

Lainie's shorts are really short, her muscular legs as tanned as a surfer's. She wears a tight suntop with skinny little straps, no bra, and no doubt Nonnie and Papa can see her perky nipples just as plainly as I can. Kateri's sporting skinny black jeans and a cropped black tee-shirt and a silver belly-ring. Maybe it's being on my grandparents' turf that makes me suddenly see the girls through their eyes, but I'm surprised at how much I want my grandparents to like my friends. Especially Kateri.

I do the introductions, Lainie first, and when I introduce Kateri, I want in the worst way to take her hand, touch her shoulder, do something to show Nonnie and Papa that we already have a connection. But I don't.

Kateri pulls off her space-age shades, and as she and Nonnie look at each other, it's obvious right away that they're somehow on the same wavelength, incredible as that sounds. "Let me get some lemonade," Nonnie says, and Kateri says, "I'll help you," and they climb the back porch steps together, already talking like friends.

Over lemonade, Kateri tells Nonnie how much she likes the house, and the yard, and the view, and the antique wicker furniture on the back porch, and the old glass lemonade pitcher, and the chewy macaroons on blue-and-white clipper-ship plates. The girl I thought I was getting to know would never notice or talk about stuff like this, but Kateri's studying everything like a traveler from another time or a parallel universe.

"You met Zach at that skate park?" Papa asks. They nod.

"Zach's going to teach me," Kateri says. "Aren't you, Zach?"

Words fail me. All I can do is smile.

༄

We leave the house in Lainie's beat-up car and drive half an hour north to a big salvage store in Mayfield, where Kateri finds a way cool pair of purple Vans. Then we hit the park, and man, what she lacks in skill she more than makes up for in guts. No matter how many times she gets bumped, banged, and bruised, the warrior girl gets right back up to do it again.

For two weeks we meet at the park to ride and hang out. At first, Lainie's right there with us every minute, but one day Kateri's alone, and after that we see Lainie less and less. Which is fine with me, because things with Kateri are going excellently.

Nonnie and Papa invite her to lunch, and it's scary how well they all get along, as though Kateri's a proper Boston debutante instead of a purple-haired small-town girl. For me, there's quite a disconnect between Kateri's punked-up appearance and everything else I know about her, the special school she goes to for gifted science students, her plans to be a geneticist, her love of J.D. Salinger and ice hockey and early Bob Dylan. Some people might say Kateri's a *poseur*, like a hodad aping the surfer look and cool but never going near the ocean. I don't think this is anywhere near that simple.

The one thing I can't figure out is what's up with her family. She never mentions them, and she never lets me pick her up at her house, always meeting me at the park or at Lainie's. I know she lives on the reservation on the road to Spruce Island, which is mainly tract houses, a store with a sign saying *Baskets for Sale*, a red brick church overlooking the ocean, and a spectacular view of the bay. I'm curious what it's like there, and I'm thinking about how to invite myself over without being a total jerk. If Lainie hadn't told me that first day, I wouldn't even know Kateri was anything other than an exotic-looking downeast girl dreaming of her small-town escape.

I've known Kateri about a month when, one rainy day while we sit in my room playing chess and stopping to make out every time one of us loses a man, she says, "My parents have invited you to dinner tomorrow night." Which is great, though I would've liked it better if she'd invited me herself.

∝

More nervous than I expected, I drive the beach wagon past Spruce Island and across the causeway to Champlain Point Reservation. I wind my way towards the water, where the Dellises live in a house surrounded by evergreens on a ledge above a pebbly beach. All I know about Kateri's parents is that her father is the tribe's lieutenant governor and her mother teaches sixth grade at the reservation school.

The front door opens while I'm parking the car and Kateri comes out, followed by her ten-year-old sister, Anna. Kateri's wearing a clingy purple dress that falls all the way to her black boots, her hair swinging smooth and shiny to the curve of her hips. We stand there looking at each other, suddenly shy, until Anna grabs our hands and says, "Come on. Moose steaks on the barbecue," and pulls us towards the house.

There's a sweet, resinous smell inside, green and spicy, and just breathing it in puts me at ease. In the living room, the walls are hung with both black-and-white and colored photographs of people in tribal dress. Ancestors and elders, Anna tells me, who guide the family and the tribe.

Kateri's mother is hulling strawberries in the kitchen, humming as she works. She's tall and serious-looking, the front of her long straight hair held back from her face with an elaborate beaded clip.

"Mom, this is Zachary," Kateri says.

Her mother inclines her head and says, "Welcome, Zachary," and almost smiles, but not quite. Her porcupine-quill earrings swing back and forth.

I can't think of a single intelligent sentence, so I dip my head like she did. "Thank you. It's good to meet you."

"Daddy's outdoors," Anna says, and I can tell from her tone that she's her father's girl.

We walk across the deck that overlooks the ocean, which tonight is flat-calm to the not-so-distant Canadian shore. Kateri's father is at the grill, turning the steaks. His hair's almost as long as Kateri's, onyx-black, pulled back and woven into narrow braids. One of the braids wraps the rest into a bundle thicker than my wrist. Anna says, "Daddy. The boyfriend's here."

As he turns, I see a profile that should be on money: hooded eyes, a proud nose, cheekbones so sharp they could cut paper. "Welcome, Zachary," he says in a deep, slow voice. Like his wife, he does not look me in the eye, which is fine because Kateri has already told me that this is the Native way. Eye contact is a challenge, it shows lack of respect. "You like *musuwok*? Moose meat?"

"I've never had it."

"A new experience, then." He spears a steak and flips it over and says, "Daughters, show our guest where his people first landed."

Anna leads us across the yard and down a footpath between two walls of ledge. Over small beach pebbles worn smooth as eggs, we crunch towards a point that curves out into the ocean, bordered by evergreens and topped by a grassy clearing. Anna says, "Champlain landed here. In 1604, before they went upriver to Saint Croix Island, they spent a week right where our house is. History books don't mention it, but it's been handed down."

History's big with the Dellis family, or, it seems, with everyone but Kateri. Before the evening's over, I've been introduced to all the pictured ancestors, seen hundred-year-old beaded moccasins and birchbark bracelets and ancient baskets made of ash and sweetgrass. I've marveled at history kept for centuries in spite of no written-down language until forty or fifty years ago. I've learned how it was before the Europeans, who took the land from the People of the Dawn and forced them onto the reservation named after the first white man here, condemning them to poverty until the 1970's land claims settlement with the state of Maine. History in school was always just a set of facts and dates, but this is different, and I'm already attracted to the Passamaquoddy philosophy: *Take care of the earth to the seventh generation, and respect all beings above, on, and below it.*

At some point during this presentation, I look up from a scrapbook kept by one of Kateri's grandmothers, and realize that Kateri's vanished. I look around the room, puzzled, and Anna says, "She went for a walk. Our history makes her sad."

I don't know what to say.

Anna leans close and whispers to me like we're conspirators. "She doesn't like talking about the past, how our land got stolen. She says the future's more important. She doesn't like to be sad."

Later, Kateri and I walk on the beach and kiss under the stars. I like her better than any other girl I've ever met, but it's not just her. It's the different world she lives in, a world I can't wait to explore.

☙

The first time I successfully caught a wave, I felt like I'd been handed the keys to the universe. That day, as usual, we'd paddled out to where the action was, Buddy and Scooter and Bimbo and I, and sat, rocking on the ocean swells with our boards pointed towards shore, Buddy looking back over his shoulder, gauging the waves. We'd all farmed it more times than I could count, though sometimes we did get a few feet's ride before the wave showed us who was boss out there. But this one morning a set built up and Buddy said, "Try this one, Zach," and I was on my feet, slicing across the face of the wave.

For the first time, I wasn't thinking about whether or not I could do it. It was suddenly perfect, everything I'd been taught fitting together seamlessly, my feet adjusting themselves almost instinctively as the wave collapsed behind me. All I could think was to do it again. And again and again and again, because I wasn't going to get any closer to Heaven in this life, and nothing would ever be the same.

☙

By the end of July, Kateri's got the basics down, ollies and manuals and flips and grabs. She's coordinated and athletic, but still hasn't gotten big air off the half-pipe and pulled a combo. I'm wishing we had more elements here, a bowl, maybe, not so high as the half-pipe, or a rail or two to grind, boxes to ollie over. Then one day we meet a dude who tells us there's an awesome park with more elements in Riverton, an hour to the south. It lightbulbs on me that Kateri could practice some slightly more advanced stuff there.

The night before we plan to scope it out, she calls to say she can't go. "There's a thing going on in Falmouth, across the border in Canada. It's kind of a big deal and everyone is going. I can't get out of it. I would if I could."

"A thing?"

She sighs. "Oh, a gathering to raise awareness about some tribal land in Canada. It was stolen from us a long time ago."

"Can you get it back?"

"Probably not. I mean, it's good that people like my parents are trying to make things right, but it seems impossible. I know it doesn't work this way, but I wish everyone would refuse to live on the rez any more and stop being limited. I mean, it's like we're in a box. The government put us here and here we stay. That's why I want to get a good education and get out of here and live a normal life. Staying here just drags you down."

Again, I don't know what to say. I change the subject. "We can go to Riverton some other time. It's cool. No worries."

"Do you like your life?" she asks, and for a moment, I don't say anything, just thinking. "Did you ever wish it was different?"

"Not really." Soul surfer and future architect. A great family. And now that I have a girlfriend, how could I ask for more?

"Well, you're lucky," she says. "I feel as though I have two lives. One at school, where no one thinks twice about my background. I'm smart and successful and that's all anyone sees. I'm just like them. But here, it's different. Some people still call us nasty names and say our people are a bunch of lazy sneaking drunks and druggies and it's a good thing we live on the rez instead of putting our problems in their neighborhoods. There are hardly any non-white people here except for us, so that's where all the prejudice goes."

She sounds angry, and that's new. I blunder into the minefield. "People who say stuff like that are ignorant. Look, in LA, you hear it, too, just substitute the projects or the barrio for the reservation. Not to say it's exactly the same thing."

"You don't get it. You just don't get it." She mumbles something else, but I can't make it out.

"I'm trying to get it," I tell her, but she says, "I have to go," and hangs up. I stand there looking at the phone and wondering if we've just had our first fight.

ଓ

Half an hour later the phone rings, and I race down the hall, hoping it's Kateri. The caller ID says it's her number, but what I hear is her father's deep voice. "Would you be interested in spending tomorrow with us?"

"Well, sure. What's going on?"

"Qonasqamkuk," he tells me. "Our capital and sacred burial ground before the English stole it and forced us out. Tomorrow, we go and protest, reclaim for a day this land in Canada that is rightfully ours."

"There are Passamaquoddies in Canada, too?"

"The land on both sides of the river and the bay was *skijn* once. There was no boundary. We were free to roam. Then we were forced into settlement camps, pushed farther and farther until the Point here is all we have left. The English did not sign a treaty with us, did not pay us for our land. Now they want to put up condominiums, violate the ground where our ancestors rest. Join us, Zachary, and see these things for yourself."

"Even though I'm not Passamaquoddy?"

"Many Euro friends come to stand with us," he says, so I agree to go.

ଔ

The next morning, Papa drops me off. I step onto Kateri's front porch and hear voices through the screen door. "I'm not telling you what to do," her mother's saying, a slight edge to her voice. "But remember, today you represent our people, not just yourself."

Anna, dressed in a fringed and beaded leather dress, comes flying out of the house and grabs my hand. We walk on the beach until she figures the argument is over. When we return, Kateri's wearing faded jeans and Vans, a fringe-cut tank top with a peace-sign dreamcatcher on the front, and wide studded black leather bracelets. I wonder what she'd had on originally.

ISLAND SECRETS

In the Dellis van with Kateri's family and her uncle, aunt, and a cousin Anna's age, she doesn't have anything to say, even to me, except a murmured, "This sucks," her head against my shoulder.

ಸಿ

Falmouth looks as if it were teleported to New Brunswick straight from the coast of England. Every house has big flower gardens, and quaint little shop after quaint little shop line a main street that eventually loops into a big flat open space overlooking the bay: Qonasqamkuk. Kinap, Kateri's little cousin, runs off as soon as we get out of the van, and I see by the back of his jacket that he belongs to a children's drumming group.

There must be a hundred or so Natives milling about at this camper park, plus the tourists whose Winnebagos and Airstreams are parked at some of the hookups. I'm just taking in the scene when Kateri says, "Look," and points past the picnic area. I see a skate park, well-equipped. A couple half-pipes, some quarter pipes, verts, rails, ramps, pools, bowls, and boxes. "Let's go," she says.

We don't have my board, but I can see that's not going to matter. I start to follow her, then stop and look back. The tribe's gathering in a circle for some kind of ceremony, and much as I want to be with Kateri, I want to be part of that, too. She runs along ahead, and I'm standing there trying to figure out what to do when I see her father walking towards me. "Where's Kateri?" he asks, and I swing my arm towards the skate park. He watches for a moment, nodding slowly, as a dude in a neon-blue shirt airs off the half-pipe in a three-sixty. "This is what you do?"

I nod. "But not today. Today's different."

"Not to my daughter," he says softly, and even though his dark eyes are shuttered, I have a pretty good idea what he's feeling right now. "She will escape us, her family, her tribe. She will make her own way."

"You want me to go get her?"

He puts his hand on my shoulder and looks at the ground. "Let her be. Her spirit is not at this gathering. You join our circle or join Kateri. It is completely your choice."

This is not how I planned on today going. Beyond the picnic tables, Kateri's talking to a couple of dudes, the one in the blue shirt and another as tall and skinny as I am. The guy in the blue shirt hands over his board and she manuals, then kickflips and ollies over a box. Like all that matters is the board under her feet and the obstacle ahead of her, not this gathering, not her family, not me.

  I walk back to the circle with Kateri's father, and Anna and her mother unclasp their hands and take us in.

ଔ

  At the welcome ceremony, there's drumming by Kinap's group, and a welcome dance. Kateri's mother tells me the drum is sacred, a living object that sends messages to the spirit world. Concentrating on the voices of those drums, I feel the vibrations in my blood more than I hear them in my head. A smudging ceremony follows, sage burned in an abalone-shell bowl, the smoke fanned with an eagle feather over each participant. I recognize that strong, resinous scent from Kateri's house, and I feel calm and open as the sage smoke drifts over me. After a couple of elders speak about the old days, good and bad, some of the Natives from Maine and New Brunswick talk about how to work together to reclaim their land, while others spread out and share information about the tribe and Qonasqamcook with the tourists and local gawkers.

  I'm having a great time, the sun on my face, the sea breeze refreshing, everyone accepting me. "People will see you here with us," Kateri's uncle told me in the van, "you and our other Euro friends, and they will see this is not just a Native issue. Good, thoughtful members of their own society are standing with us for justice."

  When Kateri comes back, I'm listening to a couple of elders tell stories while we eat lunch, burgers cooked on the grills some tribe members brought, potato salad, lemonade and iced tea. Kateri's carrying a board, and after she helps herself to food and sits down beside me, I say, "Where'd you get that?"

  "A hardware store in town. Glenn and Dickie picked it out."

  Sweet. Glenn and Dickie, friends already. I examine the board. It's actually pretty good for an off-the-shelf model.

  "I did a one-eighty off the half-pipe."

  "Well," I say. "Great. Congratulations."

  Kateri tosses back her hair and spins a wheel on her new board. "I can't believe you'd rather stay here than try out this park."

"This event seems important. And it's all new to me. I want to learn."

"You think I'm wrong for wanting to escape."

"Escape?"

"This place. This sad history. This life."

"I want you to be happy." I don't know what else to say.

"I want you to be happy, too." Her smile is warm, and we sit there for a while, staring across the dry grass and pebbly beach to the dark, flat, surfless ocean, and the American mainland bulked against the horizon. I think about boundaries, what keeps us in, what keeps us out. How Kateri's ancestors and family are completely different from mine. How Scooter and Bimbo look down on my kind of surfing, and Buddy Dexter and I shake our heads over theirs. But that's just too much heaviosity for today, so I let it go.

Anna comes to tell us it's time for the pipe ceremony. Kateri says, "Sorry I deserted you today. I'll stay for the pipe, if you want."

"I do," I say, and she sits beside me as a pipe carrier from the Owl clan performs the ceremony of assembling the pipe. It passes from hand to hand, and when it comes to me I suck in just a taste, the sacred tobacco rough and pungent against my tongue, not at all like the cigarette I once tried that made me green with nausea.

On the hour-long drive home, Kateri leans quietly against my side, her head on my shoulder, her new board between her knees. I try to imagine what it's like to want to escape your life, but I can't get to that place at all.

When the van pulls up in front of my grandparents' house, I give Kateri a quick kiss good night, slide open the door, and get out. "Zachary," her father says as I start up the walk. I turn back. He leans out the window. "I watched you today. For the government, being Native is about percentages. But for us, it's not just about the Blood, it's also about the Way. You adopt our path, you can be at one with us." He nods and smiles his slow smile, and almost meets my eyes.

I nod and smile too, and go up the walk to the house.

☙

Nonnie and Papa want to know all about the day, and I try to tell them, but getting the nuances right is like trying to grasp a handful of water. How can I explain how I felt when I was smudged with the sweet, tangy smoke from the abalone bowl of burning sage? It would feel weird to say I felt purified, swept clean, fanned by the wings of an eagle. How can I describe the way the drums spoke to my heart? It's easer to just talk about the ceremonies, so I do that, and when I'm done, Nonnie says they'd like to meet the rest of Kateri's family, they'd like to invite them to dinner.

Now, my grandparents have always known how to throw a party—we've spent Christmas with them on Beacon Hill, and let me tell you, that was straight out of Charles Dickens. So I'm not surprised when things kick into high gear, and pretty soon a couple of girls from Spruce Island come to clean the house top to bottom. The day before the dinner party, Nantucket baskets filled with dried flower arrangements appear, and a humongous glass-topped wicker table is brought down from the attic, put on the back verandah, and set with straw placemats and colorful Fiestaware.

I'm glad this isn't the formal dining room, crystal and china and three sterling forks. Nonnie and Papa don't play those "see what we have" games. They've got the true party attitude, make everyone comfortable and then make sure they have a great time. Still, when the van pulls into the driveway, I'm a little bit wound up about how it's all going to go. I'm less concerned with what my grandparents will think of the Dellises than what the Dellises will think of us.

But once we settle in on the front veranda, Anna and her father and Nonnie on the porch glider and Papa and Kateri's mother in the white rocking chairs, it's as though they've all been friends forever. As I lay on the floor with my head in Kateri's lap, shadows lengthen on the broad lawn and sunset turns the sky gold and rose and every color in between.

The adults find common ground quickly in, of all places, the Ivy League. Nonnie and Papa are Radcliffe and Harvard, and I find out Kateri's parents met at Dartmouth, which still has a mission to educate Natives. Her mother was raised not on the reservation, but in Connecticut. Kateri's grandfather, like many Natives, left the reservation for a good job building airplane engines at Pratt & Whitney and never returned. I see Kateri's desire to escape in a whole new light, now that I know one set of her grandparents also left for a different life.

After a while, we go through the house to the back veranda. A first course of crisp Caesar salad and garlic bread is followed by one of Nonnie's specialties, fresh tuna steaks broiled and then topped with Mediterranean vegetables, all sauteed together in olive oil and accompanied by a rice pilaf. Dessert is key lime pie and hazelnut coffee. Everything's so different from the food Kateri's family served, but I let that thought run out of my brain just as quick as it ran in. I don't want to think about what divides anymore, I don't want to compare.

&

The second weekend in August brings Passamaquoddy Days, a three-day celebration with activities and exhibits and a big fireworks finale. I want to experience it all, the sunrise ceremonies, the sweat lodge, canoe races, storytelling, intertribal drumming and dancing and singing. Kateri sleeps past sunrise, goes shopping for school clothes with Lainie, and leaves me to it.

The last night of Passamquoddy Days, everyone else goes to the fish pier to watch the fireworks where they can see the ground displays, but Kateri and I walk to that crescent of land where the first Euros landed. We lie on a blanket on the soft, grassy ground above the beach. The fireworks explode above us, colorful blossoms of light drifting down to be extinguished in the sea. Hard to believe it's the middle of August, summer going fast and already a little chill in the night air. Everything is starting to feel like good-bye.

In nine days, my folks will be back from Italy and I'll be heading home to California. I've been thinking about it a lot lately, wondering if this has been a summer romance, or if Kateri and I can manage a long-distance relationship. Not that I'll have anything else going. But Kateri will be heading back up north to the Maine School of Science and Mathematics with gifted kids from all over the state. I can see her showing up with her skateboard and guys who never noticed her before—if that's possible—suddenly finding her fascinating. It would totally bite to have to say final good-byes to her and to her family and to my summer world.

She pulls the blanket around us and cuddles close. "It's almost over."

I nod, my cheek against her hair. "I know."

"Senior year. College applications, all that. It'll be busy."

Does she mean too busy to stay in touch? I can't ask that, though. Instead I say, "Do you know where you're going?"

"I always planned to go to MIT. I really love Boston. But I was thinking." She looks up at me as a big bright blast of fireworks lights up the sky. "I should look at other places, too. Maybe Caltech. Or Stanford."

My heart lurches. I'm not the only one who wants to be together! "Or you might want to stick with MIT," I say. "Harlow men have been going to Harvard since 1712, and I couldn't escape if I wanted to."

She opens my aloha shirt and runs her hands over my skin. "Would you like to make love to me?"

It's so right but so unexpected that I don't know what to say. For a second or two, I remember the Ramona fiasco, and I promise myself that's not going to happen again.

We fumble around at first, but then we find our rhythm, heart to heart. Afterwards, we lie together warm and naked, wrapped in our blanket. I think about the future, another summer, then us together in Cambridge, and who knows what after that. Kateri will leave the reservation, and the world will open up for us, and whether she wants to or not, she'll carry the memory of what she left behind. And I will always wonder what's been lost.

But right now we lie here, breathing in the tang of tidal salt and balsam and sweetgrass, holding each other easy and close. In the east, over the surfless ocean, the moon is rising, not quite full yet, silver and shadow, shining across all the borders of our worlds.

ಸಂಬಂಧ

THE SEASON OF BEGINNINGS

IT WAS ORRIN'S COUGHING that awakened her. Annie slept lightly now anyway, one ear always tuned for the wheeze and hack that could make her heart almost stop in terror. She slipped into her chenille robe and followed the *tift-tift* of his slippers on the quarry-stone floor, out the back door to the screen porch. Back home in Maine, in the only 1920s bungalow on Spruce Island, she could dash around the house in total darkness, but here in Arizona, she walked carefully, feeling her way. It'd been seven months, and this house was still a stranger, one she wasn't the least interested in becoming better acquainted with.

Orrin sat in a canvas chair on the screen porch, his bare barrel chest bellowsing as he struggled for breath. Flat, infinite, the night-blooming Arizona desert stretched like an ocean to the distant moonscape foothills of the Rockies. In the wide western sky, the stars were strewn like diamond dust, cold and impossibly far away. From the front yard they could see the lights of Flagstaff, but here on the back porch this house seemed like the last outpost.

For Orrin, lungs ravaged by Maine's fog and sea and the steadily advancing emphysema, it probably was.

Annie laid a cool hand on his moist, warm shoulder. "You okay? Want your inhaler?"

He shook his head. A quiet doer, he never was much for talking, but since their October arrival he'd said less and less, wandering the rented house like a wraith. "I'm fifty-seven," he'd said once in a rare outburst. "I might as well be eighty for all the use I am." He kept to the house. The desert sun burned his fair northern skin, and he was terrified of snakes. Mostly, he sat.

Sat, and, Annie was sure, remembered.

She poured two glasses of lemonade and pulled a chair close beside him. They drank without speaking and his breathing quieted little by little. In the moonlight, his fair hair glimmered like silver. Annie, used to the silence that had bound their lives, was surprised when Orrin said, more statement than question, "You miss teaching."

It was as though the broad desert made them draw closer, made things at once fragile and strong. She had promised herself she would not be nostalgic, would not think about the students who passed through her history classes at Quoddy High, the children of fishermen and factory workers, those whose dreams burned bright and those who had already given up.

Annie remembered Miss Nichols, Quoddy High's English teacher emeritus, eighty-five years old and still as keen as a filleting knife, saying years after her retirement, "It's not so much the teaching I miss, exactly, it's being around youth. Their energy, their hopes." Annie had known, hearing it said, that it would someday be the same for her. She'd had no idea someday would come so soon.

"Well, yes," she said. "I miss it. But not as much now as in the fall. It's the season of beginnings that's hard to do without."

"Yes," he said. "The chance to start again." He nodded, looking at the floor, and Annie told herself, *Choose your words carefully. Don't summon the ghosts of things that cannot be.*

It was now, late April, that the weirmen went out to repair the winter's damage, twine-filled dories, rafts piled with poles. She remembered how he'd stow away the scalloping gear, anticipation rising in him like the high spring tide. His work the rest of the year was strictly for getting by, because it was the weir he'd loved, that huge circular maze of poles and net that trapped the herring. Boats changed, fishing gear changed, but a weir well-kept was eternal, a design that could not be improved upon, efficient and beautiful.

He looked at his watch. "It's six o'clock in Maine," he said. "Calder's likely out already."

Calder Travis was Orrin's younger brother, his partner in the Shamrock weir at Sorrell Island. Annie knew the Shamrock was considered a lucky weir, had been so since Orrin's great-grandfather first built it back in the 1930s. Most of the old weirs were gone now, the herring fishery way down, the sardine factories except for Abercrombie's a thing of the past. But the herring in Big Musquan Bay would still find the Shamrock, and the *Absarco* would come and pump them out to take them to the cannery, and Abercrombie's whistle would still blow, summoning the packers. Around the American side of the bay there were only three weirs left, a few more on the Canadian side, and Annie knew Orrin was proud that the Shamrock was one that had survived.

"Calder will take good care of things," she said.

Orrin's nostrils twitched. "Calder's right smart about some things," he said. "But he can't mend twine worth a hoot in a gale. Stuff 'll come apart on him the first time we get a good blow and a fast tide. At least Lonnie's finally got the knack." Lonnie was their son, their only child, approaching thirty now. He seemed as devoted to the weir as his father was, but Annie wondered if someday—a someday precipitated by the event she tried never to think about—he'd fly away from the weir and the island to a different kind of life.

Orrin shook his head and looked out across the desert. His eyebrows were getting shaggy, the way men's do with age, but his sky-blue eyes were still clear and bright. Except for some blurring of his jawline and the sun-squint lines around his eyes, he was still as good-looking as the boy she'd met at a Fourth of July dance the summer she was seventeen. It was opposites that attracted then, East Haven and Spruce Island, summer girl and local fisherman. She'd been planning for college; he, becoming master of his own boat.

"Everyone says you're the best net-maker in three counties," she said now, being careful to cast it in the present tense, not the past.

That brought a smile, the first genuine one she'd seen since Lonnie'd come at Christmas time. "Guess I could hold my end up with a shuttle, when I had to." It was as close as he'd ever come to a boast. "It's careful work, making and mending twine. Methodical. Takes patience." He ran blunt fingers through his still-thick hair. "I don't seem to have much of that virtue any more."

What could she say to that? Annie touched his bare shoulder, and his hand came up and covered hers. "Tell me the best day," she said, unwilling to let him lapse back into silence. "Tell me about the best day at the Shamrock."

Orrin's square-jawed face softened and became wistful. "My favorite's the days when the June fogs are in. All those fish look like the weir is full of silver. And the gulls—so many, it's like a big, noisy cloud circling. And the sound. You can hear the bell buoy off Calico Point so plain, and yet a boat passing closer hardly makes a sound at all." He drained his glass of lemonade and coughed harshly. "I talk too much."

"No," she said. "Oh, no, Orrin. Not after all these months when you hardly talked at all."

He lifted his head, as though he were reading a message in the stars. Familiar silence stretched between them once again.

Annie couldn't tell how long they sat. The moon faded by degrees, and a thin golden line grew across the eastern horizon. Orrin stood, rested his hands on the porch rail. "We're going home," he said. "I feel exactly like those herring. Netted, and ready to get sucked into oblivion."

"The doctors said—"

He struck the railing. "I don't care what the doctors said. Damn fools. They think dying's all in the body. They don't know anything about really dying, when your soul dries up from uselessness and blows away."

Annie said, "I don't want to lose you." In the dawn half-light, she could almost see his spirit take flight, a white seagull against a desert sky. What had been gained, coming to this desolate place? "All right," she said. "We'll go home. But come fall, I'll want to get away, find a school that needs a half-time history teacher. Some place warm." Where the winters would be easy on tired lungs.

"Is it too early to call the landlord," he asked. She could see the long-lost gleam returning to his eyes. "I imagine I have a lot of twine to mend."

෨෬

EVERYONE KNOWS THIS IS NOWHERE

BY EIGHT-THIRTY IT'S STANDING room only at the Rusty Scuppers. So much for my quiet little evening. I should've figured this morning's announcement about Quoddy Sea shutting down production would give everyone the same idea: get drunk and try to forget we got two more weeks and then no money and no health insurance.

They say it's some kind of salmon anemia, whatever that is, but I think maybe they were looking to close anyway. Every week, it seems like, there's another hassle with some idiot from away complaining that the cages wreck his pretty water views.

There ain't that many jobs around here anyway, and now there's a couple hundred people out of work. I don't see most of us making it. The old-timers say that when the paper mill upcountry was running full-tilt, all you had to do was get a union card and your life was guaranteed, but those days are long gone. It's a different world now, and the work we've always done is drying up bigtime. But Nana taught me to do what has to be done, and if that's driving half an hour each way to flip burgers at Mickey D's, well, that's what I'll do. I hope not, though.

I'm just as worried about the insurance as I am the paycheck. It ain't so bad for me, I'm in great shape from shoveling feed out on the salmon cages, but I don't know if I could get the kids on Medicaid or not if one of them got hurt or sick. Just one more thing to worry about, as if I didn't have enough already. Things with Tina haven't been great for a while now, which is why I'm here getting drunk and she's home doing her scrapbook pages, making it look like the perfect life none of us will ever have.

I get hauled out of my head and back into the Rusty Scuppers by Judd Merrow saying, "I bet they knew this was coming a couple of months ago. Ain't right, not giving us time to make plans. Ten years, the only job I ever had or wanted. And the baby's due in a couple months, and how'm I gonna pay for that?"

"I'm keeping the cable TV even if I don't eat," Moppet Wilson says. Which is no surprise, because when he's not working or drinking at the Rusty Scuppers, he's got his big loose self parked on the couch in front of the boob tube. "A man's got to have something to take up his mind."

"That's if he had a mind." Judd winks at Ella, then sorts out some quarters for his beer. "Sorry I can't tip you tonight. You understand, right?"

"Right," says Ella, and tucks some loose hair back into her ponytail. "You Quoddy Sea boys get too poor to drink, this place'll go under, too. Just wait."

My head's pounding, like a crew of tiny little construction workers are hammering steel in my brain. It's been hurting worse and worse since we got the news, and four beers ain't done one thing to slow it down. I'm thinking of going home and seeing if I can get laid, that might help, but then I feel these fingers combing through the back of my hair, and I think, Maybe I *am* going to get lucky.

I turn around, but it's not Tina standing there. It's Margo Burke, who was pretty much the town pump back when we were in high school. Her hair's streaked about ten shades of blonde and wound up like a bird's nest, and she's so thin her shoulders look like they could poke holes in drywall. Back before she got some worker's comp gig going, she was a spooner in the wet end, one of the shit jobs at Quoddy Sea, scraping the last bits of blood and guts out of the salmon. Not that she's got enough of a brain to do anything else. Her talents are strictly horizontal.

Judd tips his bottle and lets the last few drops fall on his tongue. "Nice," says Margo. "Want to put that to use?"

Judd gags, he truly does. Margo leans her bony old hip on my shoulder. "Don't suppose you gentlemen could offer a girl a seat."

ISLAND SECRETS

Moppet pushes back his chair and says, "Right here." Margo gives me a look like she's disappointed I didn't offer, then perches on his knee like a little bird. "Slide back here," Moppet says, pulling her by the hips. "Something's come up." Margo jumps as though she just sat on a hot stove. "Come on," Moppet says. "Give a guy a break the day his life goes to hell. I've been waiting to get into your pants since high school."

"Wait some more, then. I already got one asshole in these pants. I sure don't need two." Margo picks up her beer bottle. "See you around, boys."

"She's crazy about me." Moppet watches her cross the crowded floor. "She just don't know it yet."

Judd waves his empty for another. "I think she's crazy about something else since she got on the workman's comp gravy train. Know what I mean?"

I say, "Don't know, don't care." I had my chance with Margo the spring we graduated, but I didn't go for it because Tina was pregnant with Kady and our shotgun wedding was already in the works.

Judd shifts his butt and leans across the table. "Jan heard it at school. Those cafeteria ladies are great for gossip. Margo's on the straw diet."

Moppet drains his beer and says, "What's that?" I don't know, either, but I sure as hell ain't interested in anything Margo's up to.

"Man," says Judd to Moppet. "You really are out of touch. You got to stop playing those video games all the time while your mom's knitting sweaters. Those narcotic pills, Oxycontin? It sounds like quite a few people around here are snorting or shooting up. Margo got a scrip for her carpal tunnel or whatever the hell it is, and went downhill from there."

"That's not possible," I say. Not because Margo isn't stupid enough to get caught up in something like that, but because it's big-city stuff. It don't happen here on Spruce Island, a million miles from everywhere.

"It's happening, man," Judd says. "And I bet it's gonna be happening a whole lot more, 'cause now you got two hundred people in this town needing to get numb, and all the beer in the world ain't gonna do it for them."

EVERYONE KNOWS THIS IS NOWHERE

☙

The next day after work, I go to Nana's. She's alone on the Whitlaw home place—or what's left of it. When I was a kid, Nana and Gramp had fifteen waterfront acres, but now it's down to a postage stamp lot. Once Gramp passed on and Nana got sick with the lung cancer and it got impossible for more flatlanders to buy into East Haven, it didn't make much sense to try and pay the taxes on all that land when the out-of-staters were willing to buy it for big bucks. Acre by acre, it slipped away. Just like everything in life.

The guys on the cage site would be amazed if they saw me fixing the tea tray for Nana, but I've turned into a pretty good cook since she took sick. She's sitting at the kitchen table, looking out the window at Lambert Cove and a couple of small spruce-covered islands off in the distance. I have to shift a stack of magazines and catalogues to make room on the table, and I do that with one hand, balancing the tray in the other like some high-class waiter. Now there's a career I never considered.

Nana's house used to be so neat it made me nervous, but it's gotten cluttered since she got sick and neither one of us can keep ahead of it. I've hinted that maybe Tina could come help us swamp it out, but she ignores me, like she usually does. Nana and I ain't perfect enough to fit in her scrapbook world, I guess.

"It's awful about the layoffs," Nana says as she pours milk into her tea, and I notice, not for the first time, how thin and shaky her hands are. Nobody in my life has been better to me than Nana, and I don't know what I'll do when she goes to be with Gramp.

"Yeah," I say, "I don't know what's gonna become of us." I unwrap a store-bought donut, and the extra powdered sugar sifts down all over the tablecloth. When I try to brush it away, it sinks into the weave, and I glance at her to see if she's noticed.

In the old days, I would've gotten scolded for making a mess, but now all she says is, "Just leave it be, dear. It's not worth worrying about," and that sets me thinking again about how much we've lost.

"I'm at the crossroads of my life," I say. It came to me just like that while I was lying awake in the middle of the night last night, listening to the house creaking and settling in the August wind. A dozen years out of high school, and everything's coming unraveled.

With Nana to look after, I couldn't leave Spruce Island if I wanted to, but I don't even want to. This is Whitlaw ground, and the roots run deep. I know if I went anywhere else, I'd wither up and blow away. I say it again. "I am at the crossroads of my life."

"It could be an opportunity. You thought of it like that?" Nana dunks a piece of donut in her tea. "You ought to think about going to the technical school in Mayfield."

"I know," I say. "You're right."

She's talked about this a lot, and backalong I should've listened. *Might come a day when there's no more salmon to feed*, she'd say. *You could learn to drive a bulldozer. Or take up a trade. This town never has enough carpenters and plumbers.* I can't see myself getting into reading and studying, though. The only thing I liked about Quoddy High was baseball season.

"Promise me you'll look into it," Nana says, and I nod. I'll look into it, but that's all I'm promising. Before I can change the subject, Nana's cup rattles against the saucer as she sets it down, and I see her close her eyes and clamp her teeth together. I jump to help her as she pushes herself up from her chair. She waves me off and shuffles to the sideboard, her slippers making a soft *whick-whick* sound on the scuffed linoleum.

From the cluster beside the canisters, she picks up one amber bottle and then another until she finds the one she's looking for. "You hurting bad?" I ask, even though it's obvious, even though she's always too proud to talk about the pain.

I'm surprised when she admits it. "It feels like someone's driving a clam fork in and out of my damn lungs." She puts a pill on her tongue and takes a sip from the water glass she's carried to the sideboard with her. Then she says, "Tina's probably wondering where you are," and that's my cue to leave, her way of saying that she's ready to be alone.

I kiss her goodbye, feeling as though there's less of her than there was even two days ago. Between Nana and my job, I'm losing so much that can't be replaced. All I have now are Tina and the kids, and I've got to hang onto them as tight as I can. Sometimes I wonder, if she hadn't been pregnant and we'd gotten married only because we wanted to, would things between us be any different?

I open the front door, but this ain't "Leave It to Beaver," and June Cleaver ain't there to greet Ward and make a fuss. Tina and our three girls are sitting around the kitchen table, all of them cutting and gluing and whatever else it is they do in their paper world. Maura and Mandy, our nine-year-old twins, are making pages about a quarter the size of the foot-square ones Tina puts together, but theirs are just as happy and fancy as hers, if a bit sloppy. Kady, who's eleven, is sobbing and hiccuping as she works, big tears rolling down her cheeks. Tina's trimming a photo with wavy-edge scissors.

"Saint Paul on a Popsicle stick," I say, because she gets pissed if I take the Lord's name in vain in front of the girls. "How can you just sit there when our daughter's carrying on like the world's ending?" Which now that I think about it, maybe it is.

"I just have to finish this page for my meeting tonight," Tina says. "We've got new members coming, and I'm making the presentation."

"As if you don't have hundreds of pages already."

She flips her long dark hair behind her shoulder and glares up at me, but I give it right back and she looks away. Her nail-bitten fingers drum on the table.

"Kady's just found out her best friend's moving away. Do you even know who that is?"

A comment like that is pure Tina. If I guess wrong, I'm the one that ends up looking like the asshole who doesn't care enough to know who his daughter's friends are. I decide to go for it anyway. "Brittany," I say. "Right?"

Tina looks almost disappointed. "I'm sorry Kady's losing her friend," she says, "but I got to hand it to her father. A little over twenty-four hours, and he's got another job. He's looking out for his family instead of sitting around drinking and feeling sorry for himself."

Freddy Witham runs the box room at Quoddy Sea. He and his wife come from New Hampshire, so moving off Spruce Island is nothing for him. It ain't like his whole life's here, his family, his friends, his history. It ain't like he can't survive anywhere else.

"I already told you, we ain't moving. Practically every house in town's gonna be for sale before long. We'll never get enough to start over someplace else. And this is home, damn it. This is home. Plus, I got Nana to think about."

"We don't need to talk about this now," Tina says, which means there'll be a big go-round about it when she gets back from her meeting.

I ain't in the mood for any hassles tonight, so as soon as supper's over, I head to the Rusty Scuppers, where just about everyone feels the same way I do. Tina wants to go out, she can find a sitter. It ain't gonna be me staying home tonight while she plays cut-out with her friends.

&

Just like last night, most of the boys from Quoddy Sea are drinking their way to layoff. Margo Burke's sitting with Judd, but I get my beer and head on over anyway. "Where's Moppet?" I say.

"Watching some wrestling thing on the pay-per-view," Judd says. "He'll be along later."

Tom Estey, who runs the feed barge, joins us, and then Dunc Waycott, who drives a forklift. There are only four chairs, so Margo gets up and lets Dunc sit down—and then perches on my thigh. I don't want to be rude, so I pretend she isn't there until her bony butt starts digging into my leg and I have to ask her to change sides.

I don't know how long we sit, drinking and shooting the shit, but I'm pretty drunk when all of a sudden someone grabs the long back of my hair and the voice I least want to hear says, "So. I should've known."

"Busted," says Judd.

I stand up, almost knocking Margo to the floor. She stumbles into Tom and sits on his knee. I tell Tina, "We'll talk outside."

I follow her out, and the door to the street has barely swung shut when she says, loud enough for the teenagers hanging out in front of the pizza place next door to hear, "How could you do this to me? That bitch is a total slut."

"Stop yelling. I was just—"

"Don't say a word." Tina smacks the fender of the nearest car, and I hear sheet metal buckle.

I realize it's her best friend Shelly's car when Shelly sticks her head out the window and yells, "Hey, watch it."

"Sorry." Tina runs her hand over the fender, then slits her eyes at me. "You bastard. I felt bad about our argument, so I come down here thinking we can have a couple of drinks together and then go home and, you know, have one of those romantic moments you keep saying we don't have enough of any more. But what do I find? You with some slut on your lap and probably a big old boner." She pauses a heartbeat and adds, "Well, I guess *medium-sized* would be more accurate." That tells me she's pretty much run out, because she never plays that card when she has any others.

"It kept you happy for quite a while," I say, but I really don't want to talk about my dick in public. "Margo don't mean nothing."

"It looked like nothing." Tina opens the car door. "I'm leaving now. You go back to your drunk friends and your scrawny whore."

She gets in Shelly's car and they drive away. I don't know if I should go home now and do some serious butt-kissing, or wait until later when she might've calmed down. I stand on the sidewalk and listen to the teenagers outside the pizza place laughing. I think, *This is what I am now. A fool. A clown.* I go back in the Rusty Scuppers and drain my beer and have two more to give Tina a chance to calm down before I tell Judd I have to go.

"Tell her she looks like she's lost ten pounds," he says helpfully. "That always works with Jan, anyway."

I climb into my pickup and drive the four blocks towards home, trying out opening lines. I think I've got something figured out, but when I cut the wheels into the driveway, I realize it's too late for words. Even crawling in on my hands and knees and kissing Tina's little pink toes won't work this time.

I don't know how she and Shelly got my stuff out on the sidewalk so fast, but they did. All my stuff, clothes and rifles and tool chest and high school baseball trophies, thrown in a heap. This has never happened before, no matter how bad our fights have been. I start to hyperventilate, I can't help it, and my chest starts hurting like I'm having a heart attack. I go up the walk, but the front door is secured inside with the chain lock I put on myself, never dreaming I'd be the only person it ever kept out.

"Go away," Tina says through the narrow opening. "Go away and don't ever come back. Go stay with your little slut."

"I ain't done nothing wrong. I ain't." But I'm talking to a closed door. I stand there and look at my stuff. Is this all I have to show for my whole life, this pathetic pile of shit?

I lug most of it to the back of the truck, which fortunately has a cap on it, then put the rifles on the window rack in the cab. What's worst is that Kady and Maura and Mandy are standing in the window watching me. Kady and Maura are crying, but Mandy's dry-eyed, leaning against her mother's hip. I know it's just a matter of time before Tina has them all turned against me.

I don't know what to do. Nana's been in bed for hours, and I'm not going to disturb her. Maybe Judd will let me crash on his couch, and tomorrow Tina and I can start putting things right. I drive back to the Rusty Scuppers.

It's still crowded, and Margo's back at the table with Judd and Tom and Dunc. Judd says, "Didn't know if we'd ever see you again, 'cept at your funeral."

Margo stands up. "I better go before Tina comes back and bitch-slaps me."

I sit down. "Tina ain't coming back," I say. "And I got to find someplace to stay." I don't mean that for her, but she says, "I got room," and after a couple more beers, I figure I need to stay somewhere and Judd hasn't offered, so since Margo and me are both too drunk to do anything anyway, I decide I might as well spend the night.

છ

Margo lives in the low-income housing project out on the Remsen Road. She flips through the TV channels while I half-sit, half-lie on the couch.

"Tina ain't never gonna let me see my girls." My eyes are smarting like they used to when I was a little kid trying to keep from crying. "My life's so fucked up, nothing can make it better."

"Something can," Margo says. "And 'cause I'm feeling sorry for you, it's gonna be my treat."

She goes upstairs, and I lie on the couch and wait, wondering if she's going to expect me to try to have sex with her after all. But instead, she comes back carrying a hand mirror holding some lines of white powder and a straw cut in short pieces. She sets the mirror on the banged-up coffee table . "Here you go. Try a line of this."

"What is it," I ask, although I think I might already know.

"Forgetting powder," she says. "Oxy. Washington County heroin. If this doesn't take your troubles away, nothing will." She sticks a piece of straw up one side of her nose and hoovers up a line, then switches sides and does another. "Go ahead," she says, and hands me a fresh piece of straw.

So this is what Judd was talking about. I hesitate, but only for a second, then snort it up. It feels weird, burning its way into my sinuses and tasting bitter in the back of my throat. "Other side," Margo tells me, so I do the last line and then lean back against the couch pillows. She flops down beside me and stares at the ceiling. I close my eyes and wait.

In a few minutes this feeling washes over me I've felt only once before, calm and excited both at once.

When I was a kid, we used to hitchhike to Bryant's Mills on hot summer days. There was a long rope tied way up high in some pine branches, and you could swing clear out to the middle of the Wapatquan River and drop into the warm, lazy current. I was scared of it for a long time, but one day, instead of swinging out and then back to the riverbank like the little wuss I was, I made myself let go, and as I fell through the hot stillness to the water below, I felt exactly this feeling, finally free of everything that held me back.

I start to float, beyond the reach of gravity, no worries, no useless thoughts. Life feels more complete than it has in a long time, and I let it all go, my lost job, my lost family, my lost life.

"Feeling okay?" Margo sounds like she's a long way off.

"Great," I say. It might be a while since she asked me. I can't tell, because time seems to have stopped. "I wouldn't mind doing this regular."

"All it takes is money." She turns onto her side, her cheek against my shoulder, and I wonder if she's going to make a move on me, but she doesn't. I spin further down the spiral into nothingness.

☙

Daylight's shining around the edges of the window shades when I wake up on a strange couch. At first, I'm not sure where I am, but then I see the mirror on the coffee table and I remember. I'm at Margo's, and we snorted something called Oxy, and it was the best feeling in the world. Now it's the worst. I feel like my head's stuffed with dirty socks.

The TV clock says 8:37—and that means I'm an hour and a half late for work already. What are they gonna do, though—fire me? That's so funny I laugh out loud, which makes my head feel like someone's sunk a hatchet in it just above my eyebrows.

Margo comes down the stairs in a fuzzy old bathrobe, her hair standing up like haystacks all over her head. "What's so funny?"

"Nothing much. I got to go to work, I guess."

"Are you coming back?"

It would be sweet, snorting Oxy every night, but that would guarantee I'd never see Kady and Maura and Mandy again. "I got to try and see Tina today. Try and patch things up. For the girls, you know?"

"Yeah." Margo licks her finger, blots up the few leftover grains of crushed Oxy from the mirror, and licks her finger again. Her tongue's very pink, pierced with a silver stud. "Well, you know you're welcome here if it don't work out."

"Okay," I say. "Thanks, I appreciate that."

Judd and Moppet are already on the cage site unloading feed from the barge. "Get lucky last night, you old dog?" Judd asks.

"No. It wasn't about that." I don't intend to tell them what it was about.

"Course not," says Moppet.

He and Judd both smirk, but then Judd gets this serious look. "The only reason Margo Burke would take a guy home and not lay him is because of other—entertainments. You doing other entertainments now, Hank?"

"I don't know what you mean," I say, careful to keep my face turned away as I shovel up some salmon feed.

"I think you do." Judd takes hold of my shoulder. "I think you know exactly what I mean. Don't mess with that shit. It's bad news."

"Even I know better than that," says Moppet.

"I ain't gonna do it again," I say. I swing my shovel in an arc, so the pellets scatter all across the surface where the few remaining salmon can snap them up. "I was drunk, and curious, and—it was just a one-time thing."

☙

I'm coming through the Quoddy Sea parking lot after my shift when I see Tina's friend Shelly leaning on the front bumper of my truck. She doesn't say hello, just starts reeling off what sounds like a prepared speech. Tina's getting a divorce lawyer. I'm gonna be on the hook for max child support, so I better find another job real quick. And I shouldn't even *think* about trying to see the kids. She doesn't wait for me to say anything, just dashes back to her car and drives away, leaving me standing there like someone just hit me with the stupid-stick.

We've had our share of hassles, Tina and me, more than our share, really. But we've always gotten through it somehow—until now. I'd figured on going by and trying to start working things out, but all of a sudden that doesn't sound like such a good idea. And I can't go to Nana's, because she'll see it in my face and I don't want to talk about it. It looks like there's nowhere for me to go but Margo's. Maybe she'll give me another Oxy. One more wouldn't hurt, after this bad news. Just one more, and that'll be the end of it.

"Sure," Margo says when I ask for one. "The only thing is, it's wicked expensive, and I can't afford to give them away. From now on, you got to pay."

"How much?" It's only fair, I guess. After all, I wouldn't expect her to buy my beer.

"I'll let you have one for half-price, but just this once."

She tells me the price and my jaw drops. "People really pay that? How do they afford it?"

"Just about everyone that uses, sells. No one could afford them otherwise." She shrugs. "You got to do what you got to do. I guess you haven't used enough to understand that yet. But you will."

No, I tell myself. *I won't, because this is the last time. Forever.* I dig some bills out of my wallet, then pick up my straw and snort the lines she's laid out for me. *I can't do this again after this one*, I tell myself. *It ain't right. But why does it have to feel so fucking good?*

☙

"I'm sorry I didn't come by yesterday," I tell Nana. It's early, way too early, but despite the Oxy hangover, I'm standing at the stove cooking a poached egg for her breakfast, just like I did back in normal times. That's what I'm trying to do. Make everything I can seem like normal.

Nana dips her teabag up and down in her favorite flowered mug, then starts rubbing one side of her head just above her ear and says, "Tina called me, Hank. Not last night, but the night before. She wanted to know if you were staying here."

I feel all the blood leaving my brain. I grab the edge of the counter, positive I'm about to keel over. "What did you tell her?"

"I said she woke me up and you weren't here at the moment. I don't like this, Hank. I won't lie for anyone, not even you."

I butter the toast and flop the poached egg on it. What I ought to do is bring my stuff in from the truck right now, and tell her I'm staying. That way, I'd have to do it instead of going to Margo's. I don't know why I don't, when going back there will mean I might not ever see my kids again. But I'm caught in a bad dream and there's only one door out of it, and Margo holds the key.

Nana looks at me, and I feel like she's got x-ray vision, like she sees all my dirty little secrets. When I was a kid, she always knew when I was lying, or in trouble. Right was right, and that was it. "The truth always comes out, Hank," she tells me, just like back then. "Better now than later."

I'm doing the dishes when I happen to glance at the pill bottles on the sideboard. There it is on the label of one of them—Oxycontin. I stand there looking at it for a long time, wanting to take a few but not wanting to leave Nana short. But then she gets up and hobbles to the bathroom, and it's too easy. I hate myself for even thinking about it, but that doesn't stop me from slipping five of them into the pocket of my jeans.

෮

It's down to our last day of work. By then, I've been served with divorce papers at the Rusty Scuppers in front of all my friends. I'm still on Margo's couch, and even though I feel guilty as hell, I've had to help myself to five more of Nana's Oxys.

Our last job is cleaning up the infected cage sites, and as soon as we load the barges with the slimy nets the divers removed from the cages, we'll be done. The job I've had for my entire adult life will be over. I'm too scared to think about it, let alone make plans.

EVERYONE KNOWS THIS IS NOWHERE

We're about an hour from punching the clock for the last time when it happens. Judd and Moppet are on the cage and Tom Estey and I are on the barge, getting the last of the nets aboard, when Moppet's feet go out from under him on the wet walkway and he falls into the water, striking the small of his back on the rail of the barge.

I have to admit, I'm a little slow and fuzzy from my Oxy hangover, so by the time I realize what's happened, Tom and Judd already have Moppet on the barge. He lays there on the pile of nets, spitting and gasping, while Judd pats his shoulder.

Back at Quoddy Sea, two EMT's take Moppet away on a backboard. "Bastards probably won't give him Workman's Comp this close to shutdown," Judd says, and I figure he's probably right. I found out from Margo just how the system screws you over if you get hurt on the job, a measly wage that doesn't come close to what anyone could live on and company-paid doctors who say there's nothing wrong with you anyway.

An hour later, we punch the clock for the last time. Nobody's saying anything or even looking at each other, but everyone knows we're in for a long, hard haul. In the parking lot, I stare at the now-empty cove that was my world for twelve years. Fall's in the air, leaves turning red and yellow against the dark spruces, and this moment feels like the end of everything.

Someone yells that there's going to be an unemployment party at the Rusty Scuppers. I figure everyone's thinking what I'm thinking, might as well drink up the last paycheck and the hell with tomorrow. If we're going over the cliff anyway, we might as well go right now.

After several rounds of beer, someone gets the bright idea we should do shooters, but one shot of cheap whiskey gets my gut to roaring. I go back to beer, but Judd and Tom and Dunc keep pounding them down, until Judd does a face-plant on the table. His body-building brother, Stence, pushes his way through the crowd and slings Judd over his shoulder and goes out the door.

I figure I might as well go, too. I'm slowly working my way to the door when I hear my name. I turn around and coming towards me is the only guy in the place who doesn't work at Quoddy Sea—

Talbot Jones, son of the owner of the boatyard where the summer people store their yachts for the winter. He'd gone to some pricey college and had a fancy-schmancy job in Boston, but that didn't last long and now he's on Spruce Island, not East Haven with the rest of the family, and the gossip is that he's got a heavy drug problem like some Kennedy gone bad.

"You know where Margo is?" he asks, and I do, she's off to Mayfield scoring some Oxy, but I don't tell him that.

"I dunno," I say. "I came here right after work." Damn—it was the last time I'd be able to say that.

"I need some shit," this upper-crust loser tells me, and I think, *Man, if I had your advantages, I wouldn't be living my life like this.* But I don't, I don't have any hope at all, and that's why all I want to do is go back to the apartment and snort up another Oxy. It'll be the first time I've broken my one-a-day rule, but with my whole career ending, I think I'm entitled.

Talbot Jones wants to tag along, but I tell him I'll let Margo know he's looking for her, and stagger out to my truck and head to the closest thing I have these days to home.

☙

The next afternoon, Judd and I go to visit Moppet in the hospital up in Mayfield. "This is the first day in our adult life that any of us is unemployed," Judd says as he pulls the curtain between Moppet and some bald, wrinkled guy who looks like he's about a hundred years old.

"This sucks," says Moppet. "My back's broken, and I don't even get to miss work. And I got stuff I want to be doing."

"Besides playing video games and watching TV?" Judd says.

"That too," says Moppet. "But I got a plan, and I'm gonna get left behind if I ain't back to normal by the first of October."

Judd laughs. "Normal. You ain't had a normal day in your life."

"You got a plan," I say. "*You* got a plan. Ain't no one else got a plan yet, but *you* got one?"

"I'm gonna take that heavy-equipment course. Learn to drive a D-9. Always wanted to run one of them puppies." Moppet on a bulldozer. That was a picture. "I hope I can read good enough to keep up with it," he says.

Moppet, thinking ahead. It blows my mind. What's wrong with me? I am at the crossroads of my life, and I don't have a clue which way to go.

☙

This can't be happening. I'm getting a seasick feeling as though I'm having a bad flashback to life with Tina, but no, this is Margo standing in front of me, hands on her skinny hips, demanding that I get my shit together *right now*, no mercy.

"I know you lost your job," she says, "but you can't just lay around here all day. I got bills to pay, and it costs more to feed you for a week than it does me for a month. And as of now, your tab for Oxys is closed. I can't carry you any more. So what're you gonna do, Hank? Tell me, just what the fuck are you gonna do?"

What I ought to do is move to Nana's, but that would mean either giving up the only escape I have or feeling like shit for stealing her pills. I ain't yet sunk so low as to make it a habit to steal from my own grandmother, so I better stay put. I tell Margo, "I'll pay my tab and help out with expenses as soon as my unemployment kicks in. It ain't like I can just go out and find another job."

"Oxys are just as good as money. Get a supply going, I could overlook the other stuff." She lights a cigarette, then scales her lighter at me. It bounces off my shoulder onto the floor, and I let it lie there. She shoots me a dagger look and picks it up. "Look, I got to go meet someone. You think about things, Hank. No way this free ride's lasting forever. I want Oxys or I want money. You decide."

What a bitch. I do all the cleaning, I cook for her, and this is the thanks I get. There's only one thing that'll make this right, so I take down the cracked sugar bowl from the top shelf of the cupboard and help myself to one of the Oxys she's got stashed there. She owes me that for making me feel so small and miserable. Just for today, I'll do three instead of two, because I have to forget everything, even if it's only for a little while.

☙

Another week goes by, and even though I keep telling myself moving to Nana's is the only thing that will save me, I don't. Margo's at me about money every waking moment. Even at half-price, my Oxy habit's reached a point I don't have a fart in a hurricane's chance of paying. And now the bitch is threatening to charge me full price if she doesn't see some cash or a new source of Oxys.

Finally, I can't take it any more. While I'm cooking Nana's supper, I take ten Oxys out of her bottle. I'm thinking Margo will be happy, those ten are worth quite a bit of money on the street, but when I get back to the partment, she's gone again.

It's a warm evening, one of those the perfect summer evenings just before fall sets in for good, so I leave the front door open and let the breeze drift in.

In the old days on an evening like this, Tina and the kids and I would walk downtown and get dogs and fries at Leona's Hotdog Stand. Life seemed so simple then, a job, a house, someone to love me, and only a few beers to alter reality. Things are going out of control fast now, but I can't stop. I can't, even though I know it's wrong, it's all wrong. What kind of man steals from his own grandmother?

I tell myself the doctors will understand, she's old, and she has cancer, and it's easy to lose track. They can increase her prescription. She won't go without. It's not the end of the world. So why do I feel so crappy about it, like God's about to send a lightning bolt to end my sorry existence?

The phone rings. I listen for the message, but it's a hang-up. I notice there's a message on the machine, though, so I hit the playback. It's from Judd, around noon, which means Margo must've been here to hear it. Moppet's home from the hospital. Thanks for fucking telling me, Margo. Thanks for leaving a note.

Then this treacherous thing in my brain spins into gear. Moppet. Broken back. Oxy? It could be. He wouldn't know what they were worth, so I could offer him half price and he'd think he was making out like a bandit. And he would be, really. He would be.

When I get to his mother's house, there's a black Lexus in the driveway, looking out-of-place next to the cracked blue vinyl siding. I'm on the porch reaching for the doorknob when I hear voices through an open window, and I stand there a few minutes wondering if I should go in—until I hear Talbot Jones say, "That's too bad. I would've given you some serious cash. You think getting laid by Margo Burke is worth that?"

My heart trip-hammers. It's not true. Of course it's true. That's why Margo didn't leave me a message, she wanted to get to Moppet first. I sneak off the porch and get in my truck and drive around the block, waiting for Jones to be gone.

When the driveway's empty, I park and let myself into the house. In the cluttered living room, I move a pile of video game cases from the recliner to the coffee table, and sit down.

"I just found out you're home," I say. "Margo never told me Judd called." I look at Moppet real close to see if he reacts. He picks at fuzz on his blanket and doesn't meet my eyes at all. I push my baseball cap up my forehead and say, "What's Talbot Jones doing here? You got something he wants?"

"No," says Moppet. "I don't."

"But you did," I say. I try to keep the edge out of my voice, but Moppet must catch it, because he looks up at me, wary as a deer.

"I may only be about as sharp as a golf ball, Hank," he says. "But I'm guessing before you came in, you were listening to things that are none of your business. Is that right?"

"You let Margo have your Oxy? Why?"

Moppet turns carefully on the couch and puts his back to me. "Don't you be coming in here fighting me on the day I get out of the hospital, Hank. If it wasn't Margo, it woulda been Jones."

"But I'm your friend."

"Which is why you never woulda gotten them. Because I *am* your friend, you just don't see that right now. You got to get away from Margo, bro. You really do, before she drags you down with her and you start stealing pills from your grandmother or something."

I don't know what to say. It's been almost four weeks since Tina gave me the boot, and all this time I've been getting further and further from who I thought I was. I crack my knuckles and stare at the peeling linoleum, and wonder how big, dumb Moppet figured all this out so fast, right down to knowing I wouldn't be above stealing from Nana. That's the worst.

"I'm sorry, bro," Moppet says. "I really am. Look, you can move in here with me and Ma, if you need a place to stay. Only thing is, no drugs. And if you'd take that heavy equipment course with me and help me with the bookwork, that'd be good for both of us."

"I'll think about it," I say. And then, "I want my life back. I want my wife back." I can't believe I'm hearing myself say it, but there it is. The truest thing I've said in a long, long time.

∞

I go to Abbott's and buy a thirty-pack of Budweiser before going back to Margo's. I'm going to drink every drop of it before I say one word to her about taking advantage of Moppet, which now that I've calmed down I can see is the true situation.

She's not back yet, so I sit in the recliner and chug four longnecks as fast as I can. By the time I pop the top on the fifth one, I've got a plan. Why mention any of this? Why not just even it up? She took Moppet's pills and gave him nothing of value in return, so how would she feel if someone did the same to her?

There's got to be a stash of pills somewhere, a bigger stash than the few in the sugar bowl. I pull everything out of the cupboards, look in pots and pans and covered dishes, drive my hand into the flour canister and the sugar and the coffee, but there's nothing. It's a mess, but I'll worry about that later.

There's nothing in the TV cabinet, nothing under the couch or chairs, nothing in the bathroom. In the bedroom, I go through all the pockets in what's hanging in the closet, tumble around all the stuff in the dresser drawers, and shove the mattress off the box spring. Then I sit on the floor and chug another beer. Nothing anywhere, but there has to be a stash. There has to be. Is she dumb enough to carry it with her?

I flop over and lie on the floor. The cheap carpeting's rough against my face, and I'm about to get up when I see the only thing I haven't thought to check, the pile of shoes on the floor of the closet. When I pick up a pair of sneakers that she bought at the salvage store in Mayfield but never wore because they made her feet look big, I find pay dirt. Tucked in the left toe is a ziptop baggie holding more pills than I've ever seen.

I dump them out on the rug and count them into groups of ten. Seventy-three of them. A lot of money on the street. That would more than even things up.

I stick the baggie in my jeans pocket, pick up my beer suitcase, and go out to the truck. Talbot Jones and his spooky girlfriend are staying at a house that was built on land that used to be part of Nana and Gramp's farm. It's screened from the road, so no one will see my truck there and kick the local gossip mill into high gear.

"Well," says Jones, peering out over the chain lock on the front door, "what have we here?"

"I got something that might interest you."

"What'd you do, get a couple of Oxy from your pal Moppet?" He shakes his head, as though I'm a useless piece of shit not worth bothering with, which I am, but not for the reasons he thinks.

"No," I say. "I got a nice stash." I'm feeling pretty good now, buzzed from the beer and maybe about to make some serious bank.

Jones runs his hand over his blonde hair. "So Moppet was fibbing. It *was* you, not Margo. I wonder why he told me a wild tale like that." He looks at me like I'm a bug squashed on the sole of his shoe. "Okay. I think we can do business."

He lets me in, and calls to his girlfriend, Wynter. She wanders in, a skinny girl in a straight black dress, her long black hair hanging lank over her shoulders, and he tells her to get the bank bag.

I look around the living room while Jones counts the pills. The leather couch is draped with cast-off clothing, the ashtrays overflow on the glass-and-brass coffee table, and there's an empty pizza box on the floor by the flat-screen TV. If I had a place this nice, I'd sure as hell take way better care of it than these drug-addled fools do.

Wynter comes back. Jones counts out the money while I watch, and before I have time for second thoughts, the deal's done.

☙

Nice crispy hundreds. I divide the stack and put half under the insole in each sneaker, glad I'm wearing my old Chuck Taylor hightops. It's a nice chunk of change, a very nice chunk of change. It crosses my mind I could have my own little Oxy business, but I know my nerves wouldn't take it.

I'm just getting out of my truck at Nana's when the local cruiser pulls in behind me and Bobby Steiner, a new police academy graduate, gets out. *Oh, man*, I think, *did Jones set me up? Now my goose is really cooked.* "What's up?" I say, trying to keep it light.

"Your grandmother reported a theft," he says, and this is so far from what I expected to hear that I stand there with my chin hanging down around my knees in stupid disbelief as he walks towards the front door. When I come to my senses, which I do, luckily, before Nana answers the door, I realize there's only one theft she could be reporting. I head for the back of the house, running hard after I turn the corner out of Steiner's sight, and let myself in the kitchen and take the ten Oxy I kept out of Margo's stash and dump them back in Nana's bottle as quick as I can. Then I go outdoors and time it so I come in the back door just as Nana and the cop reach the kitchen.

"It had to be the Dowley boy," Nana's saying. "He was here to fix the faucet, and my pills were right beside the sink. He's the only one that could've taken them."

"I don't think Ronnie Dowley would do that," I say. I'm feeling pretty safe that I'm not a suspect, and I can't see some innocent kid getting his ass hauled for this.

Steiner gives me a sharp look, like he sees straight through me. "How about you, Hank? You got the straw habit these days? You boosting your Grandmother's narcotics?"

Nana raps her knuckles on the table. "I won't listen to this. Hank's a good boy. He's had some tough times, but he's honest."

"Search me," I say, and hold my arms out so Steiner can frisk me like they do on TV, but he shakes his head. "Go ahead," I tell him. "Search my truck, too, if you want to. I ain't got nothing to hide." Except, of course, all that cash in my sneakers.

He asks Nana, "How many pills do you reckon were stolen?"

"Ten."

"How can you be so sure?"

Nana holds up a sheet of paper. "I write it down when I take one. Date and time. So I don't lose track."

"So how many should be here?"

"Eighty-seven."

"You don't mind if I count them?" Steiner says, holding up the bottle, and she shakes her head. I lean against the refrigerator and wait while he counts. "I think you're right where you should be with these, ma'am," he says. "There's eighty-seven. You must've counted wrong."

Nana looks confused. "I—" she starts, then sighs. "I'm sorry. I did make a mistake. I shouldn't have accused that boy."

"No harm done," Steiner says. "I don't think I have to file a report on this. Glad it all worked out." He flicks his eyes over me and says, "Watch yourself, Hank," before letting himself out the back door. I feel as though my knees are about to collapse, but I hang on and make Nana supper, sober now, sober and scared.

☙

Margo's car is parked in front of the apartment when I get back, and I sit in my truck for a few minutes, wondering if I can face one more scene without cracking open and spilling my guts. I should've put the place back together before going out, but it's too late now.

When I open the door, Margo runs to me, tears streaming down her hollow cheeks, and starts pounding her fists on my chest. "Some bastard broke in and robbed us," she says, and again my jaw drops, and I know I've got another stupid, surprised look on my face. "They trashed the place and found the Oxys," she says. "I need one so bad, and there aren't any. Have you got any, Hank? Say you've got some, please."

"I don't," I say. "I'm so sorry."

She picks up a big glass ashtray from the coffee table and scales it across the living room. Cigarette butts rain down across the rug. The ashtray leaves a dent in the wall, but doesn't break. "Fuck," she says, "fuck, fuck, fuck. You are such a waste. I thought I could count on you, but you don't even have one little pill after all I've done for you."

"I'm sorry," I say again. Actually, I'm not the least bit sorry, and I wonder when I got so good at lying.

"You got to do something about this," she says.

"Like what?"

"I don't know. Find out who did this and kill them or something." She can't be serious. Kill someone? That's plain crazy.

"I can't."

"Then get me an Oxy. Go out and find some. I want one. I need one."

I want one, too, in the worst way, but those days are over. They have to be over. I've escaped twice in the last few hours, and I can't take the chance again, no matter what. My nerves are starting to jump, I itch all over, and I feel as though my eyeballs are jerking around in my skull, but I'm just going to have to ride it out. There's no other choice. "I don't know anyone that has any pills," I tell her, and although I want to confront her about Moppet, I don't. Best to let it all just fade away.

"I have to lie down," she says, and does. I stand there a moment while her teeth chatter and her arms and legs twitch, knowing that's where I'm headed, too. Then I cover her with the ratty old afghan and go upstairs and throw my clothes and toothbrush in a grocery bag and put the key on the table and walk out the door, glad this phase of my fucked-up life is over.

∞

"I am at the crossroads of my life, and I want to go home," I say as I drive towards town. I can't do it, though. I can't just walk up and knock on the door of the house that used to be my home and have my kids see Tina send me away again.

Instead, I park on the breakwater and watch the streetlights along the sea wall blink on as the sky turns black. Judd pulls up beside me, "Hank, you okay? You ain't looking so good, buddy. Why don't you go back to Margo's and call it a night?"

"I'm done with all that."

Judd gives me the kind of look he might if I told him I just got back from a trip to Saturn. "Well, good. Then why don't you come stay the night? Jan won't mind. You can figure things out tomorrow."

It beats sitting here. The cops have been on the breakwater twice already, turning around right beside my truck so their highbeams put me in the spotlight. Steiner probably guessed what happened at Nana's. Even though there's no way to pin anything on me, he's the kind of prick that loves to bring a guy down.

"Okay," I say. "I'll finish this beer and get my shit together."

I mean to go, I really do, but getting my shit together isn't remotely possible. I can't let Jan see me like this unless I want it all over town, courtesy of the cafeteria ladies. I can't let anyone see me like this. I feel like I'm in a world of hurts such as I've never experienced before, my heart bouncing around in my chest and my head pounding. I feel like I'm going to die and I wish I would. As I leave the breakwater behind, I try to figure out someplace to go where I can lay low and drink my beer in peace.

※

When I come to, I'm in bed, and the room is bright, so bright it hurts. I close my eyes and try to roll over, and realize I'm tied down with IV's in both my arms. Hospital or mental institution? I don't know.

A nurse comes in and checks on me, and tells me that I'm at the hospital in Mayfield. They think I passed out in the truck after drinking an entire suitcase of beer, and then threw up and sucked it into my lungs. Judd found me and called the ambulance, and it's a good thing he did, or I might be dead now, instead of just having a case of what they call "aspiration pneumonia." I figure they probably gave me a drug test, but the nurse doesn't mention it, so I don't, either. The shakes and itching have just about stopped, so maybe the worst of that part's over.

The doctor makes his rounds later that morning. After ordering the wrist straps removed, he tells me that I've been out of it for three days, three days of thrashing around so bad they thought I was going to hurt myself. The pneumonia's clearing up now, and yes, I tested positive for narcotics, but that's pretty much out of my system and the hard work of kicking the mental habit begins. I tell him I can do it, I can do anything if I put my mind to it, and he pats me on the shoulder and says as long as I don't cave, everything will be all right. Yeah, right, doc, I'm homeless and jobless, but everything will be all right.

Judd comes to visit, with apologies from Moppet, who says he'd like to see me, but the hospital would give him bad flashbacks about his broken back. I can understand that.

After Judd leaves, I fall asleep. I dream I hear Tina saying my name. Then I realize it isn't a dream. Tina's standing beside my bed, she really is.

"Hello, Hank," she says, a little cool, but at least she's here, and looking as beautiful as I've imagined her. Sure, there's that twenty pounds she didn't lose after the twins were born, but her skin's perfect and her long dark hair shines like a crow's wing in the sun.

"I missed you, Tina."

She shakes her head, not saying anything, but I know that look in her eyes, and I know it means the door's not completely closed. She still cares, at least a little bit.

"How's it going?" I say. "Are you getting by okay?"

She shrugs. "I'm back to working in the deli at the IGA. It's okay. I don't mind it." She digs into the canvas bag she carries and pulls out a stack of cash. "I don't know where you got this, Hank, and I don't want to know. Judd said it was all over the truck cab when he found you down at the Inlet. It's a good thing you weren't where other people could see it and take it from you."

The Inlet was where Judd and Moppet and I used to go drink when we were in high school, down a dirt road to a piece of shore property that would never sell to the flatlanders because of its scenic industrial view of Maine Pearl Processors. I have no memory at all of going there, no memory of taking the money out of my sneakers. No memory of anything after leaving the breakwater.

"There's an awful lot of money here. You want me to keep it for you?"

"For us. Keep it for us." I look right at her, wanting more than anything for her to agree that there's still an "us."

She looks at the floor, then drops the money back into the canvas bag and pulls out a small book like the ones she makes. "Kady put this together for you. She misses you so much, Hank."

"I miss her. I miss all of you. I miss you, Tina, most of all."

She hands me the book. I take it and look through the pages with pictures of us fancied up with stickers and colored paper and Kady's careful handwriting. The first picture of the three of us, the day we brought her home from the hospital. Picnics and fishing trips and birthday parties. I can't help it, I break down and start bawling like a baby.

"Don't," Tina says. "Please don't."

I wipe my nose on my hospital gown and swallow hard. "Take me back. I screwed it up so bad, but please take me back."

"There'd be conditions. If I did decide to take you back."

"Anything. Whatever you say."

"Well, I'd say no more drugs and no more bars. Go to the technical college and learn a trade and get a decent job afterwards."

"I can do that. I can, all of it. I'll take that heavy equipment course with Moppet. I still love you, Tina. I swear to God I do."

"Nana says you can stay with her until you get back on track. We can see each other if it works out. And sign up for that course. Will you do that?"

"Hand me the phone," I say, and she does, and gives me the number. Always prepared, that's my girl. I make the call. They tell me the course starts in two weeks and they'll mail me the paperwork so I can sign up. I give them Tina's address, so I'll have an excuse to see her again.

The big bump in the road now is staying with Nana without touching her Oxys. I know I'll have to come clean to her about what I did. And get her a lockbox to keep them in. I can't mess this up, my one-and-only chance. I got to get back to being honest.

Tina pats my shoulder before she leaves, and kisses my forehead like I'm one of the kids. It ain't much, but I'm happy with it, and I'll live for the day I've earned my way back and she kisses me for real.

Alone again, I go through Kady's scrapbook, studying every picture, every word. So this is how my oldest daughter sees the story of our family. It ain't the exact truth, but it does start me thinking. Maybe we can remember it this way instead of the way it was. Maybe it's okay for our memories to be happy ones, as long as we still hang on to the lessons we learned along the way.

ೞଓ

GONE LIKE SEA SMOKE

STEVIE'S ALWAYS HAPPY WHEN scallop season starts. The cold today feels sharp as the edge of a clamshell, but he doesn't care. I stand in the wheelhouse as he checks everything on the boat one last time, making sure the *Five Sisters* is set up perfect in every way before he takes me on a shakedown cruise. Earlier, all over Big Musquan Bay, clouds of sea smoke were rising lavender grey against the butter-colored eastern sky, but now the air is clear and dead still.

Spruce Island's to the right—I mean starboard—as we enter the channel; East Haven, the outer island, to port. At the helm, Stevie stares straight ahead, his heavy eyelids making his beautiful stargazer eyes look half-closed and sleepy, but I know better. Out here, nothing's ever lost on my husband. He can read the water and wind and sky and stars, and I never feel safer than when he's beside me.

The Caterpillar diesel, so new I can smell the paint burning off it, throbs as we push against the incoming tide, steady grey-green wavelets sparkling in the cold afternoon sun. Stevie puts an arm around my shoulders and tangles his fingers in the ends of my hair. "I love you, Heather," he says.

I say, "Love you too," and, as we swing wide around Trumbull's Head, I lean back against his shoulder and think how incredibly lucky we are, crazy in love, the *Five Sisters* and our little house both free and clear from Stevie's grandfather, a good life for a couple of kids like us. We started going out in tenth grade, got married two years ago the day after we graduated from Quoddy High. After the wedding, we danced at our senior prom, me in my white lace wedding dress, Stevie looking so handsome in his rented midnight blue tux with the ruffled shirt, his sideburns and the edges of his dark goatee shaved straight and clean.

Past Long Cove, we head towards the mainland and Little Musquan Bay, where the sweetest scallops are. I watch the shore, dark evergreens dusted with snow, reddish-grey ledges skimmed with ice. Here in the shelter of the wheelhouse, I can almost forget how cold winter on the water is. But I get chilled easy, I always have, so I keep close to Stevie's warmth, my arms around his waist and one cheek pressed between his shoulder blades, his tan canvas jacket rough against my face.

Stevie's always loose and happy out here, but now even through his heavy clothes I can feel him tensed up, and that's not normal. "What's wrong, babe?" I ask. He shrugs and fidgets, and I step away and look up at him. "No secrets," I say. We've sworn we'd always tell each other everything no matter how much it hurt or how much trouble it caused.

Stevie brushes my bangs back and looks into my eyes. "I know you won't ever tell anyone I said this. I don't think it's such a great idea, letting Tony go and taking Skip on."

That's about the last thing I expect to hear, because I know how much Stevie's looked forward to Skip coming home. I can see he's taking a chance, getting rid of Tony Readfield, one of the fleet's best sternmen. But family's real important to the Nelligan clan, Skip and Gus and my husband the only boys among the seventeen children of the five actual sisters the boat was named for, so what can Stevie do?

I've got my own reasons for wishing Skip hadn't come home after four years in the Army and another shrimping the Gulf of Mexico, but I'm not about to bring up that old stuff. Now I just want to enjoy this afternoon before tomorrow's winter work begins.

When the sun starts sliding down the sky and the gulls wing home towards Spectacle Island, Stevie lets me take a turn at the helm. As the *Five Sisters* cuts through the steel grey chop between Little Musquan and the breakwater, I pray that everything this winter will run as smooth as it has today.

༶

Not long after we get home from our shakedown cruise, Gus and his wife—my older sister, Lally—come by with a hamburger pizza and a twelve-pack. They get to talking with Stevie about the new engine, Lally asking questions about stuff I've just barely heard of. She can always hold her own with the guys.

Lally's a mechanic, the best damn mechanic on Spruce Island, gas or diesel, automotive or marine—ask anyone. She started working for Spat Putnam the day she turned fifteen and got her work permit. I have to admit, I've always been a little bit disappointed that she was born with a natural talent and I wasn't.

When the phone rings, Stevie jumps to answer it, then takes it into the living room. Gus and Lally and I sit at the kitchen table drinking our beer, and for a little while no one says anything.

"How was it up Little Musquan today?" Gus asks me.

Before I can answer, Lally says, "I'd like to see someplace else for a change." Even though our family's fished for three generations, my sister doesn't give two hoots about the ocean. She has this idea that the best place on the earth is west Texas—not that she's ever seen it. Or ever will, in my opinion.

Stevie comes back, and we all watch as he helps himself to another slice of pizza. He combs his fingers through his goatee a few times before he says to Gus, "Abner Dunbar says he'll take Tony on." Gus says Stevie's a real gentleman for finding Tony another job before he fires him.

Lally looks from Gus to Stevie, her light blue eyes narrowed. "Why would you fire Tony?"

Gus chugs his beer in one long swallow. Stevie picks at a string of mozzarella that hangs over the edge of the pizza box. Lally looks at me, and as always my face can't hide what I know. I touch Stevie's foot under the table, and he says, "Skip's coming back from Mississippi, and, well, family's family."

Lally gasps, and her cheeks get pink. "Heather, why didn't you tell me?" All I can do is shrug. We're about to sail into a northeaster, and there's not a damn thing any of us can do about it.

⁂

The next day, the sky is clear and hard, and there's no wind. Stevie leaves the house just before sunrise, and I take my mug of coffee and sit at the kitchen table where the window overlooks the channel between our island and East Haven. Roofs stairstep down the hill below me to the water's edge—one of the things I'm thankful for here in Stevie's grandfather's house, the ocean view without the waterfront taxes.

Soon I hear the heavy whine of diesels, Three boats glide into view, high bows cutting smoothly through grey-green water that looks as thick as half set Jell-O. Between the dark hulls of the other two, the *Five Sisters* is dazzling white like a bride in the dawning light.

I think about Stevie and Gus and Tony Readfield, who've worked together efficient as a well-oiled machine, but then my mind goes to Skip, who showed up last night after Gus and Lally left and surprised us by introducing a wife. With her Southern accent and curly dyed-yellow hair and lots of makeup, she was nothing like the rest of us. Together they seemed like people we'd never known, not family at all.

Before I get upset wondering if the past is going to circle around and mess things up again, I shove all that old stuff out of my mind, pour another cup of coffee, and go back to watching the boats. A whole parade passes across my window, fourteen scallopers in all, some trim and spotless as the *Five Sisters*, some nothing but rundown old tubs. I send my prayer for a safe and prosperous season for everyone, and then it's time to shower and get ready for work.

ೃ

Lally comes in the Drop Anchor after the lunch rush is over, and we sit in the back booth with our fishburgers and onion rings. She's two years older, but we've always been close as twins. Even when she and Gus eloped just a week before my wedding, so she'd be married first, I couldn't get mad.

"So what'd you think?" Lally asks as she runs an onion ring through a pool of thousand island dressing. I know she's meaning Edina, Skip's Mississippi wife.

"She doesn't seem like his type."

"Hm." I can tell by the way Lally narrows her eyes and sucks in her lower lip that she's thinking about stuff she shouldn't.

Before I can stop myself, I say, "Lally, you don't still want Skip, do you?"

She puts down her fishburger and arranges three onion rings in a cloverleaf on her plate. Then she looks up at me like she's going to pin me to the wall. "The worst mistake I ever made was letting Skip go."

This is so disloyal to Gus, my favorite Nelligan cousin, that I don't know what to say.

"Why didn't I want to leave this godforsaken island," Lally goes on. "Look at us. Living in an old trailer next to the garage, working all the time, both of us, with nothing to show for it, no way to get ahead."

I hear a slap at Stevie in those words, Stevie who pays Gus's wages, and it hurts me that she thinks he isn't treating his cousin right. "Gus gets a fair share. Stevie wouldn't cheat him."

"Oh, screw Gus. It's not about Gus. He thinks he's happy." Lally looks at me, her eyes so shiny I think for a minute she's going cry, which I swear she hasn't done since we were kids.

"Lally, you can't still be in love with Skip."

"I didn't know I was, until I heard he was coming back," she says, and for a moment I feel like I don't know her at all. "I can't even remember why I married Gus. I was awake half the night trying to figure that out." Lally squeezes my hands. "This is our secret, Heather. Okay?"

"I understand," I say. If I can keep her secret, I will. But I know if Stevie ever asks, I'll have to tell him everything, and I pray that day never comes.

☙

I'm walking home after my shift when a faded maroon Taurus with Mississippi plates pulls to the curb. "Hi, Heather," Edina drawls. "Want a ride?" It's getting colder now that the sun's going down, and there's still steep Franklin Hill between me and home. I thank her and get in. The way she says, "Come house-hunting with me," I can tell Edina's a woman who knows what she wants and plans on getting it.

We go up one street and down another, stopping at every *For Sale* sign. Nothing suits her—every house either too small, or too rundown, or too crowded by neighbors. Too ordinary or too modern. I'm about to tell her to start looking on fancy East Haven, when she slams on the brakes and says, "That's it." Big and square, it's the only house in town with tall white pillars up the front, exactly like the plantation houses people down south live in.

We're on Winfield Avenue, a cross-street between Garfield and Carlyle, the two best streets in town. Stevie and I went to school with kids from this neighborhood, kids with hundred-dollar jeans and real leather jackets and brand-new Jeeps and Mustangs.

I wonder if I should tell Edina that no one who fishes could afford to live here where the men all wear neckties to work, but when she comes back to the car after looking in the windows and starts talking about how perfect it is, I don't want to be the one to disappoint her. Instead, I tell her where the Haskell Realty office is and ask her to take me home.

✧

In less than a week, Edina gets a job, a smart person's job at the First National Savings and Loan. I watch her counting the IGA's deposit while Marla McHenry cashes my paycheck, and I can tell Edina's a girl who just loves the feel of money in her hands.

Seeing her standing there in her blue jacket and frilly white blouse, her yellow hair fluffy around her shoulders, I can almost believe she's special somehow, deserving of a perfect house in the best part of town. I'm not jealous. I love our home just as it is, our postcard view of the bay, our sweet little backyard with its hedge of beach roses and big clumps of daylilies and hollyhocks. I can't imagine living anywhere but Franklin Hill. But then I think about Lally, her tin-can trailer with tires on the roof, not fifty feet from Spat Putnam's greasy old garage right on the highway, Coastal Fuel's heating oil and propane tanks next door and nothing pretty to look at, just alders and mud on the vacant lot across the road.

Lally's already hurting that Skip didn't come back alone and try to steal her from Gus, and she'll freak out completely if Edina manages to pull off living on Winfield Avenue. I tell myself Edina has about as much chance of getting that house as I have of winning the Megabucks lottery, but then I remember the determination in her eyes.

✧

It's been two weeks, and things seem to be working out on the *Five Sisters*. Then one day Gus has to take Aunt Tess, his mom, to the arthritis specialist in Bangor, three hours away. Stevie asks me to swap days off at the Drop Anchor so I can shuck scallops and Skip can replace Gus on the winch.

Skip and I are working the boat's lines out of the maze of ropes that tie six scallop boats together when we hear a screech of truck brakes and then a shout. "Hey!" my sister calls. "Wait for me." Skip grabs a rope and pulls our bow snug against the *Christa Lynn* so Lally can come aboard. I put my hands over my ears against the loud squeal of wood as the boats grind together forward of our frontmost fenders.

"Shit," Stevie says.

My sister, who hates everything to do with boats and fishing, swings down the ladder and dashes across the four inner boats like a born sailor. "Glad I caught you. I need a day on the water."

"This is work, not therapy," Stevie mutters. Lally watches as Skip and I cast off the lines before Stevie steers past the mooring dolphins and out into the channel. As we head towards Little Musquan in the cold blue light of a December dawn, I do the sternman's chores, making sure the scallop buckets are clean and at hand, the ropes stowed in careful coils, the shucking knives sharp and ready. Lally and Skip lean against the starboard rail and chat like a couple of tourists on a summer cruise. When I tell Skip he's going to have to check the latches on the drag doors, I just don't have the strength in my hands to work them, he huffs across the deck like I have no business asking him to do anything.

Without Gus, it's Skip's job to run the winch today, putting the drag out and bringing it back. It's not exactly rocket science, but Skip just doesn't strike me as being as quick and careful as Gus. We all know stories of inexperienced winchmen swamping a boat with a bad drop or knocking off half the transom with a careless haul-up.

Stevie turns the *Five Sisters* for the first pass as the sun breaks over the hilly horizon and sends stardust sparkles across the green waves. Skip shoves the stick that puts the winch gear into neutral, and the drag freefalls to the bottom. I know that at the helm, Stevie's sensitive hands are sensing the boat's headway, the resistance of the filling drag slowing us ever so slightly. Gus would feel that through the deck, and so can I, but Skip stands there as if he has nothing on his mind at all, grinning at Lally with what he probably thinks is an irresistible flirty face.

"Any time now, Cuz," Stevie says, leaning out of the wheelhouse, and Skip hesitates only for a moment before engaging the hydraulics and putting the winch in reverse. We watch the drag rise, our winter meal ticket, and then Lally's strong hands in brown rubberized gloves release the latches and the drag doors open and the scallops spill out, shells the size of saucers, and I clutch my shucking knife as the day's cold work begins.

On our third pass it all goes wrong. I suspect Skip grabbed the wrong stick and put the winch into neutral instead of engaging the brake, but all I know for sure is, as Lally and I reach up to steady the heavy drag full of scallops, it takes off, bangs the stern so hard the transom splinters, then drops back into the water.

"What the fuck," Lally shouts. "That could've broke my fucking wrist."

Stevie throttles down and stomps back from the helm, and I know he's pissed because his eyebrows have turned into two straight lines. He slides the stick to power up, hits reverse, and the now half-empty drag rises again and stops. Then he goes astern and runs his fingers over the bashed-up wood, only a few minutes ago smooth and almost unmarked.

His eyes flash blue sparks as he turns to Skip. "What is wrong with you?" he says, so softly you wouldn't think it could sound dangerous, but it does. "We're gonna have to lay up half a day to fix this."

Skip curls his lip like Elvis. "Ah, leave it be. It ain't hurting nothing." That's the wrong thing to say. The *Five Sisters* doesn't sail unless she's completely squared away.

"I ain't running a sloppy boat," Stevie says. "Maybe you should think about that."

"Maybe you should get your head out of your ass and see that piece of wood don't have nothing to do with nothing." Skip's shouting now, but he can't scare Stevie. "Maybe if you didn't spend so much money keeping this boat looking like a fucking yacht, you could pay your crew better."

Stevie picks a big splinter of wood out of the smashed place and studies it. Then he looks at Skip, and it's not friendly. "You want to make more money, maybe you should go to Gloucester and try the long-liners. Maybe you have enough experience to be a baiter. You might even work your way up and be the master baiter."

I laugh, and even Lally smirks, but Skip looks like he's ready to punch Stevie. Then Lally puts her hand on his, and whispers something, her lips close to his ear, and Skip unballs his fists.

"Lally, run the winch for us," Stevie says.

My sister pulls off her knitted turquoise beanie and puts it back on. She looks at Skip, and then at Stevie. "I'm sorry. I can't."

If she thinks that will force Stevie to give Skip another chance, she's wrong. "Heather, come here, please," my husband says.

"I can't do this," I whisper, but Stevie bends close and says, "Stick with me on this. You can't screw it up any worse than Skip did." He gives me a hands-on lesson. It doesn't seem all that difficult as long as you keep your mind on it, and I know I can do it if Stevie thinks I can.

I look up from the winch. Skip and Lally lean close at the portside rail, watching us with their heads together, not even caring that we see. I feel as though something's been set in motion, some line crossed I didn't even know was there, and everything will be different from now on.

CR

Friday's payday, and I'm about to walk out of the bank after cashing my check when Edina calls to me. "Good news. We got the mortgage. It'll probably take all my salary, but that's all right. Now we just have to come up with the down payment."

"Where will you get that?"

Edina arches her thin eyebrows. "My parents paid our rent in Biloxi, and gave us their old car. They did their part." She takes a stack of twenties out of her drawer as she talks and pats the edges into a smooth stack, then does the same with the tens. Then she looks up at me, and her light green eyes are as serious as can be. "I figure now that we're here, Skip's family will help us, too."

"Uncle Jack's on disability. They can't afford to help you."

"Everyone says how glad they are Skip came back," Edina says. "Everyone says if we need anything, just let them know, because family sticks together."

"Good luck," I tell her, and walk out the door. I'm sure no one in the family, not even Skip, could possibly think any of us should help Edina get a dream house so far beyond what all the rest of us have.

༺

I'm stunned when Edina finds an ally, and I'm even more stunned that it's my sister. "Why should we help her?" I ask Lally as we eat lunch in the Drop Anchor's back booth the following Tuesday.

"Stevie's got assets. The house and the boat. All he has to do is cosign their loan for the down payment. It won't cost you guys a cent. They don't have a credit history, so they can't get it on their own."

"What's in this for you?"

Lally puts down her half-eaten clam roll. "Look, the only way Skip'll stay around here is if Edina gets that house. Otherwise, she's gonna drag him back down south. I made a bad mistake letting him go once, and it's not happening again."

I look out the window instead of at my sister. "Skip's married, you're married. That's crazy."

"Right now. But someday, he'll leave her, and I'll leave Gus, and everything will be the way it was supposed to be from the start."

"That is so wrong."

"Oh!" Lally crumples her napkin, then starts shredding it. Her nose is turning red, and so are the tips of her ears, and that's a bad sign. "Little Miss Perfect is telling me what's right and wrong! Well, of course, you know everything. It isn't like you live in a dump with a man you don't love while the guy you do love has this tight-assed little wife, and the conniving youngest cousin got everything in the family worth having, the house and the boat, because he happened to suck up to a dying man."

I want to tell her that Stevie never sucked up to Grandpa Nelligan, that he gave up a lot, especially the soccer team, to take care of Grandpa that last year, but there's no point. Instead, I say, "I have to go back to work," and stack my dishes and turn away.

༺

January comes in sleety and chill. Edina and Lally are still at Stevie and me about the down payment. I remember learning in earth science class that if water drips long enough, it can wear away stone, and that's how this feels. *Co-sign, co-sign, co-sign. Drip, drip, drip.*

I'm thoroughly sick of spending every weekend with Lally and Gus and Skip and Edina, and Stevie must figure that out, because one Friday when he gets home he tells me we're going out to dinner at the seafood restaurant on the mainland, just the two of us.

The Seaview's busy, but we get a booth. Stevie orders fried clams, and I go for the native shrimp. As we pick at our coleslaw while we wait for the meal, he says, "Do you think I owe them anything?"

"Skip and Edina? Of course not. You're not responsible for the whole family."

Stevie doesn't say anything while the waitress sets down our plates. Then, "It was Grandpa's free choice to leave me the *Five Sisters.* I never asked."

"And the house. I know."

"Skip thinks I should give him and Gus guaranteed wages instead of shares of the catch." Stevie drains his Coors Light and flags the waitress for a refill. "I told him, No way, that's crazy. I could end up making nothing if we had an off season. Gus agreed with me."

Stevie is perfect in my eyes, and I've never wanted to change anything about him. But right now, I wish he wasn't so dedicated to his family, in case this talk means he's running out of starch to resist co-signing that loan.

৯০

Another week goes by, and I don't see Lally or Edina at all. Then one night after supper, Stevie tells me we need to talk. We're sitting on the couch, my head on his shoulder, watching the Maine news. The weatherman says there's a winter storm watch, and I think, *Yeah, you got that right.*

"Gus thinks I should help Skip. I got the boat and all, I guess it's only fair."

"I don't see why."

Stevie leans forward, reaching for his Pepsi on the coffee table. "It isn't like I have to give up anything. Just co-sign it. Like Edina says, if something does happen, the house is worth enough to pay back both loans."

"You're going to do it, aren't you?" I feel nauseated. No good will ever come of this.

Stevie peers into the Pepsi bottle as if it's the most interesting thing in the world. "Well, yeah. Yeah, I guess I am."

That night as I lie in bed, thinking about how this could backfire, I'm scared and a little bit mad. Stevie cuddles up to my back, fits his knees into mine and throws his arm over me, but I just concentrate on keeping my breathing slow and even until I hear his soft snores.

ଔ

On Valentine's Day, Edina throws a house-warming party for the six of us. I'm getting dressed when I hear Lally's pickup in the driveway. She comes running up the stairs to the bedroom, and shuts the door. "What's going on?" I ask.

"I have to tell you something. I can't wait any longer." She looks at the floor and fiddles with her bracelets, then looks back at me so hard I feel like she's punched me. "I'm leaving Gus. We're getting a divorce."

A divorce. The word lies between us like she just spit it on the floor. "Lally, why?" I say, but she's already out the door and running down the stairs. I stand in the doorway, not quite believing she's doing this on the most romantic day of the year. Gus must be feeling pretty crappy right now, but I know he'll go to Skip and Edina's and put on a good face, never letting on a thing.

ଔ

When Stevie and I park in front of the house on Winfield Avenue, I see a triangle of light fall on the rotting snow as one of Skip and Edina's next-door neighbors checks us out. I can just imagine what all these snobs think of our old rattletraps cluttering up their fancy street.

It's been a month, and Skip and Edina still have almost no furniture. In the living room with the black stone fireplace, we sit on green resin chairs, three dollars each at the salvage store in Mayfield. The sharp plastic legs have already started to leave marks on the polished wood floor.

Gus and Lally come in, Lally grinning like a prom queen, Gus hiding whatever he's feeling behind a sweet half-smile.

Stevie and Gus talk about fishing. Edina starts telling me about everything she plans to do for the house. I just nod and say, "Nice," over and over because I'm watching Skip and Lally, I can't help it. They aren't talking—Lally keeps looking at Skip as though she's got a big, bright secret, but every time, he cuts his eyes away from her.

It doesn't take us long to go through most of a thirty pack of Coors Light. Lally's been pounding them down steady, more than the rest of us. I can't wait for this evening to end.

When Gus gets up and goes into the kitchen, I follow him. I wait till he gets another beer out of the fridge, then I say, "I'm really sorry this is happening. I wish she'd change her mind."

"Change her mind," he says, like he's not quite connecting. "What do you mean?"

"About the divorce. I wish you and her wouldn't split up."

"The divorce." His eyebrows dip together at the inner corners as he says it again, "The divorce." He sets his beer carefully on the shiny black counter and grips the edge of it as he stares out the window over the sink, into the big backyard with dead grass poking through the snow in the moonlight.

I go up behind him and touch his arm. "I'm so sorry. She may be my sister, but I'm on your side. I want you to know that."

He turns towards me and I see tears in his blue Nelligan eyes. "And when do you suppose she was going to tell *me* about this?" he says, and I realize what I've done. He brushes past me, heads down the hall and puts on his jacket and goes out the door.

I go back to the living room and tell Stevie I need to go home. He doesn't ask any questions, and I know he's as anxious to get out of here as I am. Outside, where Gus and Lally's truck still sits, I tell him what happened.

We go by the trailer, and then we drive around town checking out the bars, but Gus isn't anywhere. Stevie's not home fifteen minutes before he decides Gus is probably on the boat, so he goes out and I sit alone in the dark living room, afraid of what's going to happen next.

೮೨

I wake up on the couch when I hear Stevie come in. It's daylight, and for a moment I can't figure out what's going on.

Then Stevie says, "Gus is gone," and I remember.

"I know."

"No. I mean really gone. Massachusetts maybe, someplace far away from here. Wherever there's work."

"Fishing work?"

"Yeah." Stevie runs a finger down one edge of his goatee and says, "It wasn't right, the way he found out. She should've told him before she told you."

I nod. "I figured she had."

"Obviously." He stares off into space. "She didn't happen to tell you why?"

"No. But I know she wants Skip."

Stevie's forehead puckers, and he shakes his head. "Skip wouldn't leave Edina. He's crazy about her, that whole Southern-belle thing."

Skip could've fooled me. And did. "That day on the boat, him and Lally. Did you see them?"

"Flirting. I figured it was harmless enough."

"Lally wasn't flirting."

"Really," Stevie says, then closes his eyes and squeezes the bridge of his nose, a sure sign he's getting a headache.

I think about how Lally could misread Skip this bad, to leave a loving husband and end up with nothing at all, to be on this island and see Skip and Edina together and know that everyone's talking.

☙

Stevie tries all morning to reach Skip by phone, but no one's answering. At the house on Winfield Avenue, the door's locked, even though the car's in the driveway. When I go to cash my paycheck, Edina's not at the bank. Marla McHenry tells me she called in sick.

Stevie makes some calls, trying to put a crew together. In spite of getting replaced by Skip, Tony Readfield wants to come back, so Stevie takes him on as winchman. Tony says his wife's willing to shuck scallops if Stevie doesn't mind a woman on the boat, and Stevie says that'll be fine.

When he's done on the phone, I call Lally. I don't really want to talk to her, but I need to know how she's doing.

"Well," she says. "Thanks for a nice mess."

"I figured he knew. You should've told him first."

"Don't tell me what I should do, you little bitch." The phone clicks in my ear.

※

I'm doing lunch setups the next day at the Drop Anchor when Edina comes in. She gets right to it—she and Skip are going back to Biloxi. She can't stand Spruce Island another minute, knowing my sister's after her husband, and anyway, there's nothing to keep them here.

I don't say there's a house here she couldn't live without, and a great big debt or two.

"Now listen, Heather," she says. "This is important. I want you to interview for my job at the bank. You're the only one that's been my friend, and I want to see you get out of this dump into a better job."

I tell her I don't know anything about working in a bank. It does touch me, though, that she's trying to help. But if she really wants to help, she'll make sure the loan Stevie co-signed gets paid off. I say, "What about the house?"

"We're selling it. Don't worry. It'll be fine."

It won't be fine. Property sells real slow around here, especially in the dead of winter. All I can do is hope they get lucky. All I can do is hope we all get lucky, all this trouble soon behind us and things back to normal again. It's not too much to ask, being normal.

※

The morning Skip and Edina leave, she tells me if we're ever down south, we absolutely must look them up. I don't bother telling her we'd be as likely to end up on the moon as in Mississippi. The bank interviews me, but they don't hire me, and that's just as well. My job may not be great, but I'm good at it, and I can't imagine standing in one spot all day.

Lally refuses to see or talk to me. Before long, I hear she's left Spat Putnam's and moved away. I ask our parents where to, and they say Texas, and scold me again for meddling in my sister's marriage. They've taken her side as if I made the whole thing up, and they don't hear me when I tell them Lally talked as though the divorce was already in motion.

Skip and Edina do sell the house, to the new manager of the woolen mill, but after everything's settled, there's still five thousand dollars left on the loan Stevie co-signed. Skip says he can't pay, so now it's our debt. Stevie and the bank work out smaller payments, and I write to Skip and tell him exactly what I think of him. Outside of letting off steam, it doesn't do any good.

It's late March now, and today for the first time this winter, the sun smiles down with real warmth as I climb Franklin Hill towards home. Crocuses are poking through the melting snow, and soon the robins will come, and Stevie will re-rig the *Five Sisters* for ground-fishing. So much has happened since we took our shakedown cruise. So many changes.

At the top of the hill I stop and lift my face to the sun's heat. The sky is a fresh blue today, swept clean of clouds by a high southwest wind. What I'm thinking now is how it can all disappear so fast. All those things so far beyond reason, they slip away just when you're sure you've finally grasped them. All those things. They're like the sea smoke, if you think about it. The way it can drift right through your fingers as it obscures even the solid ground.

ABOUT THE AUTHOR

SEVENTH-GENERATION MAINER, twelfth-generation New Englander, Catherine J.S. Lee lives, writes, teaches, and gardens near the Canadian border on the island that inspired her fictional twins, Spruce Island and East Haven. While she is better known as a haiku poet and haiga artist, fiction has been her favorite form of writing since her first story was published state-wide when she was eight years old.

Many of her stories have appeared in print and online journals, and the title story of this collection was a finalist in the 2001 New Century Writer Awards sponsored by *American Zoetrope*. Lee has completed three National Novel Writing Month challenges, each time writing over 50,000 words of a novel in thirty days. In her free time, she enjoys Zentangling, playing the five-string banjo and the banjolele, hosting blues and folk music shows on a local radio station, and chasing sunsets with her digital cameras.

Island Secrets: Stories from the Coast of Maine is Lee's first published book-length work of fiction. She is currently revising a novel, *Summer's End*.

ALSO BY THE AUTHOR

All That Remains: A Haiku Collection Inspired by a Maine Childhood
Winner of the 2010 Turtle Light Press Haiku Chapbook Competition

Made in the USA
Columbia, SC
24 September 2022